Hitchhikers in Each Other's Minds

by

Jim Meaders

Argus Enterprises International
North Carolina***New Jersey

Hitchhikers in Each Other's Minds©
2011 All rights reserved by Jim Meaders

A-Argus Better Book Publishers, LLC

For information:
A-Argus Better Book Publishers, LLC
9001 Ridge Hill Street
Kernersville, North Carolina 27285
www.a-argusbooks.com

ISBN: 978-0-9842596-3-2
ISBN: 0-9842596-3-5

Book Cover designed by Jim Meaders

Printed in the United States of America

Dedication

"Aim at a high mark and you'll hit it. No, not the second time and maybe not the third. But keep on aiming and keep on shooting for only practice will make you perfect. Finally, you'll hit the bull's eye of success."

Phoebe Ann Moses ("Annie Oakley")

This sequel to *The Summer of My Fourteenth year* is dedicated to all of us who keep practicing with the hopes of hitting the bull's eye.

AUTHOR'S NOTE

Hitchhikers in Each Other's Mind is the sequel to *The Summer of My Fourteenth Year*. It picks up James' story three years later when he is in his first term of his senior year of high school. This is the Fall term of 1966. The only characters that carry over from the first book are James, his parents, and one brief run-in with another "reptilian alien thing."

As in *Summer*, some of the other characters in this story were based on individuals that I had interactions with in high school and beyond and some are purely fictional. Once again, the names have been changed to protect the guilty. Many of the names are anagrams for actual names and thus they may sound a little strange. Maybe you will find it challenging to figure those out (e.g., Mrs. Tinmoor is an anagram for "monitor"). Once again, I hope you enjoy reading my little piece of fiction as much as I enjoyed writing it.

Jim Meaders

Chapter One

"Hello?"

"Hi. It's James."

"What the . . . ? James who? And why are you calling me so early? It's only 8:00 a.m."

"James from school. You called me a few minutes ago. The phone ringing woke me up, but I couldn't get to it in time to answer. Somehow I just knew that it was you calling me"

"Oh, that James. What was it your mother used to say? You're dumber than a goat? I did not call you a few minutes ago."

"No, she said I didn't have the sense God gave a goat and I just had this feeling that it was you calling me. As strange as it may sound that thought was just there in my head somehow. And, Harmony, how did you know what my mother used to say to me?"

"You must have dreamed it, because I did not call you. I admit that I thought about calling you this morning, but I figured you were still in bed."

"Is there anyone else at your house who might have tried to call me, because I know the phone was ringing and I just know somehow that it was from your phone. And, once again, how did you know what my mother used to say to me?"

"I'm hanging up now, James. Go back to bed and dream about someone else calling you and then bother them."

"But, . . . Hello, hello, hello. Harmony?" She had hung up and I knew better than to call back until later. I didn't know what she was up to, but this was certainly not over. She had called me around 6:00 a.m. that morning and I knew it. Yes, I had been dreaming, but not about her calling me. I had been dreaming about surfing, probably because I had been to the Polk Theater earlier in the week to see The Endless Summer, again, and before going to bed it was all I could think about. And she certainly didn't have to be so mean by bringing up what my mother used to say to me all the time. *But wait a minute, she never did say how she knew about that.* We didn't know each other all that well and that was certainly something I wouldn't even tell my best friends. Talk about being called names and getting ribbed about it for the rest of my life! Maybe I should just avoid her for a few days and then when she does call I'd just ignore it for a few more days – that is, of course, assuming that she would call. *We'll see then how she likes a taste of her own medicine.*

My parents had already left for work and since it was Saturday my mother was letting me sleep in, because I would have to go to work that afternoon around 4:00 at the Star gas station that my father managed. I moseyed over to the refrigerator to get some milk out for a bowl of cereal when I heard a voice in my head say, ***I'm sorry, James. Call me tonight and we'll talk.***

Ok, where did that come from? I peaked in the refrigerator to see if some tiny gnome was in there talking to me, but didn't see anything moving around. However, I knew that it was Harmony's voice and it was in my head. So I'll just change my mind and give her a call tonight. I should know by now that women sometimes says things they don't mean and I've never been known to be so egotistical as not to be forgiving.

Thanks, James. That's what I appreciate the most about you.

Huh? Am I simply thinking the things I want her to say?

No, James. It's something I have always been able to do and now I think you have finally learned that ability as well.

Ok, let's test this theory out. Are you reading my mind, Harmony?

No, just your current stream of thought. If you are thinking it as if you were actually saying it, then I know what you're thinking. It takes many, many years to learn how to read one's deepest, darkest secrets, James.

This is kind of scary.

Don't worry, I won't tell anyone your deep dark secrets or that you have this ability now, besides you might not even be able to use it with anyone else yet. I was born with the ability and it has developed to the point where I choose who can read my mind and who can't. I have been working on you for about a year now.

Since we first met in junior year?

Yes, since the time we first met. Remember when we met in the hallway the first time and you introduced yourself? Your thoughts were revealed to me even then. That doesn't happen with everyone, but I think it was because you were imagining me naked.

That's really embarrassing. So, we can read all of each other's thoughts?

Well, not exactly, James. I can read all of yours, but you can't read all of mine.

That doesn't seem very fair, Harmony, especially since some of my thoughts about you have been a little naughty.

That's an understatement! But, not to worry, I don't mind. Just know that it isn't going to happen between us, at least not at this time.

I may not have the sense God gave a goat, but I know you could never feel that way toward me. Just friends, right?

Sure, why not?. At least for now.

Don't be a tease, Harmony.

Since this seems to be working between us now you don't need to call me tonight, James. We can communicate like this from now on and no one will know what we are saying to each other. Unless, of course, you tell them.

You know me better than that, Harmony. I'll keep our little secret. But I still don't think it is fair that you can know all of my thoughts all of the time when I can't know yours.

That ability takes many, many years, James. I have to go now so keep those thoughts clean. She giggled and hung up.

This certainly wasn't the way I imagined starting my day. I really liked Harmony (she was probably the most beautiful girl in school), but this new twist in things kind of bothered me. My immediate thought was that this was really neat. Being a science fiction fan it seemed like something out of a science fiction novel. Kind of like the machines with human brains in A Plague of Demons. Made me wonder if Harmony was from another planet or solar system. *Nah, just one of those rare human psychic abilities.*

I wasn't ready to actually "get up," so I went back to bed for a while. Being Saturday I didn't have to worry about getting ready for school. I laid there on the bed staring up at the ceiling and glancing around my poster decorated walls (Supremes, Beatles, The Endless Summer among others) not really knowing what to think or feel and being a little scared to think about anything, even if Harmony was miles away she was probably reading my every thought. *No response.* Maybe she was tuned out right then. I fell back asleep and didn't wake up until around 10:00 a.m. I wasn't sure if I had been dreaming or not, but I had already decided to go to the library that day and do some research on psychic phenomena.

I got dressed as quickly as possible, but when I had finished shaving with the rotary shaver my father had bought for me a couple of years before, I stood in front of the mirror and gazed into my own blue-green eyes for a moment. Was Harmony really psychic? Was I psychic? Or was it simply some rare ability this teenage girl had and that she used to tease boys who had no chance in hell with her? With those questions lurking in my mind, I skipped the breakfast that I didn't have earlier when Harmony first contacted me and headed straight for the library.

I wasn't sure how much had been written about psychic phenomena by 1966, but I was going to find out all that I could about the subject. Having started my senior year of high school that August I was familiar with doing research for papers in various subjects at school. It didn't take me long to find some books on the subject at our small, but well stocked, public library. I sat down at one of the big, heavy, age and varnished darkened wooden tables in a dark corner at the rear of the library to investigate psychic phenomena. I found out that most of the study done in this area had started up in the late nineteenth century with the Society for Psychical Research in England. But what I wanted to know was if any of this malarkey was actually based in fact. Now I wasn't much interested in science, or much else besides girls and cars in high school, but I was pretty much of the class of people who believed what they read and that if you could see, feel, smell, taste, or hear it then it must be true.

I discovered in my investigation that mind reading, or more correctly telepathy, is the supposed transfer of information on thoughts or feelings between individuals by means other than the five senses. I learned that the term was first used in 1882 by Fredric Myers, who just happened to be a founding member of the Society for Psychical Research. It seems, according to those who believe in this stuff, that a person who can make use of telepathy can read the thoughts and stored information in the minds of others. Although the concept isn't accepted by the scientific community, and if I wasn't dreaming, like I thought I had been doing three years ago during the summer of my fourteenth year, then I was now a believer. However, I would wait to see if Harmony actually contacted me this way when I wasn't sleeping before making a final decision on the subject. If I didn't "hear" from her in a couple of days, then I figured I could try contacting her by means of telepathy. *How does the theme from The Twilight Zone go?*

Chapter Two

My lack of interest in math class on Monday morning would have been evident to Mr. Bregala, our teacher whose face was as wrinkled as the bark of a hundred-year-old ginkgo tree even though he was only forty-five, if he could have seen past my glazed-over eyes and into my mind. I was staring in his direction, but I wasn't seeing or hearing him talk about and give an example of algebraic number theory because my mind was wandering toward trying to contact Harmony. I had not "heard" from her since Saturday morning or seen her at school that Monday morning and I had been looking everywhere for her before our first classes. It was possible that she was deliberately avoiding me so as not to reveal our little secret to anyone else or that it was just a tease, but I would keep an eye out for her anyway between classes and at lunch if necessary.

I caught a glimpse of Harmony at the other end of the hall between math and my next class, but I didn't yell out to her for fear of being struck down by some sort of mind power that she might have. Silly, I know, but at seventeen, I still had a vivid imagination and who knew what kind of mental abilities she might have developed since birth. We had study hall together during the last period of the day and if I didn't run into her or hear from her before then, I would approach her in study hall if she didn't seek me out. We had been regular "study buddies" in study hall since the beginning of the term and seemed to be drawn to each other, but not in the usual boy/girl high school situation. As I mentioned before, she was quite attractive and I was certainly drawn to her at first because of her physical beauty, but I was very shy around girls and had not had a girlfriend since the ninth grade. Harmony had that Victorian kind of beauty that I had learned about in the eleventh grade in art class: beautiful features, perfectly proportioned body, and that very mesmerizing and entrancing stare such as the woman in Edmund Blair Leighton's painting, The Accolade. It was as if she could look right through you and make you feel both her outer and inner beauty. But there had been something else about Harmony that had drawn me to her and now I was beginning to think that she had some kind of mind control over me. Maybe she only noticed guys who had naughty thoughts about her, but that would probably be every guy in school with the exception of maybe two. I was definitely going to find out in study hall that day if she was for real with this mind reading stuff and, if so, why she had contacted me.

That Monday at school seemed to drag on and on forever as I ambled in and out of the cold, white rectangles called classrooms in the long low brick buildings before I got to study hall. I'm sure part of it was that I wasn't paying much attention in any of my classes on that particular Monday. It was hard enough to pay attention to the teachers since we were crammed into desks designed for sixth graders and way too small for nearly-adult teenagers and were being subjected to their uninspired, mechanized discourse on subjects that they had supposedly studied in college, but which their lectures gave little proof of having happened. Heck, all I could think about all day was this thing with Harmony, so I didn't pay any attention to what went on in any of my classes that day. Well, study hall finally rolled around and I rushed to get there ahead of Harmony so I didn't have to waste any time approaching her about this mind reading thing that was going on between us. I was the third student to arrive at study hall and I waited by the door for Harmony to show up since she was nowhere in sight. When the bell rang we all had to sit down at one of the long, white tables that a few hours earlier had been where students ate their lunches. Harmony had still not arrived at study hall making me think that I had imagined the voices on Saturday and had simply been having a little fantasy about a hot girl at school. This little jaunt into each other's minds, if it had been real, had only happened a couple of days ago, but I was beginning to think I had either been dreaming the whole thing (1963 again) or that I had finally discovered that empty lot my father always said I had in my head instead of brains. "You got a lot up there in that head, son. It's an empty lot, but it sure is big." He would then slap me on the back with his good left hand, nearly knocking me down, laugh and then tell me to get my lazy butt in gear, to put it politely, and get to my chores.

I was seriously beginning to wonder if it had all been a dream, including knowing some girl named Harmony who had some strange attraction to me (I thought about Monica and Cookie from 1963). I mean, I had to chase girls because they never seemed to want to chase after me like they did after the star football and basketball and baseball players. It seemed that the only things I was good at were gawking, not paying attention, and sitting around on my lazy butt.

That's not true, James.

"Harmony?"

Shush! Not out loud.

Sorry.

I'm sorry that I didn't show up for study hall, but we're not ready to communicate this way when we are together in public. Other students might get the wrong idea.

You mean they might think we're a couple?

I didn't say that, James.

But that is what you meant wasn't it?

Regardless, James, you are very good at many things. You have learned my method of telepathy very quickly and I know for a fact that you excel at math, photography, and art. And, no, you can't take nude pictures of me.

I'm beginning to wish my father had been right about having an empty lot in my head.

Silly boy, your time will come. Anyway, that's why I decided to skip study hall.

Why didn't you let me know? We could have met somewhere private away from prying eyes. And what time will come, Harmony?

Your questions will be answered in due time, dear boy. Don't be too anxious about all this. You still have a lot to learn about my . . . our powers.

Don't tell me you can move heavy objects with your mind.

"Holy crap!" I nearly screamed and everyone in study hall turned to see what was happening and why I was so upset. "Sorry," I said. "My chair started to move, uh, I mean, I nearly fell over backwards in my chair. Guess I was leaning back too far." That caused several of the students to start laughing, but they quickly got back to doing whatever it was they were doing before I interrupted them.

That's why we're not ready to be seen together using these abilities, James.

That was you moving my chair, Harmony?

You brought up the subject, dear boy. We will play by my rules or you will suffer the consequences.

Suffer the consequences? What's that supposed to mean? I thought you liked me.

I like you very much, James, but we have to be careful. This ability has been in my family for thousands of years and it is now my responsibility to pro-

tect it as well as find that special someone with whom to share it.

That special someone? Can I assume that I am that "special someone?"

Yes, James. I have to go now, but we will continue our conversation and your training later, maybe even this week.

Harmony? Well, she didn't reply. I was beginning to learn that when she cut off communication it was done for the time. Period! George Orwell wrote in his novel 1984 what I was beginning to think now: "If both the past and the external world exist only in the mind, and if the mind itself is controllable – what then?" What then, indeed? Back in junior high school I started coming up with some strange ideas, probably because I liked science fiction and super hero stories. One of my ideas was that reality didn't exist – possibly influenced by Orwell. Everything was either past or future; there could be no present. The tiniest fraction of a second is gone before we can actually think about it; thus it is either past or it hasn't arrived yet. I didn't actually believe this stuff, at least not until now. I was once again beginning to doubt that any of this was actually happening and that I must be still having one of those dreams that seem to go on forever (like a certain sixteen-hour episode from 1963). It was going to take a lot of telepathic communication between Harmony and me and communication at close range so I could see, touch, hear, and at least smell her before I was going to be sold on any of this mind reading stuff. As far as I knew, if I wasn't dreaming, I was just fantasizing about being "friends" with Harmony. After all, that was as close as I had ever thought that I would get with a beautiful girl like her. And, no, I didn't take drugs! Never have and don't plan to start now over 40 years later!

Chapter Three

I only knew two kids at my high school who drank alcoholic beverages: a crippled kid who called himself Nick (short for Nicholas), but who we affectionately, alright, teasingly, called "Slushy," and who primarily drank too much beer; and a really skinny kid named Milo who was more into the hard stuff like Cutty Sark. Why do I bring this up? Because if I had to start drinking I knew where to go to get drunk. And believe me, this was starting to feel like one of those things where adults said, "I need a drink." I have always heard that waiting is the hard part, whether it was waiting for the bus, waiting for your date, waiting for a raise at work, or just waiting for a good idea. In this case with Harmony, the hard part of what I didn't know, but it had been four days since Harmony had "made contact" with me and I was becoming somewhat annoyed over the whole thing, both at myself for believing that a hot girl would ever go for me and, if it was true, at Harmony for not contacting me more often about what was really going on here. Why couldn't she "teach" someone else all this stuff and leave me to my fantasies about her and all of the other hot girls at school. What possible reason, aside from the manipulation and teasing of another human being, could she have in mind where I was concerned?

I have chosen you, James, as my student to learn all I know to do with telepathy, because I honestly believe that you have deeper feelings for me than you may ever be allowed to exhibit in a physical way. All the other boys in this school or that I have met or been around at other times in my life did not have the mental capabilities that I believe you possess. Besides, every high school boy in this school except you whose mind I have explored is nothing more than a big bag of raging hormones whose brains seem to reside in their penises. Even though you may not realize it right now, you have far greater mental capabilities than most people your age. Maybe not for knowledge, but especially for mental powers far beyond simple learning of facts.

Hi, Harmony. Welcome back, I think.

Sorry. Hi, James. I don't want you to think that I am ignoring you or doing what you call "eavesdropping."

What "we" call eavesdropping?

Don't interrupt. I do have to constantly monitor your thoughts in order to know what you need to learn about telepathy and when you don't have contact from me I am in training myself.

I thought you knew all this psychic phenomena stuff already.

No one with this "psychic phenomena stuff," as you put it, ever knows all the power that they may possess. It cannot be learned in an entire lifetime, much less a few years. Humans are the only entities in what you call the universe that use so little of their brains.

In what I call the universe? So, you plan to be teaching me to the day I die?

Only if I outlive you. That silly little giggle of hers that made her sound less than educated.

Uh, I have some questions if you don't mind, besides the ones that you haven't answered so far.

Sure, but you may not be ready for the answers at this time, James.

First, Harmony, you're talking like there are other intelligent beings in the universe. How am I supposed to believe something that most people think only crazy people believe or that we see in science fiction movies or read in science fiction novels?

Because if this relationship is to succeed you are going to have to trust that everything I tell you is the truth. Trust is more important to my kind than love or other silly human emotions.

Ok, let's say that I do trust you. Does what you just intimated about us mean that we will be together our entire lives?

Especially as friends, but that is all I even know at this time. All we know for sure is what has already past, in other words, history. We have no way of knowing what the next second will bring. We are mind readers and not fortune tellers.

That's scary!

It's only scary to humans, not to those of us who were either born this way or have learned the processes and crossed over to our side.

Crossed over to your side? What's that supposed to mean?

It is not time for you to know that, but not to worry because I will not let you perish on that side.

What do you mean, "perish on this side?" Now I'm really confused and am beginning to believe that this is all a dream. "Ouch!" Fortunately no one was close enough to hear me scream like a little baby.

How many times will I have to hurt you to make you believe?

What I don't understand is how you can deliberately hurt someone you like. Like a so-called friend.

Because I have chosen you, you are mine to do with as I please. I do not wish to hurt you because I really do like you and wish to be your friend forever.

I don't know who or what you really are, but unless this whole "process" speeds up some so that I really know what I'm getting into I'm outta here! And what do you mean you have "chosen" me, Harmony?

It is not possible for you to be "outta here," James. You have been chosen and now you have no other choice but to comply with my wishes. Cooperate and you will find much peace and joy in our relationship and the rest of your life. I must go now. You have wasted too much of my time and the Teachers over here are beginning to become impatient.

Harmony? You still haven't said what you meant by "chosen." Have you ever wondered why and what for and how and which and who all at the same time and not know what you were really thinking? Well, that's where I was at that particular moment in time, provided, of course, that there was such a thing as a particular moment in time or even time. Provided there was such a thing as me or for that matter, some exotically beautiful creature named Harmony! Could it be that my early thoughts about there not being any such thing as reality be the actual reality? Were there a few "people" in this old world who could read everyone's minds and who actually controlled everything that went on every day of every month of every year? Did the rest of us only imagine that we were real because these "others" were making us think that way? I was only 17 years old (or so I thought) and this was way too serious for someone my age to be worrying about. On the other hand, it would be kind of neat to know what other people were thinking about me, even if it wasn't always good.

I was almost scared to think about anything since it seemed that Harmony could tune into my channel whenever she so desired. If I was the "chosen one" for her to teach this stuff to then I certainly hoped that she would teach me that little aspect of her abilities as well. It would be pretty cool to be able to read the thoughts of my buddies, teachers, girls other than Harmony, and especially my parents. And if she didn't want me thinking about something then she had proven that she could "hurt" me, even if it was only a pinch or moving my chair while I was in it. That would be another cool trick to use on my buddies! I could certainly handle those things ok, so I decided I would just go about business as usual and be happy that the most beautiful and intriguing girl in school wanted to be even this close to me. I figured that eventually Harmony and I would be even closer and then all the other guys at school would see us together and think we were a couple. Now that would be just about the coolest thing ever, even more so than mind reading and moving objects with my mind.

Chapter Four

I was making my way through the crowded, narrow, gray metal locker strewn hallway the next week at school when lots of thoughts started going through my head that I wasn't thinking.

Hey there goes the kid with the kinky hair - he's thinks he's so smart just because he can do art - I saw him with that hot girl - what's her name - oh yeah, Harmony - Harmony doesn't really like him - just pretending so she can really dump him later - that one's a real nerd - what's his name again? - Jack or Joe or John or something like that - I think it might be James - oh yeah, what a really stupid sissy name that is – there's James - I think he's kind of cute in a homely sort of way (giggle, giggle, giggle) - I don't really mean that - what girl in her right mind would want to date that dork (giggle, giggle, giggle) – well, at least he's not queer like that "guy" in our English class who crosses his legs like a girl - I still think he's kind of cute – hope he doesn't get too close to me because people will think I'm his girl – ugh!

Even though I realized that I was reading the minds of the students passing me in the hallway, I couldn't take any more of this gibberish so I turned around and headed in the opposite direction to get to class. It was further to go back and around the next building, but a guy could only take so much of this mind reading stuff and not get angry and/or depressed. Hopefully my anger when "hearing" other people's thoughts would be something Harmony would teach me how to control some day. I was so angry at that moment that I stomped past a couple of my buddies and only grunted when they spoke to me. I would like to have grabbed those girls by the hair and dragged them out back like the cavemen did in cartoons and shown them that I was more of a man than there wussy boyfriends! If I had had the nerve I would have stopped the little teasing bitches right there in the hallway and asked them who they thought they were putting down quiet, shy, sensitive guys like me.

I will help you with that anger, James, and don't let it bother you too much what other people think. After all, they are just small-minded, stupid, little things who will never get anywhere in life without their precious little mommies holding their hands. I'll take care of those little teasing bitches you just heard. Talk later.

Well, no need to "think back" at Harmony because once again she had tuned me in and out like a radio station she didn't like. However, I was pretty sure that she did like me since she was going to "take care of those little teasing bitches" for me. God, I wondered what she was going to do to them? Hopefully nothing too bad. I mean, I have as many revengeful thoughts as anybody, but I rarely act on them, especially if it means actually hurting someone. I might not have the sense God gave a goat, but I was brought up better than that. Still, I will have to admit that I was intrigued by Harmony's response to those "teasing little bitches."

Well, it didn't take long to find out what Harmony had been up to with the girls whose thoughts about me were less than nice. Word spread quickly that the three or four girls who had been thinking those things about me early that morning (I couldn't be sure how many there were) had been caught smoking behind one of the classrooms by old Mr. Bregala himself. The strange thing about this was that none of these girls had ever smoked before in their lives, but had decided to borrow some smokes from another girl and "go out back" and have a smoke in plain sight of everyone who walked by them. Harmony must have put the thought in their heads and they all decided at the same time to meet and share the smokes. Then Harmony must have mentally suggested to Mr. Bregala to go outside and catch them in the act of doing one of the worst things a kid could do at school if they got caught. The girls caught smoking were suspended for a week! Well, at least Harmony didn't physically hurt them and, quite frankly, I don't think anyone even missed them.

Now I was starting to wonder how long it might take me to have that ability when Harmony chimed in on channel WJMM.

You may never be able to achieve that ability, James.

Oh, hi, Harmony. That was a pretty neat trick with those girls. Does that mean that I will have to rely on you to fight all my battles for the rest of my life?

Taking care of those little sluts was the least I could do to punish them for thinking such horrible thoughts about you and I will always be around to help you when you need help.

I would rather learn how to do that myself, but if you say I might never be able to learn that, well, then I'll let it go for now.

Once again, James, just something else that makes you a good person and someone who could use my ability in only the most correct ways.

I'm not sure what you mean by the "correct" ways. Was what you did to those girls "correct"?

Punishment has to be handed out sometimes to those who think they can treat others badly and get away with it. However, that punishment should never be greater than the bad thoughts or deeds of the one being punished.

I think I understand that and would have to say that I'm not sure I am mature enough to make those kinds of judgments against people who have wronged me. My mother has tried to teach me to suck it up and go on with my life when people treat me badly, but it is awfully hard sometimes to just let it go.

You know, James, I am really starting to like you more and more all the time. I think I have made the best choice for someone to tutor in the ways of our telepathy. Your ability to get past the bad things that happen to you and concentrate on the important things in your life is a unique asset.

Again, you make references about yourself that suggests that you are somehow different from the rest of us. Are you from another planet or something?

As of right now, that is privileged information that I have not been given permission to tell you. I told you that I was born and raised in this town. All you need to know right now is that we are somewhat different in our abilities than other people, but in all other aspects we have adapted to become as human as you.

Whoa. That may be more knowledge than I want to know. Are you saying that your ancestors weren't human?

Oops! My father always tells me that I talk too much. All I can tell you right now is that my kind have occupied earth for thousands of years and you must NEVER tell anyone about this. If you succeed in learning everything you need to cross over to our side, then you too will have become one of us.

How many of you are there and what's this "cross-over" business?

We are actually becoming near extinct in human terms. There are only a few hundred of us throughout the world, that is, earth, primarily be-

cause it is so difficult to find good male human re-
cruits such as yourself.

 Uh, does that mean your kind can't have
children and what's this "crossover" business?

 No, just that the females have outlived most
of the males and most of the remaining males have
grown too old to be of reproductive benefit, thus
young females on this side have to find suitable hu-
man males for mating.

 Well, that's one way to put it I guess. So, cre
all of the young females like you trying to recruit
young human males specifically for perpetuating the
species?

 That's too much information for now. Bye,
James.

 Harmony, wait, you haven't told me what this
"crossover" business is all about. Too late. Tuned out.
Station changed. No longer broadcasting. Ok, back to
the idea that this is all a dream. How could any of this
be real? Remember, I grew up believing that humans
have certain limited abilities and are unable to fully
utilize their brains for much more than talking with
their foot in their mouth most of the time. As my father
liked to say, "I didn't ask you to think, I asked you to
do something." But, I had had strange, long dreams
before and this seemed much more real than any of
those dreams. Of course, at the time I thought those
dreams were pretty real as well. At least Harmony
hadn't changed into a reptilian alien thing that was trying to kill and eat me. Not yet anyway. I had to stop
thinking about this too much because it was beginning
to give me a headache. Just get on with your usual boring life and see what happens, James. Who knows, if
this telepathy stuff is for real and Harmony actually
does exist outside my fantasy dream world then this
could be a pretty sweet gig in the long run. There's not
a guy in my high school who wouldn't like a shot at a

fine filly like Harmony, well, except for those two I mentioned before.

I'm certainly glad you think I am a "fine filly," ***James.***

Oops! Forgot again that I need to be careful what I think about.

Chapter Five

I guess I had pressed Harmony for too much information, because she avoided me, both physically
and mentally, for over two weeks including skipping
study hall during all of that time. Mrs. Tinmoor, our
study hall monitor/cheerleader coach/home economics
teacher, that little square shaped, big knuckled, sun-
burn colored woman with a rat's nest for hair had been
bugging me about where Harmony was since we
seemed to be "close." I honestly couldn't tell her and
Harmony wasn't letting me or anyone else that I knew
know her whereabouts during study hall either, not that
Mrs. Tinmoor believed me for one minute. Study hall
wasn't exactly mandatory, but one was supposed to
check in with Mrs. Tinmoor before cutting out to more
interesting places and activities. Some of the kids had
jobs through an after-school program mostly working
at local grocery stores and so they always got to leave
early. I had to be at work at the local Star service station that my father managed, but I didn't have to be
there until 4:00, thus I had to stay in study hall and pretend to study. Some of the more creative thinkers in
study hall could come up with some pretty good reasons, although usually lies, for skipping out of study
hall and Mrs. Tinmoor would usually believe all of
them. Mrs. Tinmoor wouldn't let you sleep during
study hall either. If she caught you sleeping she would
sneak up on you with a wooden yardstick in her hand
and bring it crashing down right next to your head
scaring the living bajeemies out of you, among other
less mentionable things. I've even seen kids fall off of
their chairs and end up cowering under the table. A

couple of times the guys she had startled awake wet themselves so much that they had to be dismissed and sent home. It's pretty funny until it happens to you.

Just as I was beginning to think that this really was all a dream or my overactive imagination running away with me, Harmony tunes in my channel, WJMM, 1666 on you're AM dial, hexakosioihexekontahexaphobia radio. Yes, I was definitely becoming somewhat phobic about what seemed to be happening to me, so why not use those three little numbers for my telepathic radio station? Of course, I knew how ridiculous that was. After all, it was also the sum of all the numbers on a roulette wheel and even has Biblical references in the Book of Revelation (13:17-18).

Hi, James. Have you missed me and what is all of this nonsense you are thinking?

I was beginning to think that maybe you had abandoned the whole idea of training me in your ways and moved on to one of the jocks and I was just being silly about the radio station stuff.

You can be amusing, but don't be stupid about me abandoning you, James. You are the one that I have chosen and that cannot be changed. I have had to avoid you for a while because the Elders called me in to discuss my choice of you for a future mate on this side. Now, don't worry, they like my choice, but they also wonder if you will be able to help us out in the distant future.

Huh?

You weren't entirely wrong when you suggested that you were picked to "perpetuate the species." There will come a time when you will be called upon to marry and mate with a female, possibly me, but only after you have learned enough to cross over to our side.

Yahoo! I could definitely go for getting it on with you, Harmony. But, what is this "crossover" business all about?

Dear, dear, James, don't be so crude! What ever am I going to do with you?

Have you been talking to my mother? That's what she is always saying to me.

No, dear boy, I have not been "talking" to your mother.

Of course, you've been reading her mind without her knowledge.

You do catch on fast!

Ok, I deserved that. But this is both exciting and frustrating information all at the same time. Don't forget that I'm a teenage boy with raging hormones just like those other guys you didn't pick and you do happen to be the most beautiful girl in school.

Thank you for that, James. I can't promise you that I will be the one, but all of the females on our side are attractive so you don't have to worry too much. And I do appreciate being compared to the woman in the Victorian painting by E.B. Leighton.

It isn't possible that they are all as attractive as you, Harmony. I made that comparison because the female model in that painting and the female models in many of the Victorian paintings are so beautiful.

Thank you again for the compliment, James, but I contacted you to let you know why I haven't been in contact with you recently. This, like all communication between us, must remain our little secret. Please always keep that in mind, James. It is of the utmost importance that you never tell anyone about how we communicate or that you have been chosen by a female of the other side to make the crossover.

Mums the word. My lips are sealed. Zip, zip. But, please tell me what you mean by "crossover."

I do trust you implicitly, James. If you ever violate that trust we will both be dealt with severely. I must go now, but I will not be gone as long this time. I may even come back to study hall if we can mostly communicate in a normal human manner. And you must be patient concerning the crossover. I will tell you when the time is right.

Ok, I think I can handle that now, however, I really do miss seeing you.

Goodbye for now, James.

And just like that Harmony turned off the channel once again. However, this time I really had some things to think about. The "other side" had chosen me to help perpetuate their species or kind or whatever they should be called. And there was that remote possibility that it would be with Harmony. I hoped that Harmony wouldn't mind too much that I would definitely be thinking about her naked now, besides it was her fault for putting that idea in my head. How could I not have such images in my head, especially after what she just communicated to me? I can tell you right now that just those thoughts and images about Harmony made me one happy camper! If this was a dream I just hoped that it would go on until the "act" was consummated. All of these thoughts would certainly make study hall more enjoyable, especially when Harmony was there for me to gaze at with that stupid, drooling look that young boys "in love" tended to have when beautiful girls were around, especially those they had a big crush on.

I wasn't sure if I was "in love" with Harmony or not or if this was just another one of those infatuation things that one's parents always seemed to be talking about. Every time I happened to mentioned to my parents, especially to my mother, that I was interested in a particular girl at school she always said it was just an infatuation and that my interest in whatever particular girl would pass just like all the others had passed (my mind drifted back to Leasure in junior high school and Christy back in the sixth grade). It wasn't until much later in life that I realized that what she was trying to do was hang on to her little boy as long as possible by discouraging my interest in girls in as polite a way as she knew how. If she even had an inkling of what was transpiring between Harmony and me at that time my mother would have had a cow and then have me committed to a work farm where I would be in charge of scooping cow poop until I was sixty. Heck, she might even have that goat she was always referring to when getting on my case about something if she had known that I had been "chosen" by some alien entity on the "other side." In charge of cow poop or goat poop. Poop was poop after all. Hopefully, my mother would never figure that out or ever realize that someone out there was reading her mind and training me to do the same and then take me to the "other side." If she ever figured that out, she would have me caged up and shipped off to the funny farm with "Sergeant Poop Scooper" emblazoned in bright red embroidery across the back of my white shirt!

It was about 7:00 the next morning and I arrived at school early hoping that Harmony might decide to meet up with me and I could walk her to her first class. I did catch a glimpse of her at some distance, but she was heading in the opposite direction so I decided to wait and see if she came to study hall that afternoon. It was lunch time and I was sitting at one of the picnic tables outside the cafeteria eating my usual brown bag lunch of a cold fried bologna sandwich and a peanut butter and strawberry preserves sandwich (two of the best things ever invented for a kid's lunch) when who should pop down next to me but Harmony.

"You don't like eating in the cafeteria, do you?" she asked me out loud.

Hearing her actually speak with a real voice kind of startled me at first, but I replied, "I don't really like the food they serve very much so I fix myself these sandwiches everyday and usually sit out here alone thinking about things."

"Things like us?" she asked.

"Yeah, among other things, but mostly about us lately," I answered.

"What other things do you think about, James?" Harmony inquired probably already knowing what I thought about.

"Oh, come on now," I said looking directly into her beautiful dark grey/green-brown eyes that had the slightest hint of azure around the irises. "You probably know everything I have thought for at least a year now."

"Well, not everything," she replied. "I'm not always prying into your thoughts, although I do find them to be quite interesting sometimes."

"Only sometimes?" I questioned.

"Ok, most of the time," she said matter of fact. "But when you meet the Elders someday you must not think those naughty thoughts about me or any other female. That could be the death of both of us."

"Not seriously?" I asked more than stated.

"Just know that the Elders always mean serious business, so don't even be flip with them."

"Don't worry, Harmony," I replied, "I will do my level best not to embarrass or hurt you in any way. If I do joke around it is only in fun."

"I know," she said. "I'm really beginning to fall for you, you know?"

"Really?" I replied in a very surprised tone.

"Really," she said. "I, too, hope the Elders pick me to be your mate. There's someone approaching our table, James, so back to normal talk."

"Right," I agreed.

The person approaching our table was none other than the old busy body, Mrs. Tinmoor. As she came up to the table she said to Harmony, "Well, hello there stranger. I hope to see you in study hall this afternoon since you haven't given me any reason for being absent. I haven't reported you yet, but if you don't start showing up on a regular basis I will have to report you. If I didn't like your little boyfriend here so much I probably would have reported you a long time ago. I'm not going to ask you for a reason for your absences from study hall, but from now on you better have some good excuses if you're going to miss. Is that clear, young lady?"

It surprised me that Mrs. Tinmoor didn't continue with one of her God awful arrogant long speeches that she liked to give all the bad little boys and girls when she thought she had caught them doing something they shouldn't have been doing.

"Yes, ma'am," replied Harmony. "It will not happen again without good cause."

"Good," said Mrs. Tinmoor. "I'm glad we understand each other. So, tell me, how long have you two been an item?"

I wasn't sure how to respond to this question so I looked at Harmony for help. "I'm not sure exactly what you mean by 'item,' Mrs. Tinmoor, but James and I are just friends who happened to enjoy each other's company. Nothing else." *At least not that you need to know about you old hag!* Harmony said to me via telepathy. I couldn't help myself and started to laugh like I had a squirming little toad in my shorts, but Harmony gently, but firmly enough to hurt, pressed her heel down on my instep and it was all I could do not to cry out.

"What are you laughing at, mister?" Mrs. Tinmoor asked in a rather demanding voice.

"Nothing," I managed to squeak out as my foot still throbbed.

"Well. lunch time is almost over so you two need to be off to your next class and I better see you both in study hall this afternoon if you know what's good for you," Mrs. Tinmoor said and then strutted off as if she had something to strut.

See you in study hall this afternoon, James, and try not to limp away from the table.

I'll be waiting in study for you and I'll do my best not to limp although my instep is still throbbing.

Poor baby!

Harmony picked up her books and strutted off to class. And believe you me, she had something to strut! After this little encounter with Harmony and Mrs. Tinmoor I was now pretty sure that this was all real and that there was such a thing as telepathy and that there could actually be beings on earth that were different from the rest of us and that I had been chosen by the most beautiful female of their kind who would hopefully someday have my children. With any luck the kids we had would have Harmony's looks and not be nearsighted and have kinky hair!

Chapter Six

If the run in with Mrs. Tinmoor hadn't been bad enough I ended up being about thirty seconds late for my American Government class and our big, red-nosed, storm-browed, half-sober, overweight, ogre of a history teacher, Mr. Kycran, lit into me like a starving coyote on a rotting deer carcass. "Just where have you been you little hard head and where do you think you're going (burp) now. mister little hard head?" he practically shouted at me in his gruffest voice in front of the whole class. Looking around the class I had a little smirk on my face and half the class was stifling laughs and the other half was cringing in fear.

With that smirk growing bigger and in the most disrespectful tone I could muster up for the occasion, I replied, "I figured I would park my butt in my usual spot over there next to the window where I could ignore you while studying the great outdoors."

"Like hell, you (burp) say," he yelled back at me. The entire class had started to giggle at my smart-aleck reply, but now all was quiet as the old coot half walked, half stumbled over to the door where I was standing and grabbed me by the arm. "You're goin' to the (burp) principal's office you little smart ass punk."

I jerked my arm free and said, "I think I can find my own way there without you stumbling and falling on me, thank you."

"Why you (burp) little snot-nosed brat," he yelled and reached for me again, but I dodged his grasp and ran off down the hallway toward the principal's office. "This isn't over you (burp) little mommy's boy douche bag," he yelled after me and then stumbled back into the classroom bumping head first into the door jamb before slamming the door behind him. I wasn't sure what a "douche bag" was, but I was pretty sure it wasn't a compliment he was paying me. I heard later that the entire class was in a riotous uproar by then and that Mr. Kycran just sat down at his desk, told everybody to shut the hell up, and to read the next ten chapters in the textbook, whereupon he leaned back in his chair and dosed off until the bell ringing to change classes woke him up. By that time, however, everyone had quietly sneaked out of class leaving Mr. Kycran leaning back with his big mouth agape and snoring and burping loud enough to be heard in the next county.

I did go straight to Miss Dutrip's office and related the whole scenario to the principle including the language he had used and the names he had called me in front of all the other students. Miss Dutrip was the fifty-something, skinny, bag of bones principal that the students affectionately referred to as Old Miss Skeleton. For several seconds, but what seemed like an hour, after relating my story to Miss Dutrip she just stood there looking like a leftover carcass from the previous century with the corners of her mouth twitching and the wrinkles in her brow getting deeper and deeper. At first I was sure she was going to send me home and suspend me from school for the next twenty years, but then she opened her mouth and the following statement issued out in the calmest yet most evil-sounding voice I think I have ever heard: "I am not afraid to say what is obvious, even if it is terribly uncomfortable to all involved. That petulant, phallic-headed, dung-heap drunk of a so-called man has made my job over the years a Sisyphean hell. He has finally gone too far and he can take his drunken carcass off these school grounds right now and never show his fat ass around here again!"

I didn't know what kind of hell she was referring to, but once again it didn't sound like a compliment. I stood there not knowing whether to cheer her own, give her a hug big enough to crush her, or run like the wind and hide in the nearest dark corner I could find. Then Miss Dutrip turned to me and with the most pleasant smile I think I have ever seen on anybody's face, including Harmony's, she said, "I am so sorry that you had to hear that vulgar tirade young man, but sometimes a person just has to finally let it all out. I promise you that your troubles with Mr. Kycran are over. Now go over to study hall until your next class and tomorrow you will have a new history teacher."

"Thank you, ma'am," I stuttered and took off as fast as I could to study hall. It took Miss Dutrip the rest of the class period to compose herself and march down to the classroom where I had had my run in with Mr. Kycran. The students who were milling around waiting to go into his next class said that he had fallen back asleep immediately after the bell quit ringing and when Miss Dutrip walked in and saw him snoring and burping she went over and pulled his chair backwards tumbling Mr. Kycran on his back on the floor. The students just outside the door said he got up yelling and screaming all kinds of profanities at her, but she grabbed a broom standing close to the door and started pummeling him and then chased him down the hallway and out the back door of the building and into the parking lot where he got in his car and peeled out of the parking lot doing at least fifty miles per hour. All the while Miss Dutrip was chasing him she was yelling over and over at him to never ever set foot on the school grounds again because he was fired immediately. And that was the last any of us ever saw of Mr. Kycran again. I later heard that Mr. Kycran had finally gotten a janitorial job at a nearby community college, but that he was fired after only six weeks when in a drunken stupor he assaulted a cafeteria worker one day at lunch for not giving him enough jello. After that

Miss Dutrip gained a huge amount of respect not only from the faculty and staff at KSHS, but from the students as well. From that day forward I never heard anyone make jokes about her or call her names.

I had left study hall and was headed to my next class when that "heavenly" voice came to me again: *I'm very proud of you, James, for standing up to that big bully, Mr. Kycran.*

Thanks, Harmony. I guess it was about time, but Miss Dutrip's the real hero here. I heard that she was really something. Wish I could have seen her chasing old Mr. Kycran down the hallway.

Yes, I think she has a newfound respect among the students. I know you like her a lot more now than before.

Heck, I didn't like her at all before. I made as much fun of her as anyone else and actually took pride in doing it. That was really wrong of me to be like that. I was brought up better than that.

I know you were, James, and I know that you will never treat anyone like that again who doesn't deserve it.

Are you saying that sometimes people deserve that kind of treatment?

Not often and definitely not because of who they are, James, or the position they hold and especially not because you assume they're mean or evil without having any proof.

How is it that you are so wise for such a young person, Harmony?

Your naïveté is a quaint trait right now, but as you learn our ways you too will gain in intelligence and the better ways of our world. I have learned these things from birth, but you have to learn them in a shorter amount of time so as to expedite your crossover.

Seems like a daunting task to me. Do you really think I am up to this crossover thing that you are always talking about?

Absolutely, James! I knew it the first time I passed you in the hallway here at school.

It really feels good to know that somebody has a little faith in me. I can only hope that I live up to your expectations, Harmony.

You will. See you in study hall later. And now for my next class. I could get through anything else the day might throw at me knowing that I was going to get to see Harmony twice in one day. With Harmony on my side the possibilities were almost endless. I felt like the frog kissed by a princess. At that moment in time there didn't seem like there could possibly be any obstacle that could stand in my way. Boy, was I wrong and it wasn't going to take long for me to find out.

Chapter Seven

When my last class was over that day I nearly ran to study hall in anticipation of seeing Harmony, but hoping to get there before she did to show how enthusiastic I was about us being "an item." I was sure that I would beat her there, but she had already arrived at study hall and was sitting in a different place than we usually sat. She saw me and motioned for me to hurry over to where she was sitting, so I walked as quickly as I could without drawing any special attention to myself and started to sit down next to Harmony when she indicated for me to sit in the seat across from her at the table.

Good idea, I thought hoping she was already tuned in to my wavelength.

Mrs. Tinmoor is already suspicious about us and you know what a gossip she can be.

No kidding, Harmony. I heard that she was spreading a rumor about Miss Dutrip and the Vice-Principle being in a romantic relationship.

Well, in all fairness to Mrs. Tinmoor, that is not a rumor, James.

No way! Miss Dutrip and Mr. Smith? Mr. Smith was almost as skinny as Miss Durip. I imagined the two of them walking down the street arm in arm. They might have taken up enough space to look like one person walking down the street. I couldn't help a little snicker at that thought.

James! That wasn't very nice, funny, but not nice. I'm afraid it is true that they are a serious couple and one of the cheerleaders said she saw them

making out in the parking lot in her car late one af-ternoon when she was leaving school after cheerlead-er practice. They are trying to keep it quiet, but it is spreading all over school and the students are making all kinds of jokes about them. I tapped into Miss Du-trip's thoughts the other day and it seems that one of them will have to resign if the school board finds out about their sordid little affair.

Wow! I don't understand why it is so sordid, Harmony. They are just two normal adult humans who are attracted to each other. Which one do you think would resign?

Well, James, based on what I have been able to get from her thoughts it would probably be him. She was thinking about some job offer he had at another school in the district to be a principle.

Well, I'm glad if it works out that way. I don't think the students would like Mr. Smith as principle. Some guys I know were actually paddled before being suspended and sent home.

You mean Kyle and Earl, James?

Well, of course you already knew that, Harmony.

They deserved to be paddled and suspended for what they were doing.

I never did hear what it was about, Harmony. Tell me.

Well, James, they were sneaking into the girls' restrooms and taking photos under the stall doors and then running out before any of the girls could identify them. They had a college friend majoring in photo-graphy that developed the film and made prints for them at his college darkroom.

So how did they get caught?

Mr. Smith's secretary, Mrs. Anskye, just hap-pened to be going to one of the restrooms that they were taking photos in and they nearly knocked her down on the way out the door, except that she is big-

ger than most of the boys here at school and they got knocked down instead.

Man, I would like to have seen that! Mrs. Anskye was not only over six feet tall, she had been a pretty good basketball player in college, she probably weighed in around 250 pounds.

Anyway, James, and Harmony gave me an exasperated look because I kept interrupting her, ***she hauled them in, one arm of each in each of her huge hands, into Mr. Smith's office and told him that she had caught them running out of one of the girl's restrooms and that they nearly knocked her down. Kyle still had his Nikon F 35mm SLR camera in his hand and when Mr. Smith asked what it was for, Earl spilled the beans because Mrs. Anskye squeezed his arm so hard that he almost cried.***

Man, Harmony, if I did something like that and my parents found out about it I would be grounded until I was at least 30.

Well, Kyle will be back at school in a couple of weeks, but I heard that Earl's parents were so embarrassed that they are moving to another town as soon as possible and that they are keeping Earl at home in the meantime.

I'll bet his butt is so sore that he won't be able to sit down for a month.

Harmony giggled at that and immediately got the attention of Mrs. Tinmoor. She waddled over to the table and asked, "Just what's so funny over here? Would you two lovebirds like to share what is amusing you with the rest of study hall?

"No ma'am," Harmony replied. "James just told a stupid, but funny joke."

"Well, little mister James, how about sharing your stupid, but funny little joke with the rest of us," Mrs. Tinmoor demanded more than suggested.

There are two things I'm really bad at: one is tel-ing jokes correctly and the other is simply remember-ing the jokes in the first place. "I really don't remem-ber what it was, Mrs. Tinmoor," I replied trying to get around Harmony's little white lie.

"You either tell us the joke, young man, or you two are separated for the rest of the semester," she said with a sly little smile on her ugly dog-faced mug.

James, that wasn't a very nice thought about Mrs. Tinmoor.

Neither was your little lie about me telling a joke. You know I'm terrible at telling jokes.

Ok, I apologize for that, but Mrs. Tinmoor is waiting for you to tell a joke, so you had better come up with something or else.

"Ok," I said reluctantly, "here's the stupid joke: What's the difference between chopped beef and pea soup?"

"I don't know," said Mrs. Tinmoor. "Why don't you tell us the difference."

Harmony and just about the whole study hall were beginning to giggle because they already knew the punch line of the only old joke I could think up. "Eve-ryone can chop beef, but not everyone can pea soup!" I answered.

"Ho, ho, ho," Mrs. Tinmoor said in her best pa-tronizing voice while the entire study hall erupted in laughter.

That's funny, James, she doesn't look like Santa Claus.

Well, that little thought from Harmony did me in. I couldn't help myself and started laughing as hard as everyone else in study hall. The only problem was that Mrs. Tinmoor didn't find any of this little scenario very funny and spun around and gave everyone else a stare that would have stopped a grizzly bear in its tracks.

When the laughing had stopped, Mrs. Tinmoor said,"Well, Mr. Funny Bones, I think you had just better go sit on the other side of the room for the rest of this period. We'll see how I feel tomorrow about the two of you sitting close together from now on. Now get your skinny little butt over there and I had better not hear one tiny little peep out of you, because if I do you'll be parading naked in front of the entire cheerleading squad!" she practically yelled while pointing to the opposite side of the room. The study hall started to crack up again, but Mrs. Tinmoor turned on them and gave them her glaring look again which made them shut up immediately.

As I was moving away from Harmony's table I looked back longingly as she thought, *I'm sorry, James. I'll make it up to you somehow, I promise.*

I know how you could make it up to me, Harmony.

Don't be silly, James. You know we have to wait until the time is right.

You mean . . .

Oh, all right, yes, someday, James, we will be together.

I can wait for you, Harmony. There isn't a guy alive who wouldn't wait for you.

You know, it might be better if we didn't sit close to each other in study hall since we can communicate without talking out loud anyway. That way, maybe you won't get in trouble anymore with Mrs. Tinmoor.

You are probably right. Anyway, I could still see you even if I couldn't be closer to you. The wretched old hag might decide to keep us apart anyway.

I wonder if everyone will be calling us "love-birds" after this, James?

Well, with as big and loud of a pie hole as old lady Tinmoor has I'm sure everyone in study hall heard her and it will be all over school by first period tomor-

row. *I don't mind, but I know you didn't want that to happen, Harmony.*

You know what, James? So what if they think that. That might just help us in our communications and it would allow for us to be seen together. I think I'm ok with it.

You're the best, Harmony. Study hall is just about over, can I walk you to your car?

Certainly. How would you like to pick me up and take me home everyday?

Really, Harmony?

Really, James. Besides, I would much rather ride in your Barracuda than drive my mom's Mercedes. You have got the coolest car in school, what with all those surf decals on that big back window. You would be surprised at how many girls think your car is the coolest in school.

If I were but a cool car.

Oh, James, plenty of girls like you, but they had better stay clear because you are mine!

As you wish, my princess.

There's the bell. We had better get going, because don't you have to be at work by 4:00?

Whereupon I sauntered over to Harmony and we strolled off arm in arm and out to her mother's Mercedes. I waved bye to Harmony as she pulled out of the parking lot and was still waving as she headed off down the road. I wondered why her mother would drive an expensive car like a Mercedes if they wanted to fly under the radar. Oh well, that wasn't my problem and, besides, tomorrow morning I would drive up to school in my "cool car" with none other than the prettiest girl in school as my passenger. I couldn't wait to see the look on all the other guys' faces, especially my buddies.

Chapter Eight

The next morning I was up extra early and had fixed my lunch and was heading out the kitchen door when my mother hollered at me to just slow down a minute. "Where do you think you're off to so early and in such a hurry, young man?" she asked in her normal suspicious tone.

"I've got to leave a little earlier now because I have to pick up someone and give them a ride to school," I replied trying my best not to reveal that I had a new girlfriend.

"Another one of your little infatuations, I suppose?" she stated more than asked.

"She is not an infatuation, Mother," I firmly stated. "We started out as just friends, but we have grown closer this semester. Anyway, yesterday in study hall I offered to pick her up and take her home everyday."

"And just where dos this little harlot live?" my mother asked.

"She is not a harlot, Mother!" I exclaimed rather emphatically. "She just happens to be a very smart and very nice and probably the most beautiful girl at school. Now, if I may, I need to get going or we're both going to be late for our first class."

"And what would a girl like that want with the likes of you? And you didn't answer my other question, young man," she yelled at me as the kitchen door slammed behind me.

I was in my car and backing out of the driveway when the door opened and my mother leaned out yelling something at me. I couldn't hear her since my windows were still rolled up, I had the radio volume turned up, and I didn't bother to wait and find out. Knowing my mother all too well, if I were to go back now she would probably take a switch to me and wear my skinny little butt out. I would certainly catch hell that night when I got home from work even though it would be after midnight. I knew that my mother would tell my father what had happened when he got home from work a little after 11:00 that night and how I had both ignored her and raised my voice to her. My father worked the 3:00 to 11:00 shift at the Star service station and I would have done the same if I could have gotten out of school sooner, but since I didn't get out until a little after 3:00 the old man let me come in at 4:00 and work to midnight. I was certainly not looking forward to getting home that night from work. With any luck they would both be in bed sound asleep when I got home around 12:30 a.m., but that was like hoping that Raquel Welch, who was only nine years older than me, would give up her acting career and move next door where she would seduce me with her charms, among her other assets.

About fifteen minutes after pulling out of my driveway I pulled up out front of Harmony's house, which actually looked more like a mansion compared to where I lived. She was sitting on the front steps waiting for me and came running down the sidewalk with her long golden blond hair bouncing behind her and jumped in the car, giving me a great big kiss. "You really don't realize what a cool car you have, do you?" she asked me out loud. "What year is it again?"

I didn't know if Harmony was simply feigning interest in my car or if she really did think it was that cool, but trying to get my composure back after the surprise kiss, I answered, "It's a 1965 Barracuda." The 1964 through 1966 Barracudas all had the same basic body style with the huge rear window and fold down rear seat, which I had hoped when I bought it would have some interesting future uses other than carrying my surfboard and groceries (my mother didn't drive and I usually had to take her to the grocery store now that I was driving). However, the 1965 model had these really cool yellow fog lights in the middle of the grill. Even though the body style changed in 1967, I liked the original body style best, besides, I couldn't afford a new car. My '65 'Cuda was a dark red with black interior, 273 cubic inch V8 with automatic transmission. Much to my father's mortification, I had removed the original hubcaps and painted the wheels black and had put a new set of wide Atlas tires on it.

"I think I like this body style better than the new style they're showing in the magazines," she told me. "The new body style doesn't have that cool wrap-around rear window like yours. Besides, no one else in school has a Barracuda."

"I'm beginning to think that you only like me for my car," I said.

"You know that isn't true, James."

"I know," I said. "It's just that I had a rough time with my mother this morning trying to leave a little early so I could come pick you up."

"I know you did, James," Harmony said, "but don't worry about when you get home tonight. Your mother will not remember a thing about what happened this morning, but she will be thrilled that you have a new girlfriend. So will your father."

"Harmony at work again on my behalf. You have got to be the best girlfriend in the history of the world!" I exclaimed. "Besides being beautiful and intelligent you are always solving my problems. Maybe someday I won't have as many problems for you to solve or maybe I'll learn how to solve my own problems."

"That's all part of the game for me, James," she answered. "It's part of what I must do to protect you, even from your own parents if necessary and, yes, some day you will be able to solve not only your own problems, but the problems others face as well."

"Simply amazing!" I replied.

"You are easily amazed, James," Harmony told me.

Well, we were arriving at school about that time and let me tell you that we were getting some mighty jealous looks from the guys in the parking lot as we pulled in. After cruising around the entire parking lot showing off my passenger, I found a good spot to park, quickly jumped out of the car and rushed around to the passenger side and opened Harmony's door for her. She handed me her books and stepped out of the car holding my hand and graciously thanking me and then taking my free arm and literally strutting onto campus with me. A couple of my friends hollered "Woo, woo" as we walked along the sidewalk, but I just ignored them and relished the moment as Harmony moved even closer and gave my arm a little extra squeeze. I walked her to her first class, gave her a quick kiss, which brought a few more "woo, woos," said bye, and turned to head on to my first class when I heard her say loud enough for others to hear, "See you later, lover boy."

Let me tell you that I got a lot of "you dog" looks from the guys that day along with a ton of questions about how did I manage to land the hottest girl in school and how far had we gone. Harmony, of course, had been "listening in" to all of this. As it turns out she could also "hear" the actual normal conversations between people when she wanted and she definitely wanted to hear what all the other guys were saying. I wasn't sure how to respond to the guys without sounding like either a puritanical wussy or, as most of them were when they were talking about their conquests, a pathetic boasting liar. I absolutely refused to lie and say that Harmony and I were doing things that we weren't, but at the same time I was a 17-year old human male with a normal ego and I didn't want the guys to think that I was hopelessly destined to be a virgin all my life and end up in a monastery somewhere in Nepal.

James, it's ok to tell them that we simply hit it off and have become very close friends. You don't need to tell them more or less. Let them have their little fantasies about us, because it's as close as any of them will ever get to knowing me. I especially appreciate your tact and manners, James.

Thanks, Harmony. I guess what they don't know will keep their evil little minds busy.

"Little minds is putting it very politely, dear James!

So, what I said to all the interested parties who wanted to know was, "I don't know how it happened, but Harmony and I just seemed to hit it off and now we have become, how shall I put this, very close friends."

The usual response to this for some time to come was simply, "You dog!"

Harmony assured me they would get over it fast and things would seem very normal in just a few days. I figured her plan was to make them forget that there had to be something "special" going on between us and to make anyone who thought something was "going on" think instead that what they saw or heard was normal. I learned at an early age that most people's lives were controlled by sentiment rather than reason. A guy was dating a hot girl, so there had to be more going on than just holding hands. Even though I usually tried to make sense of things my emotions took control most of the time and I let reason fly out the door. And on top of that, it was difficult not to let one's emotions control one's life when you had a mother who majored in "guilt trips." She could make the most pious person on earth feel guilty about not feeling guilty! But then there was Harmony. Harmony had the ability to change how people thought and what they remembered. That night when I got home from work my parents were both in bed and the next morning my mother was boasting to my father about a new and wonderful girl that I had met and become quite close to. And although my father had a strange expression on his face, because my mother never liked any of my girlfriends, he didn't let on like anything was really out of the ordinary. He simply congratulated me and hoped that it would all work out good for me.

All this telepathy stuff had started out as an unfathomable riddle to me, but it was slowly starting to sink in and I was slowly starting to really believe that I was chosen by Harmony to some day join her on the "other side," whatever that was. Heck, I thought I was ready right then, but that was no doubt those raging hormones again as I began imagining what it would be like to be intimate with the hottest girl at KSHS.

Harmony and I met up in study hall and actually sat together without Mrs. Tinmoor ever saying one word about it. *Did you "fix" Mrs. Tinmoor, Harmony?*

Let's just say that she won't be getting on our case anymore, James. From now on she will barely notice if we are here or not. And, by the way, I have a much better body than what you imagined earlier.

Blushing a bright crimson red, I tried to not think about what Harmony had just said and instead replied, *You mean that we could actually sneak out without really having to sneak?*

If we wanted to do that all we would have to do is get up and tell her that we will see her tomorrow as we walked right past her and through the front door. However, it is not a good idea to control everyone's

thoughts and actions all of the time and thus we need to play along as if everything was normal. By the way, that color red looks fabulous on you.

Thanks! So we just show up in study hall everyday like everything is perfectly normal?

Right, James. And we should actually talk to one another once in a while when we are in public where others can actually hear us.

"Well, there's the bell. Ready to head out of here, Harmony?" I asked in my normal voice and hoping that my embarrassment was beginning to fade away from my face.

"Sure thing, James," Harmony replied. "I need to get home and get started on my homework. I have a lot of homework to do tonight."

"Yeah, and I've got to go get ready for another long night at the service station." At that we got up, I took Harmony's books and she took my arm and we casually strolled out the door and headed for the parking lot where my cool chariot awaited us.

Chapter Nine

Remember how I thought a while back that I didn't think there could be any obstacle that could stand in my way now that I was "with" Harmony. We have already seen how not much had changed when a couple of different scenarios popped up and how Harmony jumped in, or thought in, and took care of them for me. Well, just because she could take care of things most of the time when trouble seemed to find me didn't mean that bad, strange, and complicated situations wouldn't still pop up in my meager little human life.

There was a girl at school who was probably seventeen or eighteen, but going on thirty-five, who was so well endowed that even the two guys who didn't like girls would stop and gawk when she sashayed down the hallways or walkways with her ample hips swaying from one side to the other. Every guy at school, including all of the male teachers, and even a few of the female teachers, would stop dead in their tracks and gawk and drool and then stumble over their own two feet when Holiday had passed by with her breasts sticking out further than that famous blond country singer that my mom liked to listen to all the time. Yes, her given name was actually Holiday and her claim to fame was that "you had never been on a holiday until you had been on her." No one really knew why she was named that and not even Harmony could dig it out of the deep, dark recesses of Holiday's mind or the chasm between her breasts. Holiday had never paid two cents worth of attention to me before, but when she found out that Harmony had taken an interest in me she decided to see how loyal I actually was to Harmony. Breaking up relationships in high school was what Holiday seemed to live for and I knew of at least five couples who were no longer couples because of her wiles. Girls just didn't seem to understand that guys liked to gawk at women with ample breasts.

I was standing outside between classes, leaning up against the brick wall just outside the boys restrooms, talking with a couple of my buddies when up waddled Holiday being preceded by her ample breasts. Actually, she wasn't just waddling. It was more like she was slithering up to my buddies and me. As she slithered up to me all three of our mouths dropped open and the drool started to flow, especially off my two buddies lower lips that were now almost resting on their shoe tops. Their eyes were about to pop right out of their sockets and they had to hold their lower lips in their hands to keep them from scraping on the sidewalk. Holiday must have had the fullest lips on the planet and they were covered in the reddest lipstick made by any cosmetics company. She had dark, deep eyes that would scare off a Cobra and her fingernails matched the color of those exquisite full lips and to top it off, her hair was puffed out in the latest fashionable hairstyle for the most expensive whores. She was being especially brazen that day by wearing one of the shortest mini skirts I had ever seen and it also matched the color of her exquisite full lips. She was the only girl in school who could get away with wearing mini skirts to school and I learned later that Mr. Smith had to sweet-talk Miss Dutrip an awful lot so that Holiday could wear short skirts. As the story goes, both Holiday and her mother paraded into Mr. Smith's office one day both wearing mini skirts and demanding that Holiday be allowed to wear her new mini skirts to school whenever she felt like it, which was almost every day. It seems that Holiday had special ordered her mini skirts from a shop in London called "Bazaar," and because they were special mini skirts, Holiday wanted permission to wear them, which Mr. Smith granted while being treated to a double up-skirt exhibition. Did I mention that Holiday had exquisite full lips? And the way that tight red mini skirt seemed to literally crawl across back and forth across her ample hips, from one side to the other, was simply mesmerizing. Pushing my two buddies aside, first Hubie and then Ronaldo, Holiday put her hands on her hips and leaned up against the wall next to me and turned toward me so that her entire body from the hips up was thrust in my direction, especially those two torpedoes that were always getting to her destination before she did.

To say that I was speechless was an understatement, mainly because there was too much drool running down my chin and the fact that I was scared witless when around females who looked like Holiday. If someone had asked me my name at that moment I could not have told them what it was. "Hi, Jamesy Wamesy," Holiday purred. "I hear you think you have a hot new girlfriend. Funny, I don't remember you telling me that I was your new girlfriend, especially since no other bitch at this school is half as hot as me."

The only response I could utter was, "Uh, uh, uh, uh," especially since those torpedoes and her ample hipbone were now pressing into various parts of my anatomy as she had turned to face me at very close range. All of a sudden there was a well-endowed, slithering, slutty-looking snake in my little paradise tempting me with her wiles.

At that precise moment, who walked up but none other than Harmony? There was a gravity in her manner and a quiet so profound that the whole world seemed to stop and turn colder than the inside of my neighbors ice truck. My buddies had now closed their mouths, although the drool still flowed freely from the corners of their mouths, but Harmony's arrival had made them literally freeze where they stood. I wasn't sure whether anything on my body was moving or not, because I felt like a stone statue in the local cemetery, but nonetheless, I could see what was taking place. Holiday had turned to face Harmony, but as soon as she did she too froze in place and couldn't even jiggle her breasts or shake her butt. Harmony reached forward, touched Holiday on the head for about 30 seconds and then stepped back, turned and walked away as quietly as she had arrived. As soon as Harmony was out of sight everything seemed to gradually warm up and return to normal except for what happened next. Remember Mr. Smith's secretary, Mrs. Anskye? Well, she was walking up about that time and asked us all why we weren't on our way to our classes. Holiday gazed at Mrs. Anskye, stuck her tongue out at her, and started stripping off all of her clothes right there in front of all of us, not that there was much to strip off. When she had removed her three pieces of clothing and was completely naked, Holiday grabbed Mrs. Anskye and gave her a big hug smashing Mrs. Anskye's less-endowed chest pretty flat, kissed her square on the mouth, and then skipped off down the sidewalk in her red spike heels with those more than ample breasts bouncing this way and swinging that way and her more than ample buttocks bouncing up and down. I looked over at Hubie and Ronaldo, but their eyes were glued to Holiday's butt and were swaying and bouncing right along with her.

Mrs. Tinmoor had witnessed most of what had happened and came running down the sidewalk with a blanket to wrap around Holiday and then led her off to Miss Dutrip's office. Mrs. Tinmoor never said one word to either Harmony or me about what she had seen take place out on the sidewalk that day, although Harmony later told me that Mrs. Tinmoor was now conditioned to only see the good in everything that Harmony or I did. Mrs. Anskye was so horrified by the naked Holiday grabbing, hugging, and kissing her that she had run straight back to Mr. Smith's office, parked her big butt in her office chair, and pretended to have been working the whole time, nor did Mrs. Tinmoor ever mention Mrs. Anskye's name in the matter. Harmony later asked me if I had "felt" anything for Holiday when she had come up to me like that. In all honesty I was too dumbfounded by the situation to have felt anything and I told Harmony just that. She told me that was the truth and she now loved me more than ever. It seems that I had passed an important test, supposedly not arranged by Harmony or anyone from her side, but simply by fate. Harmony said that fate would always be around to throw us curves, but that one of the most important lessons to be learned from her was how to handle those situations, especially when they involved other women. Knowing my penchant for attractive, ample breasted females, I could only hope that I could live up to her expectations.

Chapter Ten

Harmony and I didn't communicate much either out loud or telepathically on the way home after school that day. I pulled up to her house and she bent over, hesitated a split second, her expression hovering somewhere between disappointment and anger, gave me a little peck on the cheek, said she still loved me and would see me the next morning if all went well that evening. I started to ask her what that meant, but I just reiterated those sentiments and reached to pull her closer for a better kiss, but she dodged my reach and got out of the car and hurried up the sidewalk toward her front door. She stopped about half way and turned around staring at me with unflinching eyes and an insouciant look on her face. At first I thought that she was just checking to see if I was watching her, but then her smile widened and she thought, *I trust you with my whole heart, James, and love you more than you will ever know.* Her smile left her face and then she turned and went inside.

My mind went vacant as an erased blackboard before an algebra test and my heart felt like it was leaping over the tallest building and pumping faster than a speeding bullet (I watched a lot of Superman growing up), and Harmony's words seemed to be singing like Patsy Cline through my very soul. However, Harmony's expression and her seemingly fake smile when she looked back at me gave me second thoughts about our relationship. My past girlfriends had said "I love you" many times, but never had I ever felt those words were more than just empty talk. Harmony's words, I now knew for sure, or at least I thought I did, were true and that she was the only person I could trust completely. But, if that was true, then why was my little mind having doubts about her honesty. *Harmony, I feel like I've waited all my life to not just hear those words, but to feel them and know that they are true.* I'm glad that I didn't look in my rearview mirror at that moment because I'm sure my expression was more moonstruck than a teenage girl swooning over The Beatles. I sat there in my car for several minutes staring at Harmony's front door with the sun bouncing off the beautiful colors of the stained-glass, my gut tight with the anticipation of what would be next for us and my imagination racing wildly ahead to that wonderful day when our love for each other would be consummated. But, was all that really going to happen?

Coming out of my momentary lapse into fantasy land, I looked at my Timex watch with the simulated brown leather band and realized that I had to be at work in less than 30 minutes, so I sped off to my house to get changed into my uniform and head for work. By the time I got home I realized that I didn't have time to change into my Star uniform and get to work on time so I just ran in the house, grabbed my uniform, and peeled off down the street leaving two dark streaks of rubber on the pavement in front of our house. Say what you will about my 1965 Plymouth Barracuda, but that little 273 cubic inch V8 was pretty fast when I needed it to be. I whipped into a parking space at the station with five minutes to spare and yelled at my father that I was simply running a little late and would be changed and ready for work in a jiffy. I slammed the storeroom door shut behind me so that I could change clothes without being ribbed by the other help because I was so skinny. When I came out of the storeroom I was still tucking my white uniform shirt into my blue work pants while starting to explain to my father why I was running late, but he held up his hand and said, "No explanation needed, son. I was young and in love once myself."

"Thanks for understanding," I replied and hurried out the door and across the driveway to wait on the next customer. If you have ever worked in a gas station or service station you know how the smell of gas and oil and exhaust smoke permeates into every pore of your skin and every fiber of your clothes. Harmony had never said anything about this, but most people could tell you what you did for a living before even asking you. "Gas station jockey are you?" "Must have done a lot of work under the hood today." "Did you take a bath in exhaust fumes?" I would usually just laugh at their little harmless barbs and go about my business as usual. When any of my buddies, who were either bagging groceries at a local grocery store or flipping hamburgers under the golden arches, made these jokes I would simply ask them how much money they made the last week. They usually only got 15-20 hours a week through the after school job program and even at minimum wage 20 hours per week only paid them $23.00. I had to work eight-hour shifts at the station six days a week, but I got $1.25 per hour and time and a half for the extra eight hours earning me $65.00 per week. Of course, I didn't have much of a social life, which my so-called buddies also ribbed me about, but Harmony and I weren't officially dating yet, just seeing each other at school. Harmony and I had talked about that situation and agreed that we would get together on my one night off from work and make up for lost time together. She told me that my "training" wasn't contingent on us being together all the time, but I was hoping that our one night per week together would involve more than training. When my buddies would tease me about not being able to go out more than one night a week I would throw it back in their face and say, "Hey, but my one night a week is with Harmony!" And that brought those conversations to a close.

Well, it seemed like that particular night at work was going to be the usual boring drudgery of pumping gas, checking oil, washing windshields, checking tires, and selling cigarettes when a shiny black 1949 Mercury lead sled, with red and yellow flames painted on the front fenders and across the hood, roared into the station and came to a screeching halt at the farthest island from the front door. I had never seen a '49 Merc lead sled like this one before outside the pages of car magazines and this one was better looking than most of those and sounded like low continuous thunder while the engine was idling. The original engine was a hot flathead eight and Sam Barris built the first lead sled from one of these '49 Mercs back in 1949. Being the closest to those gas pumps, I walked out to the car all glassy eyed and in awe of the magnificent machine sitting before me. The driver hung out the window with his arm draped down the outside of where the door used to be (it was now one smooth surface and entry and exit was through the window) and told me to, "Fill 'er up, punk and make it snappy!" That wasn't the first time I had ever heard that remark since several groups of hoods (called gangs now) often came into the station for gas and cigarettes. Although most of these guys were tattooed from one end to the other and had muscles bulging out of places there weren't supposed to be muscles, they were relatively harmless and just liked to josh around with "normal" folks like me. They seemed to get a bigger kick out of acting tough around people they thought were no danger to them than causing any trouble. "And don't spill no gas on my car, punk, or I'll kick your scrawny butt into the next county!" the driver yelled after me as I walked around the car to put gas in it.

"Yes, sir," I replied and saluted him behind his back while he and his buddies laughed it up inside the Merc. There were three others in the car with him and all looked like they could have been brothers: dressed in the same white tee shirts with the sleeves rolled up on one side to hold their smokes, usually Lucky Strikes (L.S.M.F.T. – Lucky Strike Means Fine Tobacco), with a book of matches stuck between the plastic wrapper and the pack; same slicked down haircuts with a tightly greased up swatch of dyed black hair hanging across their foreheads; dark shades hanging on the front of their tee shirts; and their tight blue jean cuffs rolled up to expose their white socks and black shoes.

The driver said something that I couldn't hear to the hood on the front passenger side and he climbed out through the side window and walked back toward me. I noticed that the other three had turned around and were intently watching him with big jackass grins on their faces that showed their dirty, smoke-stained teeth. When he got back to me he bent over and closely examined the area around the gas filler cap and exclaimed rather loudly while looking back at the others in the car, "You stupid little jerk, you spilled a drop of gas on Johnny's car! He's going to beat you into a pile of pulp, roll you up in a cig paper and smoke you, you stupid little turd!"

Well, that was obviously Johnny's cue to climb out and casually stroll back to where we were standing with his thumbs hooked into the front pockets of his tight jeans. When he walked up to me, he bumped me aside with his elbow to take his turn at trying to scare the living daylights (or nightlights if you prefer) out of me. Without unhooking his thumbs, Johnny bent over and took a close look at where the other guy was pointing, stood up and gave me that "you're ass is grass" look, leaned over in my direction, and with his face in mine said in a low, yet menacing voice, "When was the last time you had your scrawny ass whupped, turd face?"

You don't have to take that, James.

Harmony?

You have the power, James. Use it to protect yourself. You do not deserve to be humiliated by anyone, especially jerks like that.

I'm not sure what came over me at that moment or if I was acting on my own or was inspired by Harmony's words, but I leaned back toward him forcing him to lean back and looked Johnny square in his bloodshot eyes and replied, "And you? When was the last time you had your ass 'whupped', Nancy?" I turned toward the other guy standing outside and raised my eyebrows while giving him the same questioning look. He turned around immediately without answering and climbed back in the 'Merc. The two guys in the back seat were watching wide eyed as Johnny just stood there staring at me.

"Well," he said taking his thumbs out of his pockets and holding them out to the side with the palms up, "I ain't never had my ass whupped before because I ain't never been in a real fight. Uh, how much do I owe you, little buddy?" I told him as I finished pumping the gas, hung up the nozzle on the gas pump, and then turned around, brushed past him, and pretended to wipe away the drop of gas that I had supposedly spilled on his precious car. He dug some bills out of his pocket and gave me the correct amount and turned to get back in his car.

"Johnny," I called after him. "Do you want your oil and tires checked tonight?"

He turned back toward me and politely said, "No, not this time, little buddy. Thanks anyway. And thanks for wiping that gas off my ride." He then climbed back in the Merc, cranked it up, revved the engine just a little and pulled out of the station driving like a very respectable old man in a 1954 Nash Metropolitan with a 1,200 cc (73 cubic inches) engine. I would often wait on Johnny and his crew after that and they were always extremely polite and courteous toward me.

Harmony, did you help me with that?

No, James. You were entirely on your own that time. I just needed to let you know that you had nothing to be afraid of with them or anybody else. You did fine. See you tomorrow. Love you.

Love you, too. And I was tuned out.

Chapter Eleven

The next couple of weeks at school went extraordinarily smooth and the entire high school now knew that Harmony and I were an item. We were constantly seen together between classes, at lunch, and especially during study hall where Mrs. Tinmoor now left us alone and kept all the other students in their place where Harmony and I were concerned. I picked Harmony up at her rather extravagant house every morning and took her home every afternoon after school before heading off to work. We had fallen into a definite routine of boyfriend/girlfriend activity Monday through Friday from the time I picked her up until I dropped her off after school. When around others we tended to talk out loud about the normal high school things that kids talked about in those days: classes, cars, dating, homework, overprotective parents, etc. But when necessary we communicated telepathically and Harmony was continually "updating" my mind and teaching me more and more about the ways of the beings on her side. My telepathic abilities and my knowledge of her kind were both growing at an astounding rate, or at least it seemed that way to me.

One day late in that second week of "normalcy" at school I had been thinking about all the strange things that I had dreamed about three years earlier: Monica, Mrs. Root Beer Lady, the old man, Mrs. Chyspo, my best buddy Roger Maleway, and especially the reptilian alien things. I was leaning back in my desk in my American History class staring up at the ceiling alternating between counting the tiles over our new American History teacher's desk and daydreaming about the summer of 1963. Mr. Kycran had been replaced by a very attractive, some of the guys even said "hot," recent local college graduate, Miss Porcoe. Just as I was getting ready to contact Harmony about 1963 my eyes roamed down toward Miss Porcoe's desk and were caught by her big dark brown, almost black, and I would swear slitted, eyes staring straight at me. She had a very insightful smile on her face as if she knew what I had just been thinking and she just kept staring at me. The harder I tried to look away the more hypnotizing and penetrating her dark, snake-like stare seemed to become.

Harmony! Help! was all I could get out into the wide blue yonder hoping that Harmony was tuned in to my thoughts.

She can't help you this time, Ja-James, because I've blocked the little bitch from reading your thoughts.

Harmony! my mind nearly screamed.

Give it up my little juicy friend! She won't come to your rescue ever again. She's just a teasing little whore from the other side who has been playing tricks on you and having fun with your little pea brain that is no doubt the tastiest part of your entire skinny little body. I would much prefer a fatter specimen, but I have been sent to eliminate you. Just my luck!

At that thought I felt like I was literally pushed out of my desk and landed hard on my skinny little butt on the hardwood floor. That drew the attention of all the other students and they started laughing thinking that I had probably fallen asleep and fell over on the floor.

Who do you believe now, Ja-James?

Is that you, Monica?

Surely you jest, little boy! That incompetent, ugly lizard was chopped up and eaten in a delicious salad that was served at the last great gathering of my kind.

Too bad we couldn't have topped the salad off with croutons carved from your bones. Never-the-less, she was a rather tasty treat!

Unable to break away from Miss Porcoe's deep, dark hypnotic stare, I literally moaned out loud, "Harmony." What happened next I still sometimes have nightmares about over 40 years later. All of a sudden I heard the harsh, jarring sounds of heads slamming hard down against the tops of wooden desks and when I stood up and looked around me all of my classmates appeared to be sound asleep at their desks. I looked quickly toward Miss Porcoe's desk and saw her floating horizontally above her desk and flailing wildly with her arms like she was drowning or trying to fly away. My first thought was that she was preparing to swoop down on me and that this was my final moment on earth. Funny thing was that my brief time on earth didn't flash before my eyes, probably just another myth perpetrated by adults to scare children.

"Help me Ja-James, that bitch Harmony is trying to kill me!" came spurting out of Miss Porcoe's mouth along with long strings of green slimy spittle that trailed all the way down to the top of her desk. Then, suddenly, Miss Porcoe's body was slammed face first down against the top of her desk and then she rose again just to be slammed down again and again and again until she lay in a bloody heap on top of the desk with her unrecognizable face dangling over the side.

I was in such a daze that initially I couldn't produce a cognizant thought, but then I thought, *Harmony, did you do that?*

I'm so sorry, James. If we had known that the Freyfacs were back on earth we would have dealt with them much sooner. Somehow they snuck back and since you are our newest recruit they logically came after you in the guise of your new history teacher. The Freyfacs are such masters at what hu-

mans call espionage that we can't always sense their presence.

Freyfacs? Back on earth? Recruit? Espionage? What is all of this about, Harmony? Are you trying to tell me that the summer of 1963 wasn't a dream? I don't know if I can deal with that or not.

Once again, I'm sorry, James, for not bringing that up sooner. We were actually hoping that it wouldn't be necessary to talk about that at all, especially knowing how it would upset you.

Were you around then, Harmony?

No, but even if I had been there wouldn't have been anything I could have done at that young age.

That was only three years ago, Harmony. If we are the same age now, you would have been fourteen as well.

That is true, James, but you will find this out when you cross over anyway, so I might as well tell you now. We don't age in the same way as humans age. We live up to four times longer than humans. I was the same age as you when those things were happening to you, but I didn't know then that you were the one that I would choose and my abilities had not yet developed to a point where I could have helped you anyway.

So, you are saying that on your side people can live to be as much as 400 years old?

That is correct, James.

That is correct, James. That's it?

The other main difference in the way we age and the way humans age is that we don't show the signs of aging as rapidly. We age about the same as humans until we are 16 years old and then our aging process slows down considerably. After you have crossed over your aging process will also slow down, so that when we are 100 years old we will only look about 25 years old by human standards of aging.

Are you allowed to tell me when my crossover might happen, Harmony?

The Elders are hoping to wait until you have reached your twentieth birthday. I must also tell you now that crossing over will not be the most comfortable experience that you will ever go through. The physiological change that happens to slow down your aging process will be very painful, but the good news is that it only lasts for a short time and when it is over you will still feel and look like you are twenty years old. Do you think that you will mind going through that for me, dear James?

Harmony, I know I won't have any problem with that as long as you promise me that it's you I will be with when I cross over to your side.

You say the sweetest things, James. Yes, it will be me and it will be forever.

It was strange, but I could have sworn on two stacks of Bibles that her response sounded "cold." No problem then. Oh crap, I forgot all about American History class! *Are the other students ok?*

Yes, they will wake up shortly and not remember any of this and you will not tell them anything about what has transpired. Do you understand that, James?

For some reason I had walked over by the window looking out toward the baseball field and hadn't been paying any attention to the awful mess on the teacher's desk, but when I turned around and looked over in that direction there wasn't any mess. It was if nothing had happened and there had never been a Miss Porcoe.

Uh, Harmony, what happened to Miss Porcoe? I felt a chill run up and down my spine as I thought about Harmony's last words to me.

While we were talking the Cleaners came in and cleaned it up. I apologize again, James, but I was told to keep your mind and eyes occupied while they were

taking care of business. There will be no trace of the Freyfac anywhere in the room or on campus.

By the way, Harmony, thanks for saving my butt again. I didn't ask who the Cleaners were and Harmony didn't offer. I figured I would find that out someday after I had crossed over and, who knows, I might not want to know who they were.

I will always be there for you and you for me as long as you never believe the lies that any others might tell you about me on your side or on my side. Although what just happened here at school in your History class wasn't planned by us, it was nonetheless a test of your trust and faith in me, James.

I will make you that promise from the deepest depths of my heart and mind, but please don't be disappointed in me if, on occasion, my human traits try to come out. I have always adapted to whatever situation presented itself to me, but not knowing yet what to really expect on your side, I can't say that I will be as adaptable.

Once you cross over that probably will not be a problem. Although our ways are very similar to yours, there are some differences that you will be required to accept and adapt to. I have to go now, James, but I will see you later in study hall. Now go back to your seat and pretend along with the other students that Miss Porcoe just up and walked out never to be seen again. Love you.

Love you, too, Harmony. And there I was sitting at my desk watching everyone else wake up and stare around like nothing had happened. It wouldn't be hard to pretend that nothing had happened, because no one would believe me anyway. Just that crazy kid, James, making up his silly ideas again and trying to get people to believe him.

Chapter Twelve

I had lots of questions for Harmony, including why she had talked to me like a little child, but would wait until study hall that day to ask them. Even if she wouldn't, or couldn't, answer them now, I was sure that I would learn the answers to all of my questions in due time. Right then I was concerned, if not scared out of my skin, about these "Freyfacs" and if they were the ones after me back in 1963, since I now knew that I had not actually been dreaming what happened back then. Harmony had told me about these "Freyfacs," but she had cleverly skirted the issue of the summer of 1963 when I brought it up. *Ok, sweet cheeks,* I thought, as one of my buddies would say, *You got some 'splainin to do.*

Not to worry, James, I will 'splain everything in due time. Do not get your bowels in an uproar!

Harmony? I still don't think it is fair that you can read my mind anytime you want and I can't read yours and your tone today has been a little patronizing!

Settle down, James. You will be able to do just that after you cross over and we have entered into a connubial state! I don't mean to sound patronizing, but you do not always seem to understand what I am trying to tell you.

"Connubial state? What's a connubial state? Sounds kind of like a place where people eat other people."

You really do need to work on your vocabulary, James! Connubial means married, silly.

Yeh, I know I'm not the brightest bulb in the pack. Married, huh?

Yes, James, married! Now, I have got to go so I will see you in study hall.

Later, Harmony.

"Connubial state." I should use that on the guys. After all, their knowledge of vocabulary was probably worse than mine. Most of the "vocabulary" we used centered around cars, girls, and sex. "How many horses you pulling out that thing?" "Can you lay down any rubber with that ride?" Did you see the rack on that babe?" Now that is one hot-looking ass!" "You get any at the submarine races down by the lake last night?" "I hear she'll do 'anything' if you get her drunk." "Hey, dude, check out my new wheels." "That ride's a babe magnet if there ever was one!"

Human Boys! You have definitely got to find some new friends, James! I heard in my head from Harmony.

I knew a response or explanation would have been futile, so I just kept thinking about the conversation that had just taken place between Harmony and me. Now, you have to understand that the guys I hung around with in high school liked to talk big, especially about their supposed "conquests." At the time, I would have bet a week's salary that, at seventeen, we were all just dreaming about "making it" with any girl. Yes, they all probably really did have a girlfriend or at least had had a girlfriend at some point in high school or, like me, even earlier in junior high school. However, I mostly just listened to their stories of conquest knowing full well that it was mostly a bunch of bull poopy and that not bragging usually made the other guys think that you were "getting some." Before Harmony "claimed" me, I dreamed of going steady with the best-looking girl in school, but for the most part I was still very shy around girls and rarely asked anyone out on a date for fear of rejection; a fear that I developed after being rejected more than once. Girls just didn't seem interested in me, that is, until Harmony came along, but now I could have gone out with the entire cheerleading squad if I wanted to, because Harmony being interested in me made other girls sit up and take notice. I would have never guessed that my wildest dream of "being an item" with the most beautiful girl in school would ever come true, nor would my buddies have ever believed me if they hadn't actually seen Harmony and me together at school. A couple of my buddies even accused me of bribing Harmony to pretend that she liked me and that we were going steady. If I had had enough money to bribe someone, I would have probably attracted a few more girls at school, since the wealthier boys never seemed to be without girlfriends or dates.

When I got to study hall that day I sauntered over to where Harmony was sitting and sat down across from her at the table to keep Mrs. Tinmoor out of our hair. Every eye in study hall was on us, but Harmony and I just looked at each other and smiled which I'm sure only intrigued everyone even more. Harmony must have worked her magic on Mrs. Tinmoor's mind because after I sat down Mrs. Tinmoor exclaimed to the rest of study hall, "What are you youngins looking at? Haven't you ever seen a cute young couple in love before?" At that the rest of the students in study hall started to giggle, but Mrs. Tinmoor came to the rescue again, "That will be enough of that! Now shush and at least pretend you're working on your homework or I'll send the bunch of you to the principal's office."

You've trained Mrs. Tinmoor well, Harmony.

You will learn in time that it isn't difficult to control other people's minds and make it appear that they are on your side. It isn't hurting Mrs. Tinmoor in the least to be nice to us.

Don't you think that the other students will think that we are the teacher's pets?

James, James, James! Think about what you just said. You can be so incompetent! After a couple of minutes had passed and I was doing my best to try and figure out what Harmony was talking about and beginning to stew a little bit about her patronizing remarks, she said, ***Well?***

I'm trying to figure out what you're trying to tell me, but sitting here engrossed in your beauty makes it difficult to think about anything else, Harmony.

If I didn't know that you really meant that I might just slap you silly! Well, have you figured it out yet, James?

Oh, wait! You've got the rest of the students in study hall under control as well.

Bingo, Mr. Brilliance! And not just in study hall.

Are you telling me that all the students in school are under your mental control, Harmony?

You can be so exasperating, James! Not just the students, but the faculty and staff as well. From now on, we will not be having any more problems with anyone here at school. That is, unless some more Freyfacs or RATs try to get to you while you are here at school. God forbid that happens, because I certainly don't feel like dealing with them anymore!

Ok, we need to talk more about these "Freyfacs." And what are "RATs," besides those ugly little furry things that crawl around on the floor?

You named them, James. We just abbreviated it. RATs stands for reptilian alien things.

Duh! Stupid me.

Duh! Another thing you are going to have to overcome, James, before you can cross over to my side is your inferiority complex. Remember, you are my chosen one and that alone among humans makes

you far superior to all other humans who have not been chosen, or least I hope so.

Thanks, Harmony, I think. I tend to forget that aspect of our relationship, such as it is. I still get caught up in the fact that I'm going with the most beautiful girl in school even if she's from another world.

Thank you for the compliment, James.

Ok, so what about the "Freyfacs, Harmony?"

God, father never told me I would have to provide an entire education to the chosen one! The Freyfacs, James, first came to Earth about 500 earth years after my kind arrived. We thought we had eliminated them completely and had established an agreement with their kind that they would never invade Earth again, that this was our domain.

Came to earth? From where might I ask?

You will learn all this eventually, James, so I might as well let you in on some of it now. The Freyfacs are from a part of what you call the Milky Way some 1.3 quadrillion earth miles away from this disgustingly backward planet you call Earth. It was very surprising to my kind that they are trying to invade Earth once again when one appeared in your History class to abduct you.

Because of an agreement that's thousands of years old, they weren't supposed to come back to earth? And why are you so down on earth when it's where you have to spend your life?

Unlike Earthlings, the beings in all other parts of what you call the universe never break agreements among themselves. It has been that way for longer than you can possibly imagine. For one of them to show up now on Earth suggests to us that there might be some renegades who are trying to do evil on other worlds, such as Earth. The Elders are looking into this and we shouldn't be bothered anymore by the Freyfacs. And, for the record, James, if I had not

been born here I would not have ever agreed to being sent here. Unfortunately, my kind are stuck here on this planet forever.

Ok, so you don't especially like my planet. How about the "RATs," Harmony?

The RATs, who are actually known in the universe as Thokiths, have been a nemesis to the entire universe since the beginning of time. After their discovery of and invasion of Earth in 1963 all of the other populations of the universe held a tribunal and voted to exile them to the Messier Galaxy which is 12 million light years away from Earth and where they will be dealt with severely if they don't behave themselves.

Are there people on Earth who know about all of this and who were involved with the decision to exile them?

There isn't a good way to say this, James, but it will take Earthlings another 10,000 earth years to evolve to even the intelligence level of the lowest of species outside of earth and be permitted a voice in the tribunals.

Well, nothing like living on the dumbest planet in the universe! By the way, you have always said "your kind." Is there a particular name for "your kind," Harmony?

We are known in the universe as Voreshas, James.

I kind of like that name. Will I be a Voresha when I cross over, Harmony?

On Earth, James, when someone from one country moves to another country they are considered an "alien" in their new country. It is much the same way throughout the universe. When someone from one species crosses over to another species they are viewed in a similar manner.

So, I would be an "alien" Voresha? Doesn't sound very appealing to me when you put it that way, Harmony.

That was the best way that I could describe it so that you would understand, James. It is never considered a bad thing, especially on our side, because Earthlings are very carefully chosen and, besides, your species is the only one in the entire universe that female Voreshas can mate with.

It may take me a little while to get over being considered by you as belonging to the dumbest species in the universe, Harmony. So, besides male Voreshas, females of your kind can only mate with human males. That must be a real disappointment for you.

We are definitely going to have to work on your self-respect, James. If you will remember, all the surviving males on my side are far too old to mate with, just the thought makes my skin crawl, thus, in order for us to exist, we have to live on Earth and hope to find suitable males here, like you. And although that is not the most desirable situation to be put in, it is what Voresha females have to accept as our destiny.

I think I may be finding out more than my little pea sized brain wants to know or is capable of keeping a secret, Harmony, but, as promised, I will not spill the beans about you and your kind or any of these other strange beings and happenings.

Not keeping secrets is a deplorable characteristic of humans, James. That is why, as you will soon discover, I have had to "program" you not to be able to disclose our little "secret."

Thanks, I think. Just call me Robot James from now on.

It's the best thing for both you and my side, James, and don't think of it that way.

"Well, James, there's the bell for school to be over for the day," Harmony announced to me loud enough for all to hear. "Are you ready to take me home?"

"You bet," I said excitedly forgetting that I had to drop Harmony off at her house and then head off to work at the gas station. We walked arm in arm out to the parking lot and my car. As usual I played the perfect gentleman, as I had been taught, and opened the passenger side door for Harmony and then got in on my side. Before I met Harmony I hadn't thought that there was much wrong with my 1965 Plymouth Barracuda. However, now that we were close and I was driving her back and forth to school every day I realized that the console between the seats in the front kept Harmony from sitting next to me. I was going to have to give some serious consideration to a car that had a bench seat in front if you know what I mean.

"A bench seat would be nice, James," Harmony piped in right in the middle of that thought, "but I really do like your car and, besides, so does everyone else."

"Is that more important than you sitting next to me?" I asked.

"No, silly," she chided me. "But as a human male, and while you are still on your side, I know that it is important for you to think that all the other guys are jealous of you because of your car and that you are going steady with me."

"Ok," I admitted, "you're right about that. Not that it would do me any good to deny it. However, by most standards, the GTOs and '57 Chevy's are considered much 'hotter' than this Barracuda."

"You're catching on fast, James, and I still think your car is much more sexy than those other cars," Harmony cooed back at me in a very sexy voice. "Now, let's get me home and you to work."

WORK! All I could think about at that moment was Maynard G. Krebs from The Many Loves of Dobie Gillis and his deep aversion to that word. WORK!

Chapter Thirteen

One of the more intriguing things about working a four to midnight shift at a gas station in a seedy part of town was all of the interesting characters that came in for gas, oil, and cigarettes, especially after 9:00 p.m. That seemed to be the hour when all the most peculiar, odd, unusual, queer, extraordinary, abnormal, eccentric, outlandish, bizarre, and freakish human creatures creeping around on the face of the earth, assuming that they were human, emerged from wherever they had been hiding during the daylight hours to prowl the byways of our little central Florida town. Of course, these individuals weren't only indigenous to central Florida; they no doubt existed everywhere there was a sizable population. Back in 1963, my father had told me that we moved from Birmingham, Alabama, because of all the weirdoes that lived there. They brought with them into the Star gas station late at night both the enchanting and vulgar scents of the evening and all of the man-made shoddiness that you could possibly imagine. Even to this day some of those scents and images sometimes just burst into my mind, reminding me of hard work and good and bad times.

I would sometimes ask my father, who usually worked with me until 11:00 p.m. when the graveyard shift came in, about some of the more "interesting" characters who passed through the station late at night. Most of the time he would just give me that "mind your own business" look and then give me some chore to do around the station with the hopes of keeping my curious little mind occupied with more wholesome things. For the most part my father was a closed book when it came to talking to me about the more interesting aspects of life. His and my mother's approach to learning about the facts of life was basically a live and learn one and to mind your own business, or to put it another way, I would no doubt learn plenty from my perverted little friends, which I did.

Most of my "street" education came from my curiosity about everything from the more scientific aspects of how things worked to the seamier side of life. In those days before computers and the internet young people garnered the seamier type of information from their peers, magazines and books their parents would rather they didn't read, and often by associating with, as my parents put it, "the wrong crowd." Working those late nights at the gas station during my senior year of high school did provide me with quite an education about what most would have considered information not befitting a young man of seventeen. As I look back on that time I have come to believe that giving me that job was my father's way of teaching me about those things that he didn't have the courage to actually tell me about and that my mother thought I didn't need to know about.

For example, across the side street from the station was another aspect of nightlife that I had not been exposed to before working those late nights at the service station. There was a small, one-story, white painted cement block building whose front two-thirds was a drycleaners during the day. The drycleaners closed everyday promptly at 5:00 and the people who worked there, I assumed they were the owners, did not hang around for even a minute after closing. On occasion they would pull in to the station after closing to get a couple of dollars worth of gas (which was about eight gallons in those days) in their white 1960 Mercedes Benz four-door sedan (maybe I should go into the dry cleaning business) and then speed off down Memorial Boulevard. I had noticed that things usually started to pick up at the back of their building around 6:00, meaning that cars usually driven only by men and men on foot would start showing up at the back door of the building. The "traffic" was steady all night and there were always several men standing around outside all evening and whatever was going on over there continued, as the guys on the graveyard shift told me, long into the morning hours. I asked my father one night what exactly went on across the street (I naively suspected gambling) and once again he indicated that it didn't concern me and I was to never go over there and if he ever found out that I had been over there he would ground me for at least forty years. Now, my father wasn't a saint, but he did not believe that people should waste their money on gambling or, for that matter, on what was actually going on across the street. Well, the guys on the graveyard shift were less concerned about protecting me from the seamier side of life than was my father, so I asked them one night after my father had left about the "activity" that went on across the street every night.

"How old did you say you were, kid?" Jack, who was around my father's age, asked me when I posed the question to him and Arthur.

"Seventeen," I responded as if that was old enough to know about things that one's parents didn't want you to know about.

"You think that's old enough for the boy to know about what goes on over there?" Jack asked Arthur.

"Hell," replied Arthur who had to be at least seventy years old, "I was goin' to them there places at least by the time I was fifteen. I betcha this here boy's still a virgin!"

Jack chuckled at that and turned to me and simply said wide-eyed with his bushy, wooly worm eyebrows moving up and down and with a stupid grin on his face, "That there's a whorehouse, boy."

"Oh!" was all I could get out and started looking around for some chore to do to get out of that embarrassing conversation. Arthur slapped Jack on the back and they both had a good laugh at my ignorance about such things. It wasn't that I didn't know about "houses of ill repute" as I had heard the Baptist minister talk about in church sometimes, that is, when I had actually been going to church. It was that I had never seen an actual "whorehouse" before. Somehow I had this idea that such places were big, two-story, Victorian houses painted pink with red curtains and fancy antique furniture scattered around inside for the patrons to relax on while waiting their turn. This was no doubt probably something I had read in one of those books or magazines that I wasn't supposed to be reading. Actually, one night I even saw the minister go in over at the "whorehouse," but he was only there about 30 minutes. Initially I figured he was there to preach to those people about how they were all going to burn in eternal damnation if they didn't change their evil ways and repent. When I mentioned this one night to Jack and Arthur I thought they would bust a gut they laughed so hard. When they had settled down enough to speak, Jack told me that the man I referred to as a minister was a regular customer across the street and that if a man wasn't "getting any" at home that he had to look elsewhere, which was probably the case with the man I referred to as a minister. They also told me that they had seen other "men of the cloth," who were regular customers, frequenting the establishment across the street. Well, once again, that was more information than I either needed to know or wanted to know, but as my father would have said, "Life can be a real disappointment sometimes."

Then there were several cars, usually Lincolns or Cadillacs, that came into the station for gas and occasionally cigarettes that were painted strange color combinations with lots of shiny chrome and usually always had wide white sidewall tires and really fancy hub caps. The men driving them were usually dressed up so peculiarly that one would have thought they were going to a Halloween party. They usually had on bright colored coats and hats (often with feathers in the hats), frilly shirts, fancy patent leather shoes, often with gold buckles, that had to have been made in Italy, often carrying a gold-topped walking cane, and about three pounds of gold chains hanging around their necks and big diamond rings on at least four or five fingers. Most of the time there were two or three women in the car with them wearing some of the shortest skirts I have ever seen, exposing more cleavage than the Grand Canyon, and with enough make-up on to make a 50-year old cow elephant look good to a sober guy. When I questioned Jack and Arthur about this they once again cracked up and laughed for about five minutes at my ignorance. When they had settled down I said, "Well, you're just going to have to bear with me because my father won't talk to me about these things and my mother doesn't think I should know about such things."

"Ain't you never heard of pimps and prostitutes before?" Jack asked.

"Yes," I said rather matter of fact, "but I don't get out much working six nights a week at this place and I have never actually seen them before working here."

"Well, boy, we get some of the fanciest pants pimps I've ever seen through here late at night," Arthur informed me. "If you want to see some really weird get ups and some really duded up pimpmobiles, you'll have to stick around some night until around two or three o'clock."

"Yeh, I can see me sneaking in around that time at home," I replied like a typical seventeen-year old boy breaking curfew. "Not only would my mother be up waiting for me to give me the tongue-lashing of a life-time, but she'd probably have the biggest switch in the county in her hand waiting to beat 'the living day-lights' out of me for keeping her up worrying about me!" Once again, Jack and Arthur cracked up and this time were still chucking about it when I got off work at midnight. Isn't education about real life a wonderful, if not humorous, thing!

Chapter Fourteen

The next morning when I went by to pick up Harmony at her house she ran down the sidewalk and jumped in the car, gave me a quick kiss, and leaned back against the passenger side door grinning from ear to ear. She was wearing one of the shortest skirts that I had ever seen her wear when we were together or, for that matter, that I had ever seen her wear at school. When I glanced down at her bare legs she giggled a little more and I noticed that she seemed to be watching me especially close that morning as we drove toward school. "What?" I asked in a rather irritated tone as it appeared that she, too, was laughing at me.

"You got quite an education last night, James," Harmony answered somewhat flirtatiously and turned toward me even more.

"I was hoping you didn't have me tuned in during that little conversation with Jack and Arthur," I replied and couldn't help noticing that her skirt had risen up a little more. "It was especially embarrassing around those two guys," as I couldn't keep my eyes off her gorgeous gams.

"First, big boy, keep your eyes on the road and second, I wouldn't have missed that conversation for anything," she managed to get out before starting giggling again.

"Ok," I said defensively, "so I'm not the brightest bulb in the pack, but I'm very shy and have been somewhat sheltered from those kinds of things all my life. If my mother caught wind of that conversation she wouldn't let me work there anymore, and, besides, how is a guy supposed to learn about those things when his parents treat him like a celibate Buddhist monk?"

"Would it be so bad not working at the service station, James?" she asked when she had composed herself some.

"Well, I'd probably have to get a job at the grocery store bagging groceries like some of my friends and that certainly wouldn't pay as much," I said once again sounding defensive.

We rode along in silence for a few minutes before Harmony said, "I know that your parents struggle to pay their bills and that they are good hard-working folks," she said sounding somewhat sarcastic, "but can't they help their baby boy out just a little, at least with gas for this so-called car?"

"What? That isn't exactly how they see it, Harmony," I answered almost ashamedly and wondering what had gotten into her. "They've had to work hard all their lives for basically nothing more than a roof over their heads and food on the table. They don't have enough education to get cushy high paying jobs like your father has, so I have to work to help out, especially if I want to have this 'so-called car'."

"What will you do when you go off to art school in Sarasota next year?" she asked matter of fact.

"You tell me. You're the mind reader," I said with a tinge of anger in my voice.

"I can read minds, not tell the future," Harmony responded coldly.

We rode the rest of the way to school in a very icy silence. I thought about our conversation the rest of the way to school and by the time I had parked my "so-called car," I realized that my stupid male ego had risen to the surface and shone brightly. Not saying anything, Harmony started to get out of the car without waiting for me to get out and open her door. I reached over and grabbed her arm as gently as I could to pull her back. Turning around quickly she yelled at me, "WHAT?"

"Harmony, I'm sorry," I said in my meekest apologetic voice. "You know that I didn't mean to get mad at you. It was just my stupid, male ego talking. Please don't be mad at me," I pleaded.

Her icy stare melted away and those eyes that could entrance me without trying began to tear up. "Oh, James," she said as the tears began to flow freely, "I don't know what came over me either." I took my handkerchief out of my back pocket and dabbed at her tears. "You know it isn't like me to get angry with you. I should be the one asking for forgiveness." At that we gave each other a big hug, kissed, and I went around the car to help her out. No one who saw us walking onto campus hand in hand that morning had the slightest clue as to what had just happened between Harmony and me. What had started out looking like it was going to be the worst day of my life now seemed like absolutely nothing bad could possibly happen. I should have known better than to start feeling good about things.

Harmony gave me a quick peck on the cheek and we both hurried off to our first class. Just as I entered the hallway of the building where my first class was located I heard in my head, *James! Help!*

Harmony?

James, that wasn't me you picked up this morning.

What? Who is this?

James, it's me, Harmony. Really! And I need your help.

If that wasn't you I picked up this morning then who was it?

Oh, James, we are so sorry, but we seem to have overlooked one of the Thokiths who were here in 1963.

WHAT? Please don't tell me that. The girl I brought to school was one of them? Why didn't she kill and eat me along the way? And where are you, Harmony?

Yes, James, she is one of them. Do you remember the one you called Monica?

Oh my God, NO!

I'm afraid so, James. She didn't kill you and eat you as you put it because she needs to gain your trust and try to make you believe that she is me.

Where are you, Harmony, and are you ok?

My parents and I are fine, but we have been locked in an old freezer in an abandoned warehouse on the north side of town. You have got to come and let us out so we can deal with the Thokith.

Ok, but exactly where are you?

Are you familiar with the old fruit packing plant just off North Florida Avenue about two miles north of the hospital?

Of course. We sometimes go out there to drag race.

You will need to come around to the back of the second building where you will see a large metal double door at the loading dock. That's the old freezer where the Thokith locked us up.

I'm on my way, Harmony. Do I need to contact the police or fire department to help me get you out?

NO! Come alone. You can do this all by yourself.

Well, I was already late for class so I took off out the door running and didn't stop until I got to my car. I hadn't even thought about a kid running as fast as he could across campus and peeling out of the parking lot attracting attention. One of the teachers had seen me and reported it to the principal's office. However, that was the furthest thing from my mind right then as I sped across town to rescue Harmony and her parents from their prison in the old packing plant freezer. Fortunately, there weren't any cops along the way to stop me for speeding and carelessly weaving in and out of traffic, although there were several motorists who honked and cursed and gave me the finger and now when I think back on it I'm surprised that one of them didn't notify the police.

I arrived at the old abandoned warehouse in what I thought was record time and pulled up behind the second building where Harmony had directed me to go. I jumped out of my car and up onto the loading dock and ran over to the large metal double doors. I started pounding on the doors and yelling Harmony's name, but there wasn't any reply. It then occurred to my slow working little brain that there had not been any communication between Harmony and me the whole way to the old warehouse and that there wasn't any telepathic communication going on now.

Harmony? Harmony? Harmony, are you in there?

In where, James?

Uh, in the freezer at the abandoned warehouse off North Florida Avenue.

I swear, James, sometimes I think you must be taking drugs. Why would you think I was there when you know good and well that you brought me to school this morning? Is this some kind of teasing little game you like to play?

No, Harmony. I'm here because you contacted me and said that the Thokith named Monica had kidnapped you and your parents and locked you in this abandoned warehouse freezer and that she or it was the one I picked up and brought to school this morning and oh crap!

James, you have got to get out of there as quickly as possible! You are in grave danger! Go! Now!

I turned around and started to head back to my car, but stopped dead in my tracks on the loading dock when I saw the same Monica from 1963 stretched across the hood of my car wearing only what we refer to as a "birthday suit."

"Hi, Ja-James," she or it cooed at me. "Why don't you come on over here and keep lil' ol' Monica company?"

"Oh crap! Oh crap!" was all that would come out of my mouth since my brain was obviously not functioning correctly.

"You know how you used to wish that you could have your way with Monica," she or it said in that sexy, hypnotizing voice I remembered from 1963.

"Oh crap! Oh crap!" once again was all that I could get out.

Oh, Harmony. Is it too late to run?

"Give it up you little bucket of camel dung!" the thing stretched out on my hood growled at me and then its smooth, pale, sexy flesh started changing into scales as one of the reptilian alien things began to emerge. "You can't hide this time, Ja-James and there is no one around to save your skinny little butt. You're all mine! That is, what there is of you." It then started crawling off my hood and all I could think was that I hope it didn't leave any scratches in the paint job, because I certainly couldn't afford a new paint job. I started backing up and looked around to see what my best chances of escape were when I remembered the freezer where Harmony and her parents were supposed to have been trapped. I turned and ran to the freezer door and pulled hard on it. It swung open freely nearly causing me to fall on my "skinny little butt," but hanging on to the door handle I didn't fall. I regained my balance, ran inside and slammed the door shut behind me hoping that the Thokith couldn't get in. I looked for a way to lock it from the inside and then realized that no one would have designed a freezer to be locked from the inside and realized that I had probably picked the perfect place to finally die at the hands or claws of the

Thokith. I jumped back about two feet when I heard scratching on the other side of the door and thought that this was finally the end. *Good bye, Harmony. It was nice knowing you.* Then I heard what sounded like a lock being thrown and a deep growling voice say, "I'll be back for you later, Ja-James, but right now I have some other unfinished business to take care of back at your school with your slutty little girlfriend."

I started pounding on the door and screaming at the top of my lungs, "You leave her alone you ugly rotten stinking beast! Leave her alone, you hear me?"

HARMONY! Please be there.

I'm here, James. Don't worry about me, I can handle the Thokith without any problem, that is, if it decides to show up here. I have contacted my father and he is going to pick me up in a few minutes and we will come and get you out of the freezer. I pretended to be sick and have already signed out of school for the day.

Is that really you, Harmony? I don't know what to believe any more.

Yes, it is really me this time. Always remember that I will never abandon you. I will always be there for you and to help you.

I should have known that it wasn't you with that emphatic NO when I suggested bringing the police or fire department. I should have also known that you wouldn't have allowed yourself to be put in that situation.

It takes time to learn everything you need to know, James, but you will learn in due time as you will find out once you have crossed over to our side. Here's my father. We'll be there soon. Love you.

About 20 minutes later I heard a car pull up outside and a couple of minutes later the freezer door opened to reveal Harmony and her father, a tall, blonde-headed man with a full beard. Since we had never met, Harmony's father extended his hand and introduced himself as Harmon Beckham. I gave Harmony a quizzical look and she apologetically confessed, "Yes, I know. My father wanted a son named after him, but got me instead."

"Glad to meet you, sir," I said as I took his hand and shook it. "I'm sorry that you had to come to my rescue. I should have known better than to get myself in this situation."

"Not a problem, James," he assured me. "Harmony has told me a lot about you and we are very happy that she has chosen you. You make a splendid couple. And don't be fooled by what Harmony said, we love her dearly and I wouldn't trade her for two sons." Harmony and I were now standing close with our arms around each other's waist trading little squeezes.

"What about Monica or whatever that thing was?" I asked remembering who or what had locked me in the freezer.

Mr. Beckham hesitated for a moment looking like he was in deep thought. Harmony spoke up and informed me that her father was communicating with the Elders to get an update on the Thokith that called itself Monica. After a couple of minutes he looked at both of us and reported that the Thokith had been apprehended by the Elders and disposed of in the most appropriate way. "Does that mean I don't have to worry about her or it anymore, Mr. Beckham?" I asked with the nervousness starting to subside from my voice.

"Well," he replied, "as you folks say, that's a big 10-4!"

"Oh, father," Harmony chimed in, "James is perfectly used to the way we talk. You don't have to pretend to be like you're from his side."

"Well, little darlin'," he said, "you know how I like the vernacular of this country."

"Yes, father," Harmony said turning red with embarrassment and turning to me, "You will have to forgive my father his little idiosyncrasies."

"Actually," I said, "it makes me feel more like a part of the family."

"Well, if it makes you feel good, James, I'm all for it," Harmony said while holding me at arm's length and smiling at me like a bear that has just caught a big trout.

Mr. Beckham broke in before Harmony and I had a chance to start smooching, "Harmony, you riding with me or James?" Harmony just turned her head ever so slightly and smiled at her father. "Gotcha," he said and got back behind the wheel and drove off down North Florida Avenue in a brand new white 1966 Chrysler Imperial Crown convertible with the new 440 cubic inch engine that was introduced that year.

I hadn't really noticed their car until that moment and all I could say was, "Wow! Your father has got one fine looking set of wheels!"

"Boys and their cars!" Harmony exclaimed as we strolled back to my Barracuda.

Chapter Fifteen

As we pulled out of the old warehouse parking lot and headed back south on North Florida Avenue, Harmony asked, "What would you like to do for the rest of the day, James?"

"Uh," I started trying to decide why she would ask me that question, "I guess I should go back to school and try to explain why I skipped out so quickly."

"That has been taken care of, James," Harmony informed me. "No one at school will remember that you weren't there today. Besides, what exactly would you tell them? That you skipped out to go rescue your girlfriend and her family from a reptilian alien thing?"

"Cool," I replied, "and I didn't have a good excuse made up yet for skipping. What have you got in mind for us to do then, Harmony?"

"Well, your parents are both at work all day, so we could go to your house and spend the day together," she coyly suggested. "We have never had the opportunity to spend that much time alone together before and I'm sure we could find something to do to occupy our time."

"Harmony, I think you have just made me the happiest camper on the earth!" I exclaimed loud enough for passing motorists to hear.

"Don't get too excited, silly boy," Harmony said. "I didn't say we were going to be engaged in sexual activity all day."

"Part of the day?" I asked pitifully.

"James!" was all she said.

At that moment I was pretty sure that I truly loved this beautiful being who called herself Harmony Beckham. Heck, I was so taken by her that if she had turned into a reptilian alien thing and eaten me on the spot I would have gladly given myself to her without putting up a struggle.

Forgetting that Harmony could read all my thoughts when she wanted to, she said, "James, as unromantic as that might sound to everyone else, I think it may be the most romantic thing you have ever thought or said about us, but you certainly don't have to worry about me turning into a RAT."

"Well, that is really good news. I don't think I could exist anymore without you, Harmony," I replied in as meek of a voice as you might hear from some love sick, shy, little puppy dog.

Harmony just smiled at me, reached over and placed her hand on my thigh and gave it a little squeeze as we drove on toward my house and I don't need to tell you what kind of message that sent coursing through my hormonally overtaxed libido. Then, as we were getting closer to my house, it occurred to me that some of the neighbors might see us pull up or wonder why my car was there in the middle of the day when I was supposed to be at school, especially the more nosy ones.

Harmony broke into that thought with, "Don't worry, James, they won't remember even if they do notice. The last thing we need right now is to draw attention to our situation and we certainly do not want your mother finding out that we were at your house alone."

"Sorry, Harmony," I replied, "I keep forgetting that you are always taking care of that kind of thing. You're the best girlfriend a guy could have."

"I hope that it's not just because I keep you out of trouble and have to rescue you all the time," she said.

"You know better than that," I said as she continued to give my thigh little electric squeezes.

"Just testing you to see how you are coming along with that part of your training," she responded.

"Harmony, I need to ask you a very important question," I said in my most serious tone.

"Yes, James?" she asked me.

"What are we going to do if I go off to art school next year?" I inquired. "I mean, I don't know if I can be away from you for weeks at a time."

"Well, James," she said very coyly, "there is no 'if' about you going to art school next year. That will be taken care of by my father. And, not only will you be going to art school, I will be there as well."

You will remember that I'm not the brightest bulb in the pack and I said rather excitedly, "You mean your parents are moving to Sarasota so we can continue be together all the time?"

"No, silly," she replied exasperatedly. "Do I have to explain everything in minute detail to you? I am going to attend art school, too, and we will be able to be together most of the time. We will even take the same classes together so that I can keep an eye on you."

"Yeah, I'm afraid I do need constant care. Are your parents ok with that situation for us?" I asked still not convinced that what I was hearing was real.

"Remember, James, that my parents are mind readers as well and they know at all times what we are up to and what we are thinking," she reminded me. "And, yes, they are ok with everything that has gone on between us so far. My father is not even upset about the naughty things you sometimes think concerning me. He says that he was young once, too, and that he understands the urges of adolescent males, regardless of their species. Besides, my parents completely trust the decisions I have made where you and I are concerned and whatever decisions I make for our future together."

"Have I told you lately how much you mean to me, Harmony?" I asked in my most sincere, yet puppy dog, voice.

"All you have to do is be patient, James," she once again reminded me. "We are together now for all time, but you will have to have patience about some things."

"Yeah, I know," I replied with that same exasperation in my voice that she had had in hers a few minutes earlier. "But don't get too frustrated with me while I'm still on this side. I am still a teenage human male with urges you know."

"Yes, I know," she replied. "Cars, girls, and sex!"

We were pulling into the driveway at my house about that time and I said, "Well, with me now it's one girl, whatever car, and anticipation."

Without another word we got out of my car and went into my house, which compared to where Harmony lived looked like the servants quarters. I was waiting for Harmony to comment on our simple little one-story, two-bedroom, one bath house, because she lived in what would have been considered by my parents to be a mansion. However, this time she never even hinted at the fact that my parents weren't as well-off as her parents. When I had closed and locked the door I turned to Harmony, took her hand, pulled her to me and kissed her like I knew what I was doing.

When we broke for air she exclaimed, "Wow! Where did you learn to kiss like that, James?"

"I have no idea," I said turning red. "Maybe it was latently hidden in the deep, dark, recesses of my being."

"Whatever!" she said and then planted one on me that ignited those raging hormones.

When we broke for air again I asked, "Would you like to go to my bedroom and listen to records?"

"Listening to records would be fun, but I don't think we should do that in your bedroom," Harmony answered very matter of fact.

"Yeh, I know, be patient, James," I replied in the saddest voice I could muster up. Tell that to a certain part of my anatomy!

"James! You are so naughty! Now, I noticed a large stereo in the living room" she said somewhat apologetically. "We could listen to records in there and snuggle on the sofa."

"Ok," I readily agreed hoping that snuggling might lead to some more serious activity. "You make yourself at home and I'll pick out some good albums and join you in a few minutes."

I headed back to my sad, lonely bedroom to select some albums for us to listen to while Harmony sashayed into the living room. I know she "sashayed," because I paused long enough to watch her walking away from me. I selected a couple of my favorite albums by The Beatles, Rubber Soul and Yesterday and Today, and headed back to the living room. I briefly paused in my bedroom before going to the living room to join Harmony wondering, in my usual paranoid frame of mind, if this was maybe another set-up by one of the Thokiths to get me alone and once again try to eat me. If it was, she/it was certainly going to a lot of trouble to get me alone.

No, James. It really is me, Harmony, and nothing bad is going to happen to either of us. Please trust me when I tell you that.

Gathering up my courage I strolled into the living room like a pimp with a gold-topped cane and said, more to convince myself than Harmony, "I do trust you, Harmony, with all my heart and soul."

"I understand your anxiety about the Thokiths, James," Harmony replied, "but my father and the Elders are now positive that there will not be any more trouble from them. When the Elders are angry about something they usually dole out a severe type of punishment."

"Thanks," I said, "but my paranoid little mind wonders if there will be other aliens who try to do me in or put an end to our being together. I don't mean to always sound like a cry-baby, but there is only so much evil doings that a person can handle."

"The Thokiths were the greatest danger for you, James," Harmony informed me. "They were the most difficult to keep track of because of their ability to blend in by assuming the form of any human as well as their mind reading ability. What you didn't know during the summer of 1963 was that your mind was being constantly monitored and controlled by the Thokiths. That is how they always knew where you were and what you were doing and why you sometimes acted the way you did. And, unfortunately, there will be other dangers that arise for both of us, which is why it is so important for you to learn our ways as quickly as possible."

"You think I could have figured out back then that I was being manipulated," I said with my head bowed down feeling sorry for myself.

"You were only fourteen, James, and you had your mind on making money to buy that first car, not to mention the fact that the Thokiths were constantly pursuing you," she reminded me.

"I'm sure glad you're on my side, Harmony," I said as I looked up and smiled at her. "Do you like The Beatles?"

"Love The Beatles," she answered. "I hope one of those albums is Rubber Soul. That is now my absolute favorite of all time!"

"Then that's the one we'll play first," I said and opened the lid on our 1962 Delmonico Stereo Console, Model Number TW 504 S. My parents had briefly gone in debt for it in 1962, because all I had in my bedroom was a RCA portable phonograph (although it was still rather large and heavy) from the late 1950s. When my mother wanted to listen to some country music she would have to get me to lug my portable stereo into the living room, so that she wouldn't bother me in my room with that racket she called music. Of course, that left me without a way to listen to my rock 'n roll records. I was hoping one day to get a new and smaller record player that was easier to move around, but money was always tight in our family and I would just have to wait and maybe ask for one for Christmas. The Rubber Soul album started playing and as I gazed into Harmony's eyes I started signing, if you could call it that, along with The Beatles, "I've just seen a face, I can't forget the time or place that we'd just met, she's just the girl for me and I want all the world to see we've met."

"You are a hopeless, hopeless romantic, James," Harmony said with the strained caring of a woman trying her best to be patient with one of the less intelligent humans on the planet, but at the same time gazing back into my eyes with the same intensity.

I continued signing, "Falling, yes I'm falling and she keeps calling me back again." We embraced, kissed and reclined back on my parents' gold colored sofa and with my arm around Harmony's shoulders we listened to the rest of side one of Rubber Soul.

Chapter Sixteen

The Beatles music kept playing on the stereo and Harmony and I seemed to keep getting physically closer and closer as we slipped down on my parents' sofa and started to doze off, traveling down that dreamy path of half-sleep. I remember us giving each other another kiss and gazing at each other with eyes of unfulfilled longing as drowsiness crept over us as the music began to make a low, dull, continuous humming sound in the background. Harmony and I must have dozed for about two hours when I woke up feeling a cool breeze that seemed to be flowing through the house. The Rubber Soul album had obviously finished long ago and, as my senses started to come awake, the house seemed not only to be getting colder, but there was a feeling of heavy silence that seemed to be enveloping us. All I could hear at that moment was Harmony's shallow breathing, but in that peculiar silence it sounded more like someone beating on a kettledrum. My arm was still wrapped around Harmony as if I thought I could actually protect her from some unseen danger and it had fallen asleep all the way from my shoulder down to my fingertips. I sat up slowly trying to work my arm from behind Harmony and not wake her up, but as I did so she started to stir. When I had finally gotten my arm out she was beginning to sit up and then reached over and took hold of my still tingling arm. When I turned to say something she placed her hand over my mouth and shook her head. ***Don't say anything out loud, James.***

What's the matter, Harmony?

Don't you feel it, James? The silence and the cold breeze?

I did think that it seemed awfully quiet and a little chilly when I woke up. What do you think it means?

This particular kind of silence is highly unusual, James, especially on earth.

You're scaring me, Harmony. What are we supposed to do now? Do we need to get the hell of here?

Just don't say anything out loud, James, and sit very still for a few more moments. It will take me a few minutes to determine if we are in any kind of danger, but my guess is that we are.

You got it, sweetie. Is there anything I can do in the meantime?

We need to stop our communication so I can concentrate, James. We were both sitting straight up on the sofa now and were very close together and holding hands. My arm was almost fully awake now, but I felt helpless, like I did most of the time when I was around Harmony. I wanted to be able to protect her, but I knew it would be some time before I would be in that position, if ever. Five or six minutes passed, although it seemed like an hour, when Harmony opened the channels again. *We must get out of this house now, James!*

At that I increased my hold on her hand, pulled her up off the sofa, and led the way toward the kitchen door. I unlocked the door and let Harmony go out ahead of me, but then something seemed to grab hold of my entire body and pull me roughly back into the kitchen where I fell on my butt on the linoleum floor flailing like a drowning man. I was being slowly dragged backwards across the kitchen floor and toward the hallway that led to the bedrooms. Although there wasn't any sign of anything having hold of me, I felt something like a giant hand was holding me as I was being pulled backwards across the kitchen floor. I confirmed that fact when I turned around to see what had hold of me and there really wasn't anything there.

***James! James! Can you hear me*?**

Yes. What the heck is happening to me, Harmony?

I'll tell you later. Right now you must do what you can to resist the power that has hold of you, James.

By this time I had been dragged backwards onto the hardwood floor in the hallway and was starting to pass by the bathroom door, so I grabbed at the doorjamb with both hands and held on for dear life. *Harmony, can't you come in here and help me?*

No, James, I have been frozen in place in the carport by whatever this power is that has hold of you. I am trying to do what I can to break loose and get in there to help you break free, but it seems futile at this moment. You must hold on!

Well, if nothing else had given me any extra strength in my puny little arms and determination to hold on to the bathroom door jam, Harmony's encouragement did. Whatever this "power" was that was trying to drag me back toward the bedrooms didn't seem to be that strong as I seemed to be hanging on pretty good.

What is this "power," Harmony?

I believe that eerie silence and unusual feeling that we were experiencing when we woke up is an invisible entity in the universe that some think was the first life billions of years ago. Many believe that it is just a long gone legend, but Voreshas have always believed that these entities were real and I am convinced that one is trying to get you now and pull you through the hole it has created in the atmosphere to come to Earth.

Get me? Hole in the atmosphere? Oh crap!

You must continue to hold on tight to the doorjamb, James. They have been around for so long that

we believe they have lost some of the power they once had. The fact that you are still here seems to prove that hypothesis. I believe that I can break free of this frozen state since it is probably some type of mind control. Just hang on, love! Know that I am doing the best that I can!

No problem there. As a matter of fact, I was now trying to get to my feet and seemed to be slowly succeeding in doing so. I imagined my squirming and getting to my feet must have been what Fay Wray would have felt like while squirming around in King Kong's grasp in the 1933 movie. When I was finally in a standing position I swung out behind me and my arm did seem to come in contact with something even though I couldn't see what it was that I had hit. There wasn't any sound from the invisible, cold entity that was holding me, but I gave out a loud grunt when I made contact with this invisible entity. *Are you ok, James?*

Yes, I have managed to stand up and I hit whatever this is that is trying to hold on to me. That was me you heard grunt.

Can you break free of the entity?

I gave a very hard jerk with my whole body away from what felt like King Kong's hand wrapping around me and to my surprise I stumbled forward and nearly fell down on the hardwood floor in the hallway. Stumbling, I regained my balance and ran faster than I thought I could for the kitchen door which was still standing open and jumped over the two steps landing in the middle of the carport close to where Harmony was frozen in place. I was ready to do whatever I could to help Harmony break loose from whatever had frozen her there, even if it meant caring her like a manikin and stuffing her in the back of the 'Cuda. But when I landed on the pavement in the carport I saw that she was beginning to move, if somewhat stiffly, so I ran up to her and grabbing her by both arms began to shake her gently, because I didn't have any idea what else I might do to help. Harmony seemed to loosen up and we both headed for my car without wasting time to say anything. I laid down a lot of rubber in the driveway backing out as fast as I could, and when I was out in the street I threw the 'Cuda into drive and peeled off down the street.

"Oh, crap!" I exclaimed. "I left the door standing open."

"The entity closed it, James," Harmony informed me. "It seems that they never like to leave any evidence of having been somewhere."

"Do these entities have a name?" I asked.

"You are not going to believe this, James," Harmony started, "but they are known as Semaj."

"Semaj?" I repeated more as a question. "Why would I not believe you, Harmony?"

"Think about it, James," she replied.

I gave it some thought and then it hit me like a ton of bricks! "That's James spelled backwards," I acknowledged. "Does that mean something where I am concerned?"

"I really do not think so, but it is strangely interesting," Harmony said. "I will have to confer with my father on that one."

"It's a little too interesting if you ask me," I replied matter of fact. At that moment I realized that I didn't know where we were going, so I asked Harmony where we should go that would be safe from this invisible entity that she was trying to explain to me.

"The Semaj has now left your house, although I do not think it has left earth, so I think you should take me home and then you need to go home and get ready for work," Harmony reminded me.

"You want me to go back to my house? Are you absolutely sure that the Semaj won't be there?" I asked with a tone of doubt in my voice.

"Absolutely, James," Harmony said with confidence. "You can trust me."

"No need to say any more, love," I said as confidently as I could. "If you say I'm safe, then I will believe you. Can I ask you another question about the Semaj?"

"Absolutely," she replied.

"What would have happened to me if the Semaj had won the tug-of-war?" I inquired.

Harmony began to tell me about the Semaj, which was also the plural form, kind of like one sheep or twenty sheep. "I am a little afraid to tell you, but it is time that you learn about the methods and dangers of things that try to harm you until you cross over. Once you have made the crossover, there will be far fewer dangers like this to bother you. From now on, James, I promise you that there will be no more secrets between us, not that the Semaj were meant to be a secret. The Semaj seem to be able to enter a planet's atmosphere through invisible holes they create in that atmosphere. Since no one has ever seen one, because they are as invisible as the holes they enter through, this is only speculation. But I am convinced that what grabbed you today was definitely a Semaj and that the silence and strange feeling we each experienced was caused by that hole in the atmosphere. It is almost like that hole lets in the cold from the universe while sucking out the sound from its immediate area. At least that is what I have been taught about the Semaj. Their abduction method seems to be that they try to pull their chosen victims through the hole in which they came."

"No offense," I interjected, "but I'm not too keen on being 'chosen' anymore."

Harmony giggled that cute little giggle of hers and continued with her explanation. "There have been thousands of people on earth alone over several millennia who have never been found after disappearing when there have been suspected visits by Semaj. Regardless of these suspicions, most beings throughout the universe are still not convinced that Semaj actually exist."

"But it seems that if people resist they can break free of the hold the Semaj has on them," I offered.

"I think that is especially true of the older Semaj," Harmony said with conviction. "We do not know if there are younger Semaj or if there are only a few who have been in existence for all time and who are immortal."

We had arrived at Harmony's house by then and she got out of the car when I came around and opened her door. She headed inside after we hugged, kissed, and she assured me that everything would be ok now at my house. I drove back home and when I cautiously tried the kitchen door it was locked. Unlocking it I went in confident, though with some trepidation, that nothing bad would happen and it didn't. I changed into my work clothes and headed off to work since it was nearly 4:00. I wish that I could tell you that it was a peaceful night at the station, but that wasn't to be.

Chapter Seventeen

I got to work with five minutes to spare and since my father was busy at the front desk with some sort of paper work from the eight to three shift, he barely noticed me when I pulled in and said "hi" to him when I walked through the front door. I knew better than to interrupt him when he was doing business paper work, so I went out to the first car that came in, a red and white 1959 Edsel Corsair convertible. Now, like most people, I wasn't much of a fan of the Edsel, but this was one fine looking automobile. I was a little freaked out, however, when I walked up to the driver's side and saw a beautiful blond woman sitting behind the steering wheel wearing a fairly short, flowing skirt. When she glanced up at me it took me a few seconds to get my wits about me and ask if I could fill' er up. She simply smiled and winked at me and told me to do just that with high test and then she started searching through her purse for something. Although this blond woman was young, attractive, and had ample breasts, I was relieved that she didn't look anything like Monica from 1963. It also gave me some comfort to remember that Harmony had reassured me that I would never be bothered by the Thokiths again, so I was pretty sure that she wasn't a Thokith. I finished filling up the Edsel, collected the money for the gas, and as she pulled out she turned and winked at me again. Reassurance from Harmony or not and some 40 earth years later I still get the willies when I encounter young, blond, attractive women with ample breasts.

Business was brisk at the station, although un-
eventful, for the next several hours. A little after 8:00
that night things settled down and Arthur, with his dai-
ly newspaper tucked under his arm, made his usual trek
to the men's restroom where he would spend up to half
an hour "doing his business" as he put it. I figured he
had also read all of the newspaper that he cared about,
because he always tossed it in the office trash can
when he came back from the restroom. Jack and Arthur, who both usually worked the graveyard shift from
11:00 p.m. to 7:00 a.m., had traded shifts with the other
two men on the 3:00 to 11:00 shift, as they often did,
for a couple of weeks. We never checked on Arthur
because he always returned after 20 to 30 minutes, but
when Jack mentioned to my father that it was almost
9:30 and Arthur was still in the restroom my father
immediately got the spare men's restroom key and
went around the corner of the building to check on Arthur. Being as old as he was, my father was always
worried that the old guy would have a heart attack
while on the job, so Jack tended to keep a close track
of Arthur on their shift. Jack and I were right on my
father's heels when he knocked on the restroom door
and called out Arthur's name. My father did this three
or four times, but got no response from within the restroom. My father inserted the key into the lock and
unlocked the door being careful to open it slowly in
case Arthur was lying on the floor of the small, white,
cinder block room with one small toilet and an even
smaller sink. The door opened without meeting any
resistance and when it was open all the way we were
all surprised to see that Arthur wasn't in the restroom
even though the door had been locked. His newspaper
was scattered all over the floor and one piece was
hanging out of the toilet.

Jack exclaimed, "What the hell? Where do you
think that old man got off to? And why was the door

locked? And why is his newspaper scattered everywhere?"

"This isn't like Arthur," my father replied. "I didn't notice him that much when he came in this afternoon, but did either of you notice if he had been drinking again?"

"I didn't notice anything unusual," said Jack, "but I wasn't working that close to him."

"I was working pretty close to him during the big rush around 6:00, but I didn't smell alcohol on his breath," I offered. "I didn't even know that he was a drinker."

My father asked us, "Did he seem to have his wits about him? He does sometimes seem a little tetched, if you know what I mean."

"He seemed normal to me," Jack replied.

"Arthur seemed normal to me, too, Dad," I answered. "Like always, he was constantly ribbing me about something and cracking his usual corny jokes. Now, that I think about it, he did mention something about a dream he had last night. He told me that in the dream he had been abducted by this beautiful alien girl who took him back to her spaceship and made him her sex slave."

"Sounds like a far fetched story that old coot would come up with. Now where the hell is he?" my father exclaimed more to himself than directing the question toward Jack and me. "I've been worried about that old man for some time now, but I didn't want to let him go. I know he needs the money so he can keep that room in the boarding house downtown. He keeps saying that if he misses even one week's rent, the people he rents from will ship him off to an old people's home."

"Maybe he decided to go for a walk and got lost," I offered. "Or, maybe he decided to visit the whorehouse across the street." And trying to add a little levity to the situation, "Maybe that beautiful alien woman did abduct him and take him away." My father only glared at me after that remark.

Jack chuckled at this remark and said, "Hell, that old coot couldn't get it up with both hands in either case!"

Although my father chuckled at Jack's remark, he was still giving me a cold stare at the same time. "And just how do you know about the place across the street, young man? Been over there, have you?"

Not wanting to get Jack or Arthur in trouble with my father, I lied and said, "I overheard some of the fancy pants customers than come in here late at night talking about it. After all, it's no big secret what goes on over there."

"It may be time for you to find another job, James," my father seriously informed me. "You seem to be learning a little too much about too many things you're too young to know about." I would pursue that line of thought later when this mystery surrounding Arthur was settled. Not pulling the night shift at the service station might give me more time to be with Harmony. "We had better call the police." At that my father hurried back to the office and called the local police to report a missing old man. About ten minutes later a policeman pulled into the service station in his 1967 Plymouth Fury black and white police cruiser and parked next to the building on the restroom side.

My father knew several of the policemen on the local force because they fueled up their cars at the Star service station. A tall, dark-haired, tanned, 40ish, blue uniformed policeman got out of the police cruiser and casually strolled into the office. He walked up to my father and they shook hands. "What's up Slim," he asked. Slim was everybody's favorite nickname for my father because he was tall and thin.

"Boys, this here is Sergeant MacPileno," my father said and the sergeant shook our hands as well. "The sergeant and I have known each other for many years, almost since we moved here back in 1954. He is one of the city's best policemen and don't either of you ever forget that. Got shot up pretty bad a few years back, but that didn't stop him from coming back to do his job. Takes a hell of a man to go through what he did and still want to be in law enforcement."

Looking at me, Sergeant MacPileno said, "I have a feeling that your dad would say that about whatever policeman showed up. I guess that's why all of us on the force like him so much. Now, back to why you called, Slim."

"It seems that we have misplaced Arthur, sergeant," my father chuckled as he replied.

"Care to elaborate, Slim?" the sergeant asked.

My father, Jack, and I each in turn related the story about Arthur announcing that he went to the restroom around 8:00 and that Jack noticed he hadn't returned for nearly an hour and a half. We related to the sergeant that my father decided to call the police and see if they would help look for him, especially when we didn't find him in the restroom and his newspaper was scattered everywhere. Knowing Arthur, Sergeant MacPileno agreed that it was strange that Arthur had been in the little boy's room so long and was glad that we had called the police. The sergeant went around to the restroom and gave it a thorough inspection. He then returned to the office and said that he didn't find anything unusual besides the newspaper being all over the restroom, but that he would also cruise the neighborhood to see if Arthur might be wandering around somewhere and got lost. However, first the sergeant was going to check the "business" across the street on the rare chance that Arthur had "gotten the urge." Sergeant MacPileno got back in his black and white Plymouth police cruiser and pulled across the street to start his investigation into Arthur's disappearance at the whorehouse. It was funny to see all of the patrons of the business who were standing around outside quickly disappear into the dark night behind shrubbery and down the alley behind nearby bungalow style houses on the side street. In a few minutes the sergeant came back out of the building across the street and looking over toward the station where we were all watching waved the all clear signal to us. He then got back in his black and white police cruiser and headed off down one of the side streets to search for Arthur.

It was almost 11:00 and time for my father to get off work and head home when Sergeant MacPileno pulled back into the service station. He pulled the Plymouth Fury up in front of the office and rolled down his window. All three of us went out to the car to hear his report. "I couldn't find any sign of Arthur anywhere," the sergeant told us. "It's like he disappeared into thin air."

"What do you think we should do next?" my father asked.

"Well, that's the sixty-four-thousand dollar question, isn't it?," the sergeant replied. "I'll get the department to put out an APB on him and hope that someone sees him wandering around here somewhere. Now, you boys need to go home and get some sleep and leave this up to the police to solve. We'll find him sooner or later. I'm sure he probably just wandered off to a neighbors house."

"10-4," my father replied. "Maybe you can let us know something tomorrow."

"Will do, Slim," the sergeant said and then rolled up his window and pulled out of the station heading west.

My father turned to me and said, "I think you had better come on home with me, son, the graveyard shift gets here pretty soon. No need for you to hang around here with all this funny business going on."

"That's a good idea, James," Jack added. "The night shift can take care of themselves and Sergeant MacPileno will thoroughly investigate this. Maybe he will have some news for us tomorrow."

A few minutes later the graveyard shift arrived and my father related what had happened earlier in the evening concerning Arthur and told them to be on the lookout for him or anything suspicious looking. If they noticed anything out of the ordinary they were to notify the police immediately. Shortly thereafter my father and I and Jack left the service station and headed our separate ways home. On the way home all I could think about was my little episode with one of the Semaj and I wondered if that was what had happened to Arthur. Being older it was likely that he wouldn't be able to resist their power like I did and, besides, he didn't have Harmony looking after him. It was going to prove to be a restless, sleepless night for me and I suspected my father wouldn't get much sleep either.

Chapter Eighteen

Amazingly enough I slept pretty well that night, but before I dozed off to sleep I thought I would try to contact Harmony and see if she had any information about Arthur's disappearance. *Are you tuned in tonight, Harmony?*

Yes, James. I was just getting out of the shower to get ready for bed before you interrupted me.

Well, excuse me for interrupting you, but you walking around naked is an image I could dream about all night.

James! You are so bad! You have got to quit having naughty thoughts about me!

Ok, so I'm a bad little boy with a vivid imagination, but the real reason I contacted you was to see if you knew about the disappearance of Arthur at the service station tonight?

I was listening in to all of the conversations you and your father and Jack and the policeman were having and got my father involved in listening as well. My father contacted the Elders and they are now looking into the matter. You are probably right when you were thinking on the way home that one of the Semaj abducted him. My guess right now is that the same one followed you and when it saw Arthur, it figured that he wouldn't be as hard to abduct.

So, in a way it's my fault that Arthur was abducted?

Yes and no, James. The Semaj probably did follow you and then select Arthur, but you should never feel that it was your fault. You were able to resist, but the Semaj only followed you hoping to make its search easier for a weaker person to abduct. We will probably never know why the Semaj entered the earth's atmosphere and ended up at your house and picked on you. It just as easily could have entered on the other side of the world, or even another planet.

Thanks, Harmony, but I will have to think about that for a while before I quit blaming myself. Just a human thing I guess.

Yes, James, I know. I can't wait for you to finally cross over to our side so that you will better understand that you aren't responsible when things like this happen.

And I'll be able to watch you when you get out of the shower!

Boys! Go to bed, James, and have sweet dreams and try not to think about Arthur. Goodnight!

Goodnight, Harmony. I didn't want to come right out and say it, even though I was sure Harmony would read my thoughts anyway, but I was not thinking about Arthur when I fell asleep that night. Imagine if you will, falling asleep with visions of the woman in E.B. Leighton's painting or John William Waterhouse's Psyche or one of his water nymphs stepping naked from her bath. My dreams that night were of me romping around with one of those naked beauties from Victorian paintings. Arthur who?

The next morning the conversation at the breakfast table, which was also the dining room table since that part of the big room where the kitchen was located served as the "eating area," centered around the events of the night before at the service station. My father was anxious to get to work that morning with the hope that Sergeant MacPileno would come by with news that the police had found Arthur and that he was ok. I wished that I could tell my dad what Harmony and I were afraid had happened to Arthur, but the telepathic communication that was going on between Harmony and me and the fact that she was not human would be things that my parents would never be allowed to know. It was very difficult not to confide in the two people who always tried their best to trust me and believe in me, even though I had often betrayed that trust and, according to them, failed them miserably.

The one revelation at the breakfast table that morning was my father telling my mother and me that I no longer would be working at the Star service station, because he didn't want me hanging around a place where so many strange things happened and so many strange people were always passing through. Besides, he didn't want me being tempted by "that place across the street." My mother didn't question this at all, which suggested that they had talked about it before retiring for the evening. I did ask him, before he left for work, what I was going to do for spending and gas money, especially now that I had a very steady girlfriend. He told me that he and my mother had been discussing that for some time now, and that they had decided that morning before I got up that, since it was my senior year of high school, I wouldn't have to work until I went off to art school, provided I got accepted. If I didn't get accepted at art school, then I would have to get a job, at least part-time, and go to the local junior college. Without sounding too cocky, I assured them both that I would get into art school and make them proud; just showing off some of that self-confidence that Harmony was trying to teach me. At that my father left for work and I headed off to pick up Harmony for school. My mother headed out shortly after that to catch the city bus to go to work at S.H. Kress downtown where she worked in the notions department.

Harmony must have been watching for me to come down her street, because she was already opening the passenger side door almost before I got the car completely stopped. She jumped in before I could even get my door open to go around and open the door for her. Harmony gave me a kiss, and told me to get going because we were going to make a little detour that day before going to school.

"What's up, Harmony?" I foolishly asked, knowing full well that it probably didn't matter to her whether I agreed with her plan or not.

"First, James, that was a very naughty little thought you had about water nymphs before you went to bed last night."

Blushing as dark as a red delicious apple, I replied, "I was just using the images from the paintings, but I was envisioning you, Harmony."

"I know," she replied, "and that is very sweet of you."

"Where are we headed before we go to school?" I asked, this time trying to pin her down on our current destination.

"We are going to spend the day trying to find out what happened to Arthur," she answered.

"But what about school?" I asked.

"Already taken care of, sweetie," she replied as if I should have figured that out by now.

"Of course," I said in my most apologetic voice. "You're the navigator. Where to first?"

"The man with a thousand questions this morning," Harmony said, but this time with her little coquettish smile that drove me crazy. "Do you remember that warehouse where the Thokith nearly got you?"

"Yes," I said coldly, "how could I ever forget that evil bitch."

"Such language," Harmony reproved me. "My father hasn't heard anything from the Elders yet, but it is always a very sticky situation when dealing with the Semaj. Anyway, my father thinks that warehouse would be the perfect place for a Semaj to hide if it didn't want to leave Earth yet, because we do know that the port of entry, in other words, the hole in the atmosphere, stays open as long as they are on a planet. And since no one really knows how they operate, it is possible that the Semaj could have swept up Arthur and taken him somewhere like that to hide him while it continued to hunt for more humans too weak to fight back."

"And we really don't know what the Semaj do with humans or other species after they take them back through the hole?" I stated more than asked. I was trying my best to understand all of this and not sound completely stupid to Harmony.

"Correct," Harmony said, "and you are not stupid, James. You have got to have more self-confidence if you are ever to make the crossover. How many times do I have to tell you that?"

"I know," I said, "but it's hard when you've been criticized and corrected all your life and your father is always telling you to use your head for something besides a hat rack or your mother keeps telling you that you don't have the sense God gave a goat!"

"I understand all of that, James," Harmony replied, "but keep in mind that I am patiently waiting on the other side for you so that we can be married and unless your self-confidence level goes up you will never make the crossover."

"Please don't say 'never'," Harmony, I pleaded. "All I want now is to be able to crossover as soon as possible so we can be together forever and ever."

"That is my wish, too, James," Harmony stated, "but our work together on this planet will only have just begun when you do make that crossover."

I moved that thought aside as we were getting closer to the warehouse off North Florida Avenue and so I asked Harmony what our next move was going to be when we did pull up to the warehouse. She suggested not going all the way back to the building where I had almost been captured by the Thokith disguised as Monica, but rather we should park about two hundred yards away and sneak up on the building.

This idea made perfect sense to me if we had been sneaking up on a sleeping shoplifter, but I had my doubts about sneaking up on a Semaj. "Isn't the Semaj able to detect when someone or something is sneaking up on it?" I inquired.

"Once again, we do not know what all of their abilities are, so it is quite possible that the Semaj already knows that we are coming," she answered.

"Should we go into "thought mode" only?" I asked.

Harmony gave me that look my mother always gave me when she was getting totally frustrated with all of my questions and said, "Honestly, James, you are going to have to also learn to make some of the decisions where we are concerned."

"Yes, mother," I said as sarcastically as I could.

"Do not ever call me your mother again," Harmony said trying to sound sincere but with that cute little smile on her face and then she started to giggle.

I parked the 'Cuda two buildings away which was somewhere in the neighborhood of two hundred yards from the building where I had the run in with the Thokith. Without saying or thinking anything, Harmony motioned that we should creep along the backside of the buildings with the hope that if the Semaj was here it wouldn't be able to sense or hear or see us approaching. Of course, this whole idea was just a long shot based on what Mr. Beckham thought might be the case. I was willing to take the chance because I was with Harmony and had the highest respect for Mr. Beckham. Harmony was letting me lead the way, I suppose to help boost my self-confidence, but being the timid soul (sounds better than chicken) that I was I would have gladly relinquished that position. As we came to the end of the first building we scurried as fast as we could go to the side of the second building and stopped to catch our breath.

All of a sudden I began to feel a slight chill in the air even though the sun was shining as brightly as it could making it was a warm day. I turned toward Harmony and she knew what I was trying not to think and nodded her head and wrapped her arms around herself and did a fake shiver. Holding my hands out with the palms up and close to my shoulders, I shrugged and gave Harmony a quizzical look without thinking "what do we do next?" She tilted her head ever so slightly, which always drove me crazy, too, and gave me that "you decide" look. Well, self-confidence, bravery, or stupidity, I had an idea and motioned for Harmony to quietly follow me. If I had looked back at that moment I would have seen a very satisfied expression on her face.

There were some crumbling concrete stairs next to the loading dock at that end of the building where we were supposedly hiding and I led her up them. Staying close to the building we moved toward the large, gray, metal double doors associated with the loading dock. Harmony was so close behind me that I could feel her warm breath on the back of my neck and, yes, it was driving me crazy and not helping as far as me keeping me focused on the business at hand. I tried the left side of the double doors and it didn't budge. With my heart sinking and my plan starting to fade I tried the right side door and it swung open with just a slight creak. That froze us both in our tracks and we quickly glanced at each other and I could see for the first time a little nervousness in Harmony's eyes. But now, being the leader of this expedition, I took her hand and moved cautiously through the door and inside the building. As soon as we were inside I gently closed the oversized door and this time it didn't creak. Without looking back at Harmony and with her hand in mine, we started walking as quietly as we could through the enormous cave-like interior of this second warehouse building. Having been abandoned several years before there wasn't much in our way in this cavernous structure of mostly concrete and steel. As we moved in the direction of the third building, I began to definitely feel the air getting colder and colder as if someone had turned on a giant air conditioner and it was blowing directly on us. About two-thirds of the way through the structure I stopped and turned to see if Harmony was looking chilled or whether it was just my imagination. She was shivering slightly and I knew that was not a good sign as we were no doubt getting close to the Semaj.

At that moment, Mr. Beckham's voice came through loud and clear to me, and I assume to Harmony as well. ***James, you must get out of there as quickly as possible! Get Harmony back to your car immediately and head straight back to our house. The Semaj is closer than you think and he is having a very bad effect on Harmony's ability to think straight. Now, GO!***

Without saying or thinking anything I squeezed Harmony's hand a little tighter and began to pull her at a jogging pace back through the empty warehouse and to the door where we had entered the building. Harmony almost seemed to resist me, but with a very disoriented and scared look on her face she followed after me anyway. When we were back outside in the warm sunshine, Harmony started to respond better to my pulling her along and picked up her pace as we ran toward the 'Cuda. When we got to within about ten feet of my car the sand in the parking lot started swirling around it so hard and fast that it looked like a small tornado. I kept urging Harmony on anyway and to the passenger side of the car. With the sand blowing so hard around the car that it stung our skin like a million bees attacking us, I opened the door and literally pushed her inside. Slamming the door shut I fought against the mini-wind and the blowing sand storm to get to the driver's side and I jumped in slamming the door behind me. I was so scared and at the same time so pumped up that I fumbled my keys getting them out of my right front blue jeans pocket and dropped them on the floorboard.

Finally getting her wits back, Harmony yelled at me, "Hurry, James, the Semaj is getting very close to us!"

"I'm trying," I said with that tinge of fear in my voice, "but I can't reach my keys." At that Harmony bent over my lap pressing her upper body into me and searched around my feet for the keys. It was certainly hard to concentrate on what I was doing when Harmony was always pressing up against me. She sat back up and instead of handing the keys to me she inserted the key into the ignition and turned it until the car started I shifted the floor-mounted gear shift into drive and peeled out of there creating almost as much of a sand storm as the Semaj had stirred up. As I was pulling back out onto North Florida Avenue we both heard, in our heads, but not out loud, what sounded like a giant, dying owl screeching. Harmony turned around and looked out through the large rear window of the 'Cuda and I was looking in my rear-view mirror when we witnessed the entire second building, where we had just been, seem to instantly implode. We then heard that horrible screeching in our minds one more time as I speeded south down North Florida Avenue and back toward the Beckham's house.

Chapter Nineteen

Before arriving back at Harmony's house Mr. Beckham tuned in and told us not to discuss anything either mentally or out loud just in case the Semaj happened to be following us. Harmony and I looked at each other with blank stares and blank thoughts, but we knew that if her father had contacted us to keep silent that things must have gotten pretty serious. I sped on toward Harmony's house doing my humanly best not to say or think anything about what had just happened to us, although I couldn't help running all these recent events through my head. It was only a matter of a few more minutes before we pulled up in front of Harmony's house, jumped out of the car, and ran up the sidewalk to the front porch with its Victorian railing and that stretched across the entire front of the house. Mr. Beckham was waiting for us on the porch and opened the large front door and ushered us inside into the two-story foyer. I stood there in awe looking around me at this huge entrance that looked like something out of Gone with the Wind and in which my entire house would probably have fit. As long as Harmony and I had been going steady this term at school, this was the first time I had actually been inside her house or, for that matter, any house this large. All of my other friends lived in houses similar to my parents' house, with maybe one or two more bedrooms and a second bath. I stood in the foyer wide-eyed and staring at a white, heavy, ornate staircase that curved upward to the second floor on both sides of the elaborately flower-covered wallpapered foyer. Without speaking

Mr. Beckham motioned us to the right side stairs and guided us up to the top landing and then down a well lit hallway to a large room at the end of the hall that served as his office.

We entered Mr. Beckham's office and he closed and locked the door behind us and motioned for us to sit in two chairs in front of his dark mahogany desk that was as big as my car and ornately carved on the front and sides with what looked like hunting scenes. The top of his desk was so highly polished that you could see yourself in the finish. My guess was that it had never seen one speck of dust. Not yet having learned to choose my thoughts carefully, Mr. Beckham communicated to both of us, *If the desk were to get dusty, James, I would probably have to fire the housekeeper and the desk is probably about two feet longer than your car.*

Oh, father, do not tease James like that. You know good and well that you would never let Mrs. Bishaga go. She has been with the family since before I was born. I do not think that anyone knows for sure how old she might be. Besides, father, James and I have both just been through a very scary ordeal. What can you tell us about what happened at the warehouses?

I apologize, James, my daughter does not share my sense of humor.

No problem, sir. I didn't think you were being serious and I appreciate a good sense of humor.

James, I think you and I are going to get along just fine. We will have to go deep sea fishing on my yacht sometime and share humorous stories.

Father, can we get back to what just happened to James and me at the old warehouses?

Of course, Harmony. First, let me tell you that we are communicating this way because the Elders and I now believe that although the Semaj have many unknown abilities, we do not think they can read minds, but we do think they have extraordinary hearing. That ability may have evolved over several millennia or it may be something they have had since time immemorial. James, I unfortunately have to tell you that your friend Arthur is no longer alive.

Although Arthur wasn't a close friend, he had proven to be a good buddy at work and this news did bring tears to my eyes. I took my handkerchief out of the back pocket of my blue jeans and wiped the corner of my eyes as Mr. Beckham continued.

There is, as far as we can determine, only one Semaj here on Earth at this time, at least in North America. The Elders are conducting a thorough search of the entire planet, however, just to make sure. It seems that this particular Semaj did abduct Arthur and take him to the abandoned warehouse building where the two of you were and hid him there in an old chest freezer. One of the abilities of the Semaj seems to be the ability to will people to do what they want them to do, including Voreshas, who have the ability to block most such powers by other species. The reason the two of you ended up at the warehouse is because you were willed there by the Semaj. The Elders and I believe that you were only going to be the first three of many that the Semaj planned to take back through the hole it made in the atmosphere upon leaving earth.

I had been taking all of this in and trying to wrap my puny little human brain around it, but I just had to ask Mr. Beckham one simple question. *Did the Semaj kill Arthur before he put him in the chest freezer, Mr. Beckham?*

No, James. As far as we know the Semaj take live victims back through the hole with them. The unfortunate things is that Arthur died when the Semaj destroyed the warehouse building.

Mr. Beckham?
Yes, James.
Can the Semaj be killed?
Not to any knowledge that we or any other species has about them, James. The best that we can determine, they have always been, meaning that they are as old as time itself. Some of the species in the universe actually believe that the Semaj, because no one has ever seen one, may have actually been the creators of the universe.
Do you know why they take other species away from their home planets, Mr. Beckham?
Well, James, since no one has ever come back after being taken through the hole created by the Semaj when they enter a planet's atmosphere and because the hole closes after they go back through, we have no idea why others species are taken or where they are taken. Our best guess is that all other species in the universe may serve as food sources for the Semaj.

Harmony had kept quiet through all of this, but she now had a question for her father. *Father, if I understand what you are saying, James was not specifically selected for abduction by this Semaj.*
That is what we think, Harmony. We believe that the Semaj selections are completely random and that is why we believe that this Semaj was here because it just happened to be in the neighborhood.
You mean Earth , Mr. Beckham?
Yes, James.
That is such a relief, father, that James was not especially chosen for abduction. I was beginning to believe that some of the different species were getting together just to ruin my plans. While looking at me with those entrancing blue-green eyes she said to her father, *If James had been chosen for abduction, I do*

not think that I could bear to continue with this training in order for him to make the crossover.

Harmony! I will endure whatever is necessary to be with you forever!

Oh, James, I know that you say that now, but humans can only endure so much pain and suffering in their lives. However, I would be willing to sacrifice our life together to protect you from any unnecessary suffering at the hands of other species.

And I would devote the rest of my life protecting you, but I realize that I can only do that if I make the crossover.

Harmony, I believe more than ever that you have chosen well in this human. The Elders are going to do their best to keep the Semaj away from you and James while it is still here on Earth. Although it is extremely angry about losing the two of you, not to mention this man Arthur, it probably will not stay on Earth very long after it figures out that the Voresha Elders are trying to force it to leave.

I apologize for all the trouble I seem to be causing Harmony and you and the Elders, Mr. Beckham.

None of this trouble, as you put it, is your fault, James. Something that you are going to learn when you make the crossover is that the Voreshas are on Earth to help people just like you with their problems.

Maybe you should elaborate more on that, father. I am afraid that I have been somewhat remiss in explaining everything to James that I probably should have explained to him by now.

Well, I suppose now is as good of a time as any, James, for you to learn the Voreshas' true mission and why we are permanently on Earth.

Mr. Beckham, could I ask a couple of more questions before you start?

Yes, James.

Please excuse my hopeless human curiosity, but is Mrs. Beckham somewhere safe and why is your house a safe place for us to be if the Semaj can go anywhere it wants to go?

You do have a lot of questions for such a young man. Harmony said that you were always more concerned about others than yourself, James. Thank you for being concerned about Harmony's mother, but my wife is elsewhere in the house right now advising the cook about our dinner, to which you are invited.

Thanks, Mr. Beckham. I will have to let my parents know that I'm staying for dinner.

My wife has already been in contact with your mother at her workplace and she has graciously agreed to allow you to dine with us this evening. As to your second question about our safety, all of the homes of Voreshas are protected from any kind of harm by an invisible barrier which is even hard to explain by our most brilliant minds, but which is something the science fiction writers of earth might refer to as a "force field."

That's pretty cool, Mr. Beckham. I always kind of dreamed about being in a science fiction story or at least writing one.

Well, unfortunately, my young friend, this is quite real. Now, if the two of you can listen for a while, I will get back to my explanation of the Voreshas mission on earth.

We will be quiet, father, will we not, James?

Yes, Harmony.

Good. A large group of Voreshas were selected many millennia ago to go out into the universe and find the planet that had the most crime, poverty, anger, depression, and anything else bad, with the charge to help as many of its inhabitants as possible. As our ancestors traveled from solar system to solar system they found many bad places, but they wanted

to continue their journey until they were sure they had found the absolute worst place in the universe. As you have probably guessed, that place unfortunately was Earth, even thousands and thousands of years ago. The hard part for the Voreshas was trying to adapt to the extremely backward ways of earth's inhabitants at that time. No other place in the universe was as undeveloped technologically as Earth and, to this day, Earth is still several millennia behind technologically.

The group of Voreshas who came to Earth numbered in the thousands and those who sent them thought that would be enough to help any size population of any planet. However, even thousands of years ago Earth was already what we consider to be overpopulated. There were far too many people on Earth then and certainly too many now for the number of us who were and are here to help. However, we have never wavered in our charge to help the people of this planet. We do what we can for as many as we can with the meager number of us who remain. Fortunately, Voreshas live far longer than humans and that at least gives us the opportunity to help more than we would be able to do if we only lived the average life span of humans. That, James, is what you are getting yourself into when you crossover. I hope that it doesn't give you second thoughts about being chosen by Harmony to be her mate on our side.

Not at all, sir. As long I am with Harmony, I will gladly join forces with you to do whatever good I can on Earth.

I do believe you, James, and am very happy about Harmony's choice of you. Now, I believe that dinner may be getting close to being ready and you, my young friend, need to meet Harmony's mother.

At that, we all got up and went back downstairs to the dining room.

Chapter Twenty

I wasn't sure what to expect either about Mrs. Beckham's looks (she had to be beautiful to have a daughter as beautiful as Harmony) or what Voreshas ate (hopefully it wasn't human males!). At school Harmony always ate the same things the rest of us ate, usually composed of what appeared to be kitchen scraps, so I had always assumed that the rest of her kind ate the same foods that all humans consumed. But now that I was in Harmony's house and was getting ready to have dinner with her and her parents my curiosity was beginning to run wild. Did they have strange and exotic foods imported from other parts of the universe and, if so, what would they look and taste like? The three of us entered the dining room, which had to be as long as my parents' entire house and in which was a table large enough to probably seat 40 people. The dining room table was as elaborately carved and highly polished as Mr. Beckham's desk and the three chandeliers hanging over the table appeared to each be at least six feet in diameter and made of the most sparkling crystal imaginable. However, there were only four large chairs arranged at one end of the table, two at the end and one on each side at the same end. Mr. Beckham motioned for Harmony and I to sit together at the end of the table and then he left the room. Being the gentleman that my mother had trained, I pulled one of the heavy ornate chairs out for Harmony and then sat down in the other chair next to her.

Thank you, James. My parents would be impressed with your chivalry.

My father isn't much into that kind of thing, but my mother has tried her best to instill some manners into me.

Well, she has certainly done an excellent job from my viewpoint.

At that moment Mr. and Mrs. Beckham both entered the dining room and my suspicions about Mrs. Beckham's beauty were far more than justified. She was not only as beautiful as Harmony, but moved with the same ease and effortless charm. Trying not to gawk too much and getting my wits about me I immediately rose to my feet and stepped out from the table to greet Mrs. Beckham.

As we clasped hands Mrs. Beckham communicated to me, **James, it is such a pleasure to meet you and may I say that you are more handsome than Harmony said.**

Trying not to stammer, but feeling the blood rush to my face as I began to blush, I communicated to her, *The pleasure is undoubtedly all mine, Mrs. Beckham. I can certainly see where Harmony gets her beautiful looks and grace.*

And such the gentleman and flatterer you are, James.

Ok, Mr. Beckham broke in, **enough of this bowing and scraping you two. Shall we be seated as I believe dinner is about to be served?**

As I was already up and close to where Mrs. Beckham was going to sit, I pulled the chair out for her as well. *Allow me, Mrs. Beckham,* I said.

Why, thank you, James.

I returned to my seat next to Harmony just as the first course of dinner was being brought to the table. Up to now I had not paid much attention to the table setting, but based on the amount of silverware (real silverware, not stainless like at home) and glassware arranged around each setting I was guessing that this was going to be an elaborate affair, even though none of us was formally dressed for such a dinner.

You will have to excuse us for skipping the aperitif, James, but we do not drink alcoholic beverages in this household. As a matter of fact, Voreshas are discouraged from imbibing. We are having a special sweetened tea that Mrs. Mescotid makes and claims to be an old family recipe made from a secret low-country tea grown in the Sabaragamuwa Provence of Ceylon. So, if you don't mind we will move directly to the appetizer. We do hope you enjoy crab cakes and dim sum.

I have never had any alcohol either, I lied, *even though a couple of guys at school I know can't seem to live without it. We almost always have sweet tea at home for dinner, but I'm sure it isn't as good as Mrs. Mescotid's tea. I'm not sure what dim sum is, but crab cakes are one of my favorites.* I didn't mention that at my house crab cakes would have been the main dish and not just an appetizer.

Tonight the dim sum will be egg rolls, James, and, just between you and me, I have a sneaky suspicion that the tea comes from the local grocery store and is called Lipton.

Great! I love egg rolls, too! The dinner continued with a simple green salad topped with a dressing that I was unfamiliar with and too embarrassed at this point to admit or ask about. This was followed by a clear soup that tasted a little like plain old beef stock like my mother would use in some of her recipes. Conversation up to now had been limited to telling the cook how good everything tasted and confirming this among ourselves.

Well, Mr. Beckham broke in after the soup bowls were removed from the table and the cook went back to the kitchen, *Mrs. Mescotid informs me that the filet mignons will not be ready for several more minutes, so I guess we could have a conversation about the two of you,* as both he and Mrs. Beckham looked at us questioningly.

What would you like to know, father, that you do not already know?

Actually, dear, your mother and I would like to ask you and James what you think about an idea that we have been considering for some time now.

And what might that idea concern, father?

Would you like to present our idea to them, Hollace? Mr. Beckham asked his wife.

If that is what you want, Harmon, I will pursue this subject with Harmony and James.

Nothing like being included in the conversation, huh, James?

Now, Harmony, don't be rude, Mrs. Beckham said. *Harmony and James, how shall I begin? I am always at such a loss for words when it comes to trying to explain things to people*.

Just tell them, Hollace, and quit beating around the bush for crying out loud!

You do not have to yell, Harmon. Harmony, your father and I have been discussing bringing James over before he turns twenty years old.

Really, mother? Why? How soon? What is your reasoning?

I was so surprised and confused at both this idea and Harmony's response that I couldn't even stammer out something mentally in reply.

Well, dear, we were thinking that this should happen as soon as possible. You see, we, your father and I, as well as the Elders, are afraid that maybe James is being targeted by different entities in the universe because of who you are and that you chose him. It has been known to happen on occasion over the course of our history on this planet.

Oh my God, no! Then it is true that the Semaj was here specifically for James!

Mr. Beckham broke in here, *Yes, we are now convinced that this is the case and we apologize to you both for the deception. It is becoming harder to protect James on his side, as you well know from your experiences with him so far, and we are very concerned that if he doesn't crossover soon that some entity out there is going to succeed in getting to him and then, my dear little girl, you would have to go through all of this again. And as much for your sake, Harmony, as for James', we think it best to move forward with his crossover.*

Harmony looked over at me with those entrancingly beautiful eyes and asked, *How do you feel about this, James?*

It had sounded like to me that I was being talked about as if I weren't even there. But trying to put that thought aside, I replied, *First, I wish we could talk out loud. But since we can't, I'm flabbergasted to say the least. And at the same time I feel very privileged to have you as my girlfriend and honored to even be in your house and talking about this with your parents. How soon is soon, Mr. and Mrs. Beckham?*

Mrs. Beckham picked up where she left off, *Well, James, that is kind of up to you, but the longer you wait the greater the danger to you and the more stress this situation will put on Harmony. Although you haven't learned all that you need to know for the usual crossover, the Elders are willing, in your case, to make an exception. You can make the crossover at any time, but you do need to know what is involved in the process. Ah, here comes Mrs. Mescotid with the filets, so let's talk more about this after dinner.*

Mrs. Mescotid approached the table with a sterling silver tray containing four large filet mignons and proceeded to give each of us one starting with Mrs.

Beckham, then Mr. Beckham, Harmony, and lastly me. I would have thought that she would have started with the guest first, but since she had not seemed to make eye contact with any of us I guessed that this was the way they did things in the Beckham's house. I supposed that servants weren't allowed to say anything to or make eye contact with guests. Mrs. Mescotid left the dining room and without anyone saying anything during her brief absence she returned momentarily with a dish from which she served each of us a helping of barely cooked asparagus. After dishing out my serving she then returned to the kitchen and didn't come back until it was time for the dessert course.

Mr. Beckham broke the silence, **Shall we enjoy our entrée and afterwards we will continue our conversation over dessert.** As formal as the Beckhams seemed to be about most things they seemed to have a voracious appetite when it came to eating. Now, I'm a pretty fast eater as I am usually grabbing something on the run or having to scarf something down in a few minutes at work, but I was only a little more than half way through my steak when the other three were finished.

I'm sorry to be taking so long to eat, but the steak is so good I'm just trying to savor it.

No problem, James, Mrs. Beckham said, I apologize for our seeming to be in a hurry. Harmon always seems to eat and run around here, so Harmony and I have learned to eat faster if we want to have any time with him at the dinner table. Now, you just take your time and enjoy your dinner. The steak was especially tasty tonight. I think that Mrs. Mescotid must have gone all out for you, James.

Well, I had speeded up and finished my steak and asparagus by the time Mrs. Beckham had finished apologizing. One of the Beckhams must have been in mental communication with Mrs. Mescotid, because within thirty seconds of finishing my steak she was collecting the dirty dishes from the table and placing them on a fancy cart with wheels. *I hope that you like crème brulée, James. Mrs. Mescotid makes the absolute best crème brulée! She likes to serve it with the custard cold and the caramel warm, she says it, too, is based on an old family recipe. I just know that you are going to love it!*

Sounds delicious to me, Mrs. Beckham. Everything else was so good that I can hardly wait to dive into the dessert. And about ten seconds later Mrs. Mescotid was at the table placing fancy crystal dishes with the dessert in them in front of each of us, me being last of course. I have to admit that before that very moment I had no idea what crème brulée was since it wasn't something that would have ever appeared on the dinner table at home. I'm also pretty sure that my mother didn't know what it was either. Now, banana pudding was another story. Nobody, but nobody, made better banana pudding than my mother. It was an old family recipe, too! I waited for one of the others to begin eating their dessert so that I didn't do something wrong or look really stupid and when Harmony had started I began eating mine. As it turned out, it was very tasty although it would never replace my mother's banana pudding. *This is very good, Mrs. Beckham. I must confess, however, that this is the first time I have ever had this particular dessert.*

Well, that is ok, dear. It is just one of many fancy desserts that you will enjoy at our dinner table when you and Harmony are married. Mrs. Mescotid will be so pleased that you liked it, James. She does worry so about how guests like her cooking.

Well, you can tell her for me that this was probably the best meal I have ever eaten, which was, of course, a lie since no one could cook better than my mother.

I'm so glad that you enjoyed it, James. The meal this evening just happens to be Harmon's favorite meal.

When we had all finished our dessert Mr. Beckham suggested that we retire to the library to continue with our conversation about me crossing over to their side. The library was about five times larger than Mr. Beckham's office and all four of the walls were lined with dark mahogany bookcases with elaborately carved Corinthian columns separating each section. There didn't seem to be any place for even one more book anywhere in the bookcases and all of the books appeared to be very old. I couldn't help myself and said, *Wow! There must be a thousand books in here! This is an awesome library, Mr. Beckham!*

Mr. Beckham chuckled out loud and then put his hand over his mouth, Oops! ***There are actually 3,579 books in the room, James, and all are arranged alphabetically according to subject. I have a cross referenced list of authors arranged alphabetically so that I can find a book by a particular author in case I can't remember a title.***

Father is extremely proud of his collection of books, James. Maybe someday he will actually let you look at some of them. Most are very old and have to be handled very carefully. That is why there are always fresh white gloves laid out on the library table by the door. This room is kept closed up all the time because it has to be kept at a certain temperature and the humidity level has to be kept very low. Otherwise, books this old would deteriorate in no time.

Please be seated, James, and Harmony, you sit next to James. There were two extraordinary, deep burgundy, leather sofas facing each other in the middle of the library and a large, elaborately carved coffee table with a matching leather top between the sofas. Harmony and I parked together on one of the sofas and

Mr. and Mrs. Beckham parked on the opposite sofa, but not as close together. *As we indicated earlier, James, Mrs. Beckham and I have been seriously considering yours and Harmony's situation, as have the Elders. Let me reiterate that we are extremely pleased with Harmony's choice in you and we know how much she really seems to care for you. Because we believe it to be in your best interest, we are hoping that you are ready to make the crossover. Of course, this would also be in Harmony's best interest.*

I guess the next question from me, Mr. Beckham, is what exactly is involved in this crossover?

Well, James, I think that Harmony has touched on this subject with you, but it is important that you know what happens to you both physically and mentally in the process and after you have made the crossover.

Don't be so frightful, father. If you scare James away I will never forgive you. No matter how much you may want grandchildren, I am not going to go through this so-called "choosing" rigmarole again!

Harmony! James, I hope you will forgive Harmony's tone. I also hope that you do realize how very lucky you are to have been chosen by the most beautiful young lady in the entire universe.

Yes sir, I am aware of how lucky I am and I can't imagine that there is any girl more beautiful anywhere. Even if you didn't say so, I would still believe that.

Oh, James, you are embarrassing me in front of my parents.

You should be glad that the boy you have chosen feels that way about you, Harmony.

Yes, mother, you know I am. Should I jump up and down on the sofa and cheer?

Ok, ladies, may we get back to the business at hand.

Yes, dear.

Yes, father.

I don't mean to scare you, James, but you must be made aware of what is to come before you actually begin the crossover. Are you ok with me continuing with this discussion, Hollace?

Yes, dear.

Harmony?

Yes, father.

Well then, James, I will try to keep this simple and to the point so as not to confuse you too much.

James is not totally stupid, father.

Thanks, Harmony, I think.

I apologize to you both, but it is just my way. First of all, James, the crossover is somewhat painful during the actual crossing over process. The good news is that it only lasts for about ten minutes. Mr. Beckham hesitated a moment looking at me for some reaction to his last remark. However, I sat there on the big, plush leather sofa holding Harmony's hand in mine without showing any reaction to what he had said, but instead gave him a serious, yet quizzical, look. *I guess that means I can continue. What causes the pain during the crossover, James, is that your brain has to be made to convince your body to make the transformation to its appropriate aging process on this side. As Harmony has indicated to you, Voreshas age much slower than humans after they turn 16 years old and our aging process slows down considerably compared to humans. The pain, if brief, is rather intense, almost excruciatingly so, because the physiology of your body has to make this tremendous change without changing your external appearance. Are you with me so far, James?*

Yes sir, Mr. Beckham, I think so. Would I be awake during this crossover?

I think your question is if you would be aware of the pain during the crossover, correct?

Yes, sir.

I am afraid that is the case, James. Although we are highly developed mentally, we do not have any special magic or technology that would make the crossover any easier or less painful. Unfortunately, it is also somewhat humiliating because you have to be strapped down during the process.

Why is that, Mr. Beckham?

It is to keep you from physically hurting yourself because you will be reacting to the process as if you are having seizures.

Mr. Beckham paused for a moment and searched my face for some reaction. I was very deep in thought about what he had just explained to me and I knew that he, Mrs. Beckham, and Harmony were all reading those thoughts. I wasn't having second thoughts about the process, but simply running all of the information through my puny little human brain. I looked at Harmony to make sure that she didn't think I was having second thoughts and her look assured me that she wasn't. Her look also told me that she was becoming somewhat impatient with both my questions and her father's going on and on about the crossover process.

Harmony interrupted my thoughts at that moment, *James, if it makes you feel any better, I will be by your side through the whole process. I will even hold your hand if you would like that.*

You know I would like that, Harmony. I just hate for you to see me like that, having seizures and screaming out in pain.

Although I have never seen this process, James, I understand it because my Voresha education has included such things, as will yours when you cross over. There is much more to being a Voresha than just mind reading.

Turning back to face Mr. Beckham, I said, *I don't have any qualms about going through the process of crossing over, but I do have one more question?*

Of course.

Harmony! Ask your question, James.

Will my parents know that I have made the crossover or will things go on as usual until Harmony and I are old enough to be married? Harmony giggled at my question. *Do you know something I don't, Harmony?*

Mr. Beckham didn't give Harmony a chance to answer, **Everything will continue just as it is now, James, and, yes, we have talked this part over with Harmony, but only recently, so she has not had time to discuss it with you. The main difference will be that you will continue your mind reading training, but in a more accelerated manor. At some point you will have to be especially careful not to give your parents any indication that you have changed. The hardest parts of that will be that you will soon be able to read their minds and you will have to be very careful not to react to some of their thoughts. In addition, there will come a point in time when they might question how young you continue to look while all of your friends are looking older and older. That may well be the hardest thing for human males to work out with their parents, but we will help you in whatever way we can. Voresha children are trained, for lack of a better word in your vocabulary, from birth to respect their parents' thoughts and to know that no matter what we may think between us that it always kept between children and parents. To answer your question about when you and Harmony will be married, the normal age that Voreshas are married is twenty years old. It is a custom that has, as far as we know, always been. However, Mrs. Beckham and I have had several conversations with the Elders about our concerns for yours and Harmony's safety and have asked them to** *agree to Harmony and you being allowed to be married when you both are eighteen. That would be on July 21st next year for you, but Harmony will not be eighteen until August 3rd based on your earth calendar. How do you think your parents would feel, James, about you and Harmony being married when you are only eighteen?*

Well, let me tell you, Mr. Beckham, nothing could make my mother any happier than to see me get married. But, I was considering going to art school after graduation. Does Harmony and I getting married mean that I will have to get a job and stay around here instead?

Good question, James. That is something my parents didn't discuss with me.

Would that be a problem, James?

Of course not, Mr. Beckham. I will do whatever is required to be with Harmony.

That is good to hear, James. However, Mrs. Beckham and I are going to send both you and Harmony to art school as planned. The expense will be taken care of by us so that your parents will not have to worry about where they will get the money. When you graduate from art school you will go to work for me, which will be in the company that I use as a front to hide our identity. In reality, you and Harmony will be doing the work that all Voreshas were charged with thousands of years ago.

Wow! was all that I could think at that moment.

Chapter Twenty-one

The rest of the evening at the Beckhams revolved around simple social conversation and then it came time for me to leave. Mr. and Mrs. Beckham wished me a good night at the front door and then left Harmony and me alone to say good night to each other. We took each others hands and stared into each others eyes for a few seconds before I pulled her close and kissed her. Although our kiss seemed to be passionate, I also felt like Harmony was resisting me a little.

James, are you sure that you are ok with all of this business about the crossover?

Of course, Harmony! I can't wait to be with you on your side and I am especially excited about us getting married when we are eighteen!

Yes, I know what you are excited about, but I just want to be sure that you are absolutely sure about going through with the crossover, especially now that you know what you will have to endure.

I readily admit that I am looking forward to having sex with you, Harmony, but being with you in your world for the rest of my life is the most important thing to me.

I do believe you, James, especially since you did so marvelously during my father's explanation of what will happen to you during the crossover, but I do think you should think about it a little more. Well, as much as I would like for you to stay all night, I think that you should get on back home. I do not think that you will be bothered by any other malevolent beings for a while.

You're right about me getting home, because my mother is going to have more questions about dinner and your parents than I'm going to be able to remember. We hugged and kissed one more time and then I got in my car to head for home, but because it was still a little early, I thought I would just cruise around town for a while and think about what Mr. Beckham had told me about crossing over to their side.

I still got home around 10:00 and my mother was still up, because she always waited for my father to get home around 11:30, and she wanted every detail about dinner, the Beckhams, and their house. Amazingly enough, I remembered all the details of the meal and tried to describe the Beckham's house without making it sound like the mansion that it was, but at the same time making it sound nice. I feigned being really tired and went to my room to get ready for bed. I had changed into my pajamas and had climbed into bed when my mother peaked in and asked, "This is really serious with Harmony isn't it, James?"

"Oh yes!" I exclaimed. "It couldn't be any more serious. Why, we are practically engaged already."

"Well, don't rush into anything, but your father and I are really happy for you, James. I hope you believe that."

"I do believe you, mother. I know you always say you only want what's best for me."

"Good night, son," she said and left me alone.

It didn't take long for me to get to sleep even though my mind was racing with all the information from that evening that Mr. Beckham had imparted to me. My dreams that night centered around Harmony and me and our future life together. I don't know whether it was just my normal mind causing my dreams or if Harmony was somehow placing those sweet dreams of our life together in my head. Either way, it was a very peaceful sleep and my dreams were the best I think I have ever had or at least better than I had had in a long time.

I awoke the next morning feeling very relaxed and refreshed and since this was an unusual state of being for me over the past few months my suspicious little mind started to work. By the time I was dressed and ready for school my father had already left for work and my mother was putting my breakfast on the table. She told me that my father had left early because the police wanted to meet him at the service station early that morning and give him an update on Arthur's disappearance. If nothing else got my brain cranked up that morning that little bit of information certainly did the trick. I wondered if the police had found Arthur's body buried in the collapsed warehouse on the north side of town or if they had given up the search for him altogether. I finished my breakfast of bacon, eggs, and fresh homemade biscuits and since I was running a little late, I headed on out to pick up Harmony at her house and try to get to school on time.

I was one of those semi-nerdy teenagers who actually liked school and usually tried to do my best in my classes. Up until my senior year I had a 3.85 grade point average, but that had sunk to near a 3.0 because I had lost interest in some of the subjects that one had to take their senior year. My least favorite class was probably Senior English, which was taught by Miss Mutchan, a 70-plus year old spinster with dyed dark brown hair, who believed that all students had an innate interest in Shakespeare and Macbeth in particular, which we spent half the school year reading about and studying in some depth and the other half of the year acting out bits and pieces of the play. I can still see to this day her favorite student, Ron Cotworthy, standing erect at the front of the class and reading from Macbeth in his best English accent, "So foul and fair a day I have not seen." Compared to Ron's eloquent recitation, my reading sounded more like the monotone prattle of a shy six-year old. Of course, History hadn't been the best course that school year so far either with all that had happened in there, although I still kind of liked it, probably because our new teacher, Miss Norriso, seemed to be a real human being who didn't imbibe and who had a knack for making history actually interesting. Part of that "interest" in history with her was no doubt that even though she was in her thirties, she was still quite attractive as any of my buddies would have readily told you if asked. Although math had been one of my favorite and best subjects from the fourth grade through the eleventh grade, Mr. Bregala and his version of algebra left me just not feeling it. Although he was very intelligent, his approach to polynomials, equations, and algebraic structures, with geometry, topology, and combinatorics thrown in for good measure, left most of us walking around counting on our fingers and toes. Of course, there was always art class. Even though we weren't being taught anything, by Mr. Carter, affectionately know as "Old Man Carter," I still enjoyed creating my work and getting as good as I could before heading off to art school the next year. And my favorite time of the day, as you might have guessed by now, was study hall, especially since that was when I actually got to spend some time in Harmony's presence.

Harmony was already waiting for me by the curb when I pulled up in front of her house that morning. She jumped in without waiting for me to get out and open her door for her. "Good morning, love," she beamed and bent over to give me a big kiss.

"Good morning to you, too," I responded. "I assume it's now ok to talk out loud?"

"Yes, James, father told me this morning that the elders had worked hard all night to drive the Semaj back through its hole and away from Earth," she informed me. "They do not think that one will be back here for a very long time."

"That's the second best news I've heard recently," I told Harmony.

"And what might be the best news you have heard lately, James?" she asked rather coyly.

"As if you didn't know," I replied.

"I just want to hear you say it, James," she suggested to me.

"The best news that I have heard recently, Harmony," I began, "is that you and I are going to be married next year and spend the rest of our lives together!"

"That is the best news I have heard in a long time, too, James," Harmony said, but not with the conviction in her voice that I would like to have heard. "My father wanted me to ask you when you thought you might want to make the crossover?" she asked me next with a little apprehension in her voice. "I do hope that you gave it some serious thought last night."

"The sooner the better," I stated matter-of-factly. "I didn't have to give it much thought at all and I really do not have any reservations about doing this, Harmony. However, I would be lying if I said I wasn't afraid of the physical pain involved, after all, I am only human and humans, with a few masochistic exceptions, don't especially like pain."

"I talked to father about an idea that I had concerning that, James," Harmony informed me. "I asked him about hypnotizing you so that you wouldn't be aware of the physical pain or even realize afterwards that you had had pain or seizures."

"Sounds like a painless plan to me," I said. "What did he say to your idea?"

"Quite frankly, he had never thought about that, but it would be easy for us to hypnotize you so you wouldn't be aware of what was happening to your body during the crossover process," she said. "Father said there was no precedent for hypnotizing someone who was crossing over, but that he did not see anything wrong with it. He was going to check with the Elder that he had in mind for conducting the process to see if it is ok."

"Would that make your father think less of me as a man?" I meekly asked.

"Of course not, James," she said without hesitation. "My parents think very highly of you and, as they told you last night, they are both extremely pleased with you as my choice. Besides, Voreshas aren't especially fond of pain either."

"Well, then," I said trying to sound as confident as possible, "tell your father that I'm ready whenever the arrangements can be made." We were pulling into the school parking lot about that time, so I found a good parking place as close to campus as I could and Harmony and I strolled onto campus arm and arm as we usually did these days. I walked Harmony to her first class, gave her a big kiss, and then headed off to my first class. I was so pumped up that morning that I could have given Ron Cotworthy a run for his money with a reading from Macbeth. Fortunately, however, Miss Mutchan didn't call on me that day in class, probably because she didn't care much for my childish renditions of her favorite Shakespearean play; as it turned out, it seemed to be "pick on the girls day" in Senior English. Ron sat up front, of course, and I sat back in the corner next to the windows so I could keep an eye on the lack of activities outside, but I could tell that Ron was stewing about not getting to read from Macbeth that day.

James, Harmony here.

Hi, love. What's up?

James, Ron is very, very upset about not being called on to read from Macbeth today. He is not a very stable person mentally to begin with and right

now he is seriously thinking about harming Miss Mutchan for not calling on him.

No way! I admit that Ron may be a little eccentric, but mentally unstable?

Yes, James, unstable! Please believe me when I tell you that his thoughts right now about not being chosen to read from Macbeth are not very nice where Miss Mutchan is concerned.

Can't you do something about it, Harmony?

No, James. I am currently having to deal with another problem with one of the girls in my class who is acting really strange today. You are going to have to deal with Ron yourself.

I don't mean to sound stupid, Harmony, but what can I do about his instability?

James, you are now ready to communicate tele-pathically with others without them knowing it. You must refocus Ron's thoughts so that he doesn't hurt Miss Mutchan. I really have to go now, so good luck with Ron.

As I have said, I could tell that Ron was stewing about not getting picked to read from Macbeth, but I had seen him get angry before, especially in art class when one time he broke the canvas in half that he was working on. Every time that I had seen him get angry about something he always took it out on some inanimate object, like the painting. Once in the parking lot I saw him get angry when he discovered that one of the tires on his 1964 Ford Galaxie was flat. Instead of cursing about it and then changing the flat out with the spare in his trunk, Ron took out a pocket knife and poked holes in the other three tires and then opened the trunk and did the same to the spare. He then threw all of his books as far across the parking lot as he could, actually being careful not to hit any other cars in the parking lot, and then stomped off in the direction of his house, which was about eight miles away. I don't know how he got back and forth to school for the next few days, because his car sat there with four flats and the trunk open. No one offered to help Ron, because we were all afraid of him when he was like this. Now that I thought about these occurrences, I guess Harmony was right about him being unstable. However, I had never known Ron to actually hurt anything that didn't belong to him and, especially not anyone.

I could tell from my vantage point back in the corner that Ron was getting more and more upset, because his face and neck were turning a bright red and the veins in his temple were starting to throb. If Harmony thought that he was a danger to Miss Mutchan, then I figured I had better keep an eye on him for a while. Since we both had art class next it would be easier for me to watch him and try to intervene if I thought he was going to actually hurt Miss Mutchan or anyone else for that matter.

When English class was over, Ron stormed out of the room bumping into several desks and knocking over one that had just been vacated and without speaking to anyone. I had to practically run down the hallway to keep him in sight. I had always heard that when the adrenalin gets pumping that people can perform great feats of strength, but I had never seen this happen until Ron and I got outside the classroom building. Ron had stomped out into the grassy area and taking his English tome on Macbeth, he held it out at arms length and with it spread open and clasped in both hands ripped it in half. He then started tearing the pages out one by one and slinging them into the air. Since it was a windy day, Macbeth was being blown all over campus. As this act was taking place a crowd had gathered and was now chanting, "Tear it up! Tear it up!" I figured this was as good a time as any to try and get into Ron's head and see if I could actually read his mind and change his thoughts to more peaceful ones.

Much to my surprise, I was able to easily read his thoughts although they were speeding randomly through his brain like a runaway locomotive. Heck, I even imagined smoke coming out of Ron's ears while he was ripping the book to shreds. What I pieced together from his thoughts, however, was very scary. As he was destroying the book page by page, Ron was seriously putting together a plan in his mind on how he would kill Miss Mutchan. It was at this point that he started chanting over and over, "Fair is foul, and foul is fair: Hover through the fog and filthy air." That got the crowd of students standing around watching into it even more and they started chanting with Ron, "Fair is foul, and foul is fair: Hover through the fog and filthy air." The term that Ron was using for Miss Mutchan in his mind was "that ugly old Macbeth whore" and the plan that was forming was to seduce Miss Mutchan after school and take her someplace where he would tie her up and chop off her head. If Ron had been saying that out loud as he was tearing up the book, the crowd might have given it a second thought, because even though we knew he ranted and raved about doing a lot of things to a lot of people, that was a plan to actually murder someone. However, now that I could read minds and get into the deep dark recesses of people's brains, I knew that he was very serious this time about his plan to kill Miss Mutchan.

Up to now I had relied heavily on Harmony to come to the rescue in situations like this, especially where I was concerned, but I was now beginning to understand what the Voresha's purpose on earth was all about. I concentrated all of my metal ability on Ron's mind and started trying to implant in his mind more peaceful thoughts and images. All of a sudden, Ron seemed to start calming down and relaxed, dropping what little remained of his English book to the ground. He didn't turn around, but just kept standing there and started staring up at the sky. Since he had quit his violent rampage against the book, the crowd was beginning to disperse, giggling among themselves about another of Ron's little temper tantrums. My next thoughts to Ron were to calmly go back to Miss Mutchan's classroom and quietly apologize for getting upset and storming out of class and for tearing up his English book.

At that, Ron turned around and walked back toward the classroom building where I was standing just outside the door. He walked right past me as if I didn't even exist and entered the hallway and headed toward Miss Mutchan's classroom. I figured that since I wasn't completely sure that my ideas had sunk into his head that I should follow him closely to make sure everything went ok, although I didn't know at that moment what I would do if he actually attacked Miss Mutchan. I stopped just outside the classroom door after Ron had entered. I both listened as closely as I could and sneaked a peek around the corner of the door in time to see Ron hugging Miss Mutchan and apologizing profusely about his actions. He dropped down to one knee and even promised to never get angry at her again and to be the model student in all of his classes. I stepped aside as Ron left the classroom and passed by me again as if I weren't even there. I peeked into the classroom one more time before heading off to art class to see Miss Mutchan wiping tears from her eyes and muttering to herself that Ron was such a nice young man.

Chapter Twenty-two

I had arrived at the portable building that served as the art classroom and settled into my spot at one of the eight-foot long folding tables to work on an abstract painting of a cityscape in yellows and blacks I had started during the last art class when Harmony tuned in, *James?*

Yes, Harmony.

What you did with Ron was excellent! I could not have done a better job myself. Although he was a little too ingratiating for my likes, your influence on his mind worked just fine.

Thank you, Harmony. I wasn't sure at first what I should do, so I just tried implanting the idea in his head to calm down and go apologize to Miss Mutchan. That seemed to me to be the best suggestion since it would not only calm him down, but, hopefully, make him a better person for everyone else to be around.

Father will be very impressed with what you did today to avert what could have turned out very badly for Miss Mutchan. I think that you are progressing with your telepathic training at an exceedingly fast pace, which should also impress the Elders.

You make it sound like it is unusual for humans to learn so quickly.

It is usually a very slow process for most humans, James, but you seem to be learning faster than normal.

Harmony, how is it exactly that I am learning telepathic skills when I wasn't even aware that I had them in the first place?

My charge for having chosen you, James, is to implant these skills in your brain without your knowledge of it happening, similar to what you did with Ron. Most humans, as I have been told, usually take several years to get to where you have come in a matter of weeks. Father and the Elders have told me that they believe you may have had a Voresha as an ancestor at some point in history. It may have been thousands of years ago or only a few hundred years ago, but the Elders are actually doing research on this to find out if you actually do have Voresha blood running through your veins.

That would just be too cool, Harmony. I don't have to submit to any kind of blood test, do I?

It would be very cool, James, and, no, you do not have to submit to any blood tests. I, too, am very excited about the possibility that you are part Voresha, because even the tiniest percentage would make your crossover much easier and make our relationship go much smoother.

Will I have to wait until the Elders figure out whether or not I am part Voresha before I can make the crossover, Harmony?

No, James. We absolutely believe in your conviction to crossover to our side and serve with us in our quest to help everyone we can to be better people and live more peaceful and enjoyable lives. If we had any doubts about you, then the Elders would have erased any memory of us from your mind by now and you would go back to living your ordinary, boring human life. My parents and the Elders all trust my decision to choose you as you have heard my parents say and I could not be happier with my decision.

Aw, you say the nicest things, Harmony.

Do not go getting all mushy on me, James. You know what effect that has on me.

Ron just came into the room and he looks more at peace with the world than I have ever seen him, Harmony. As a matter of fact, he's smiling and I can't remember him ever smiling. I hope that's a good sign and that he's not just having evil thoughts.

I assure you that it is a good sign, James. The ideas that you implanted in Ron's mind will remain there forever. No one can change that except another Voresha and once good has been accomplished, we do not change it back to evil. It may take some time for others at school and especially his parents to get used to him being nice and cheerful, but in time his life and all those whose life he interacts with will be much better for what you have done.

Is what I did today with Ron what being a Voresha is really all about, Harmony?

It is but a small part of the good that we are charged with doing here on earth, James, but it is a great start for you as a Voresha.

You know what, Harmony?

No, but I have a feeling that you are going to tell me anyway, James?

I don't think I have ever felt so good about doing something as I do about what happened today with Ron. Voreshas must be the most contented species in the universe, Harmony.

I am not sure that contented is the right word, James. Although we deal with many problems throughout our lives, they are mostly other people's problems and we are happy to help in whatever way we can to make life better for as many people as we can. I guess you could say that we are content with what we do and happy in our lives as Voreshas.

Harmony, I had better get to work on my painting, because old man Carter just showed up, late as usual and looking like he has a bone to pick with the world. See you in study hall later.

Bye, James. See you later.

Old man Carter had his usual 'what are you staring at you little pip squeak' look on his face with his deeply furrowed brow. From my experiences in his classes so far, I knew he was out to pick on someone today. For a man in his mid-thirties he must have had a lot of stress in his life and the way he treated students made him one of the most disliked teachers at school, to put it mildly. The only reason I was in his art class was because it would look good on my application to the admissions people at art school. Most students didn't give a flip one way or the other about art, but endured old man Carter's maltreatment with the hopes of getting an easy A. I started to wonder if maybe I should try to change him and make him a more pleasant person to be around, but before I took that step I would confer with Harmony first. Preventing violent acts and making people forget bad things was one aspect of being a Voresha, but changing someone's attitude because you didn't like it might not be a chapter in the books.

Old man Carter, as everyone in art class or who had ever been in one of his art classes, referred to him behind his back, slammed some magazines down on his desk. Two of the magazines slid off the desk and crashed in a wrinkled up heap on the floor causing him to utter, "Damn it!" Without bothering to pick the magazines up off the floor, he started his brief walk around the room to see if anyone was actually working on something or just pretending to work. The most talented student in the class was undoubtedly George Potus and old man Carter moseyed up to him first. Standing next to George and looking down at what most of us thought was a fabulous landscape that George was working on he said, "That's the worst mess I've seen in a long time! I thought you were going to actually accomplish something with that painting, Mr. Potus, but it just gets worse every day!"

"Everyone else thinks it is pretty good, Mr. Carter," George politely replied.

"Well now," old man Carter began, "do you think these jackasses have any clue as to what art really is? Take James over there for instance. He thinks he knows something about art and so he's going to apply to art school next year. They wouldn't take him at art school if he owned it." Old man Carter started to laugh and then grabbed up George's painting and holding it above his head showed it to the rest of class saying, "See this piece of trash? Now where do you think trash is supposed to go? Why, in the trash can of course." He then walked over to the large trash can in the corner of the portable building where he tossed George's painting. George wasn't a big guy, but he didn't usually take anything off of anyone. He got up and walked over to the trash can and retrieved his painting. "What the hell do you think you're doing, Mr. Potus? old man Carter yelled at him.

"I'm going to continue to work on my painting," George stated.

"If you are going to do anything, Mr. Potus, you are going to start over on your painting and you're going to pick a decent subject to paint, not some stupid landscape from some farm in Iowa that your grandmother grew up on! I'd bet the old hag is probably dead now anyway!" old man Carter continued yelling. "Now put that piece of crap back where I put it and go sit down!"

Standing up, I said, "Mr. Carter, why not let George finish that painting and then if you don't like it you can give him a lower grade? Besides, George is painting it for his mother, who also grew up on that farm."

"Well, if it isn't Mr. Know-It-All who thinks he's going to art school trying to give advice to the teacher," old man Carter replied to the entire class. "What do all of you little goof-offs think about that idea? All in favor of letting George finish his so-called painting raise your hand." Much to my surprise and I'm sure to old man Carter's surprise as well, every student in the class raised their hand. The look of surprise on old man Carter's face was priceless as everyone continued to hold their hands up high. "Well, never let it be said that I don't believe in democracy. You go ahead and finish your pretty little painting, Mr. Potus, but know that it probably won't get a very good grade."

George, trying to hold his temper, said, "Thank you, sir," and sat back down at his spot.

Old man Carter walked back to his desk in defeat, picked up the two magazines that had slid off his desk, and sat down to read them. The rest of us in class then got down to working on our paintings and nothing else was said during the rest of the class period. When the bell rang for us to change classes, old man Carter never even looked up as we all exited the portable building. Since that was my last formal class of the day I quickly headed to study hall to be with Harmony. I was about half way there when I heard George call my name from behind me. I stopped, turned around and waited for him to catch up figuring that he was going to get on my case for interfering in his business in art class. When he caught up to me he said, "Thanks for sticking up for me, James, in art class I mean. At least I'll get to finish that painting for my mother for Christmas."

"Some of us, George, have to stand up to ogres like old man Carter once in a while," I said. "Getting your painting out of the trash can was very brave considering the mood he was in today. I really admire you for that and your mother is going to love that painting regardless of what old man Carter has to say about it.

For what it's worth, I think it is great and I also think you are the best artist in our class."

"Well, I don't know about that, James, but thanks anyway. And I know that if any of us can get into art school, it would certainly have to be you."

"Thanks, dude," I replied. "Listen, I have got to get to study hall, so I'll see you later."

"Later," George said and then headed off to his last class. As I was watching him walk away he stopped, turned around and said," By the way, buddy, you have got to be the luckiest guy in school to be going steady with Harmony Beckham! What a doll!"

"Thanks, George," I said. "I'll tell her you said so," although I knew that she had heard every word of what had been said over the past hour or so. I then headed off to study hall and met Harmony at the door as she was just arriving as well. She gave me that approving smile of hers confirming what I had suspected.

When we had settled into our places in study hall, she communicated, *Standing up for George in art class and making that suggestion to Mr. Carter was very brave, James. I'm very proud of you for doing that. Standing up for others is one good trait that a few humans, like you, have.*

Thanks, Harmony. I couldn't just sit there and let old man Carter run rough shod over George like that and I especially couldn't let him throw George's painting away like that. Fortunately, old man Carter didn't break the painting in half before throwing it in the trash can. I did notice that it got a few smudges and scratches on it, but George can easily fix those. Old man Carter is always so mean to all of his students. I don't think he likes anybody or has any friends at all. By the way, George said you were a doll.

I know, James, but I appreciate you telling me so anyway. Back to Mr. Carter, he does have some atti-

tude problems and your idea about adjusting those might be a good one.

Really, Harmony, I wasn't sure that was an ok thing to do just because I don't like him. However, I would love to try and give that sorry rascal an attitude adjustment.

As you know, James, none of the students in his classes like him because of the way he acts toward everyone. Wouldn't it be better for the student's and their work if he were nicer and more accepting of what they are creating?

So, you are saying that it's more for the students than for him?

Absolutely, James. And besides, it probably wouldn't hurt if Mr. Carter's life was more enjoyable from his viewpoint. You probably don't know this yet, but Mr. Carter has been having trouble at home with his wife for a long time now, which is probably why he is so miserable at school.

No, Harmony, I did not know that. I'll give some thought to giving him an attitude adjustment and maybe it will not only help him and the students, but maybe things will improve for him at home as well.

That sounds like a wonderful plan, James. Father has been in touch and he and the Elders think that maybe this coming weekend would be a good time for you to make the crossover, especially since you are not working at the service station any more.

Really? Wow! I'm ready and willing! What time should I come over to your house on Saturday? Assuming, of course, that the crossover will take place there.

The set-up and process, as we have described to you, doesn't take very long, but you will need a few hours to rest and recuperate from the crossover and, yes, it will be at my house. If you could come over to my house around 10:00 Saturday morning you could

spend the rest of day there with me and I could aid in your recovery from the crossover.

How long will it take for me to "recover," Harmony? That doesn't sound very appealing.

Your crossover should be completed by no later than 11:00, depending on when you arrive and the set-up time and you should be fully recovered by 3:00 or maybe 4:00 Saturday afternoon. My mother is making arrangements with your mother for you to spend the day with me and then have dinner with us again as well.

Well, it all sounds pretty good to me, Harmony! I can't wait to be a full-fledged Voresha!

Neither can I wait for you to be on our side, James! I am quite excited to know that you are so willing to become one of us and live the rest of your life with me.

No more excited than me, Harmony.

Chapter Twenty-three

Saturday rolled around and I was wide awake that morning long before the alarm went off on my Lone Ranger alarm clock that my parents had bought for me one Christmas back in the 1950s. I hadn't slept much that night, but it was only because I was so excited about what was going to take place that day with my crossover at the Beckham's house. I had never met one of the Elders, but Harmony assured me I would not want to meet any one any kinder than them and especially the one who was performing the crossover. She had also told me that the Elder who was going to perform the crossover on me had done several crossover procedures over his 378 Voresha years (making him about 94 1/2 in human years). This particular Elder was the most advanced mentally of all of the Voresha and Harmony assured me I had nothing to worry about. Once again I assured Harmony that I wasn't worried about anything and was actually looking forward to making this transition so that she and I could always be together.

I wasn't supposed to eat anything before the crossover process took place, so I lied to my mother and said that Harmony and I were going to get something for breakfast at a local café down on South Florida Avenue that was always open early. My father had left early again for work and my mother left at her usual time around 7:20 to walk to the corner and catch the 7:30 bus to work downtown at S.H. Kress in the notions department. My father kept hoping that Arthur would turn up or that the police had some new information about his disappearance. Of course, the police, nor anyone else, would find Arthur's body for a long time to come in the pile of rubble that used to be an abandoned warehouse. Several years later while the pile of twisted steel and tin that was the old warehouse building was being removed, the workers found some human bones and did contact the police. Arthur had never been to a dentist in his long life, so there were no dental records to match and the police never did identify the body. Rats and bugs had eaten away at Arthur's clothes and the few scraps that were left gave no clues to having been a Star Service Station uniform. My father never believed that the body could possibly be Arthur, because he could never have wandered so far away.

Since I didn't have to be at the Beckham's house until around 10:00 that morning, I just hung out at my house watching cartoons until it was time for me to head out. I arrived at the Beckham's house around 9:45 and Harmony was waiting for me outside on their front porch in one of their rocking chars. Per Harmony's instructions, I pulled into their semi-circular driveway that morning instead of parking on the street and parked in the area paved for parking at the front of their house. I got out of my car and walked up on the front porch where Harmony motioned for me to sit in the large white rocking chair next to her.

She leaned over and gave me a kiss and then informed me that the Elder had already arrived and that her father and the Elder were preparing the game room on the third floor upstairs for the crossover procedure. "Are you nervous, James?" she asked me.

"I would be lying if I said that I wasn't a little bit nervous, Harmony," I replied, "but I think I am just as excited as nervous."

"My mother will come downstairs and let us know when my father and the Elder are ready for you," she said. "Are you sure that you are ok with being hypnotized?"

"Although I have never been hypnotized, or for that matter have never believed that it could really be done, I trust you and your father completely in this matter," I replied. "Are you still going to be there with me during all of this, Harmony?"

"Of course I am, James," she answered. "Besides wanting to be there with you, this will actually be part of my training. I am anxious to learn about conducting the crossover procedure."

"You must be very highly regarded by the Elders to be allowed to study the crossover process at such a young age." I stated.

"I am very honored to be allowed to do this, because there has never been a female Elder and the current Elders have decided that it may be a good time to start training a female who might someday become an Elder."

"And they have picked you?" I asked.

"Yes," was all she said, because Mrs. Beckham had just come out on the porch to let us know that her father and the Elder were ready for me.

Harmony took my hand and we followed Mrs. Beckham into the house and up the left side curved stairway this time to the second floor, but this time we turned down the hallway in the opposite direction from Mr. Beckham's office. At the end of the hallway was a narrow stairway that led upward to the third floor and to what Harmony had referred to as the game room. This room was so large that it stretched almost all the way across the third level of the house. It was impossible to tell that this huge room in the house even existed from the street level. One might have guessed that there was an attic in the house, but not that there was a room as large as this one used exclusively for an elaborately carved billiards table and several other types of tables used for different games that I had never seen before.

There was so much open space in this huge room because it had no center supports anywhere. There was a large full bed-size table that had been set up at one end, where some of the game tables had been moved out of the way, and with Harmony's hand in mine I was guided by her over to the table where Mr. Beckham and a very old-looking man I assumed to be the Elder were standing. This elderly, 378-year old man was slim but muscular looking and stood about six feet tall. He had a long, snow-white beard and long matching white hair that was braided and hung over his left shoulder almost down to his waist. Although I was prepared to see someone dressed like the Dalai Lama, the Elder was dressed in normal everyday Levi blue jeans, a dark brown wide belt with a fancy silver buckle with strange symbols on it, and a red and black, long sleeve, plaid shirt with pearlized buttons. In later years I would think of this Elder every time I saw a picture of Willie Nelson.

Mr. Beckham spoke first, "James, I would like for you to meet the Great Voresha Elder, Cudur Mus Noslen."

The elderly man moved forward a couple of steps and extended his hand in greeting and in a very deep voice said, "It is my great pleasure to meet the man Harmony has chosen to join her on our side."

As I took his hand and shook it, I replied, "I assure you, sir, that the pleasure and honor are all mine."

Cudur Mus Noslen looked over at Harmony and said, "As you indicated young one, James is a most courteous man and I see in his eyes the love that you have only begun to know and which will no doubt increase a hundred fold after his crossover."

Harmony only blushed at the Elder's remarks and didn't say anything, but her father told me to get up on the table, but to remain sitting up as Elder Cudur Mus Noslen would begin the hypnosis process. I did as Mr. Beckham instructed and sat on the edge of the table with my feet not quite touching the floor while the Elder moved in front of me. I could see the Elder's legs and feet moving, but it was almost as if he were floating along the floor instead of walking. The Elder's movements didn't resemble those of a human or even those of the Beckham family, but were so smooth that I didn't notice his head or shoulders move at all. He moved in front of me and told me to look deep into his eyes and tell him what I saw in the depths there.

After staring for a few seconds into the nearly black irises of the Elder's eyes, whose pupils I couldn't see in that blackness, I heard myself say in a distant sounding voice that I didn't recognize, "I see the universe, Great Elder Cudur Mus Noslen."

"And what do you feel as you look out into that vast universe, James?" the Elder asked me.

My eyelids were refusing to stay open, but I did hear myself say in that distant sounding voice, "Sleeeeeeeepy."

"You may now lie down, James, and you will sleep and not feel anything while I perform the crossover," I heard the Elder say, but was unsure if I were actually hearing him or if it was telepathic. "You will wake up only when I tell you to wake, James," and I felt myself being gently lowered onto the table by several pairs of hands. "James, can you count backwards from 100 for me?"

Again, I heard that distant sounding voice say, "What's the first num . . . ?"

I have no memory of what took place during the crossover procedure, which was supposed to only take about ten minutes, but Harmony offered to explain it to me in detail the next day if I so desired. I do remember looking at my watch when the Elder brought me out of hypnosis and thought that it was strange that it was still 9:45 a.m., which is what it read the rest of the day. However, the next morning when I put my watch on it showed the correct time. I forgot to ask Harmony the next day about what happened to my watch and it mysteriously slipped my mind until I just wrote about it over 40 earth years later.

The next day Harmony and I took a picnic lunch of cold fried chicken, homemade potato salad, and banana pudding my mother had prepared and we drove out into the country south of town where I took her to one of my favorite quiet places so that we could be alone. Besides my bedroom at home, with the door closed, and my posters to look at and collection of albums to listen to, there were several places in and around town where I liked to go when I wanted to be alone. One of my favorite spots was a grassy hillside behind a row of buildings downtown that overlooked a small, concrete surrounded lake where one could catch a glimpse of a very large alligator. I remember rolling down the hill many times as early as eight years old.

My favorite spot that I was taking Harmony to on that Sunday morning was at an old mined-out phosphate pit that had been filled with water and stocked with a variety of fish many years before. This particular man-made lake was one of my father's favorite fishing places for bluegill and bass, although he didn't know about my using the area for one of my "quiet spots." The spot that I refer to was toward the back of the man-made lake and was amongst a literal forest of huge live oaks that had to be at least 200 years old and which were profusely draped in grey-green Spanish moss. There was a smooth, grassy area under one of the largest of the live oak trees that I was taking Harmony to and, when we finally got back to this spot, we spread out an old blanket with deep intense colors and an unusual abstract design that Harmony's mother had given us to use for our picnic. Harmony told me that the blanket was at least 300 years old and that it was made with special fibers that the Voresha scientists had developed over a thousand years ago. It had been in her family for at least that long and familial legend said that blankets made like this one often exhibited magical powers.

After spreading the blanket out we sat down and Harmony gave me a long kiss and then reclined on the blanket and said, "James, this is a very romantic place with these beautiful old trees and the musical sounds of nature. Thank you for bringing me here to your quiet spot for our picnic."

"Your presence in this spot has made it more beautiful than I could have ever imagined," I told her.

Harmony blushed and asked me, "Do you really want to know what happened during the crossover yesterday, James?"

"Right now, Harmony, all I want is to be with you and enjoy this time alone together in this quiet spot without having to worry about getting to work on time," I replied. "And I am not sure that I do want to know what happened during the crossover process. I mean, if I had been aware of what was gong on and saw you there I would probably have been very embarrassed both during the crossover and right now."

James," Harmony said, "Nothing happened yesterday that you should be embarrassed about. The process is not a physically pleasant one for humans and we are very sensitive about that, but father, the Elder, and I all now believe for sure that you must be part Voresha, because you exhibited very little physical discomfort and didn't seem to have any seizure-like reactions at all during the crossover. Hypnosis might not have even been necessary for you, but I'm glad we used it just in case."

"Thanks, Harmony," I said, "but I am still glad that I was hypnotized. Are you ready for some lunch? My mother made us some fried chicken, homemade potato salad, and her famous banana pudding"

"I'm starving, love!" Harmony exclaimed. "It all sounds yummy! I know how much you love your mother's cooking and I think I have seen you swoon when talking about her banana pudding." Harmony started giggling at that.

"Just wait until you taste her banana pudding," I said. Harmony got everything out of the picnic basket and laid it out very precisely on the blanket between us. We both woofed down the fried chicken, potato salad, and banana pudding like we hadn't eaten for a week and washed it down with a couple of bottles of Coca-Cola. Harmony told me that I would have an unusually big appetite for about a week or two after the crossover. It was due to my new physiology trying to "catch up" with being a Voresha, even though I may have been part Voresha before the crossover. My body didn't actually "feel" any different, but I knew now that my aging process would be much slower and I have to admit that I was still having trouble wrapping my mind around that idea. The aging process would be extremely hard to explain to my parents if I ever had to do it. Reading my mind, Harmony assured me that I would never have to explain it to my parents, but she didn't elaborate and I didn't ask why not.

We finished our lunch and together packed up the dirty dishes. I sat the picnic basket over to the side of the blanket and scooted over closer to Harmony and put my arm around her waist. She suggested that we snuggle up and take a little nap and then maybe go for a short hike afterwards in the nearby woods. For a piece of cloth that looked very thin, the old blanket was amazingly comfortable and seemed to have a tranquilizing effect on us. We snuggled up as close as two people could get, closed our eyes and fell fast asleep to the sounds of a gentle breeze blowing through the moss and a variety of birds singing in the branches of the live oak trees. When we woke up we discovered that we had been asleep for nearly two hours and sounding somewhat groggy, I said, "Those heavy meals can sure knock you out, but I feel really refreshed from the nap. Do you think the blanket had some magical effect on us, Harmony?"

"My mother told me that these blankets are rumored to have special attributes," Harmony reminded me. "It certainly did not take us long to fall into a deep sleep."

Do you feel refreshed as well?" I asked.

"I do feel very alive and I am convinced that the blanket had something to do with the way we feel," Harmony responded. "Are you ready to go on our hike, James?"

"Did your parents give you a certain time that you had to be home?" I asked not wanting to get Harmony in trouble with her parents for getting home too late.

"My mother told me that I could stay out all day, but not to be home any later than sunset," she answered. "We have lots of daylight left, James, so let's go for that walk in the woods."

We got up and both of us stretched before heading off on our walk, but we left the blanket spread out on the ground. Hand in hand, we started off down a path that didn't appear to have been used very much in the past couple of years, but which was still very passable with only a few weeds growing in the path.

"I wonder where this path leads?" I said more as a statement than a question.

"Haven't you ever ventured down this path when you have been out here by yourself, James?" Harmony asked.

"To be honest, love," I started, "I don't remember ever having seen this path before. However, it must have been here all the time and, besides, I love to explore these woods when I'm out here, so now is as good of a time as any to see where it goes."

"Lead the way, James," Harmony instructed.

Still holding Harmony's hand in mine, I took the lead and cautiously watching where I stepped, and warning Harmony when she needed to pay special attention to where she was stepping, headed off down this formerly undiscovered path. We had probably walked down the path for about two hundred yards when I came to an abrupt stop and motioned with a finger to my lips for Harmony to be quiet. I quickly squatted down behind a low bush and pulled Harmony down next to me. *Be quiet, Harmony, because there is a couple about thirty feet away making out like there is no tomorrow.*

Peeking over the top of the bush with me, she said, ***Cool! Is it anybody we know?***

I don't think so, but they are sure going at it pretty hot and heavy! The guy is almost to second base!

At that remark we both watched wide-eyed to see how far the guy would actually get, but today wasn't going to be his lucky day. At the precise moment when his left hand was almost to second base there was a noise on the other side of the couple opposite of from where we were hiding and watching. Whatever was causing the noise sounded big and wasn't trying to be quiet as it was crashing rapidly through the underbrush. The couple had stopped making out and were standing now, the guy bare-chested and the girl down to her bra and both barefoot. In a panic-stricken voice the girl yelled at the guy, "What is it, Johnny!"

"Sounds like a damn elephant charging this way!" Johnny replied and then I recognized him as the hood that was driving the '49 Mercury lead sled that came into the service station on a regular basis. "Get your shoes and blouse, Wanda, and let's get the hell out of here!"

However, they both continued to stand there staring wide-eyed into the woods in the direction of the ruckus that was getting closer and closer. All of a sudden Wanda screamed loud enough to be heard in the next county and that sent Johnny running, leaving her standing there to fend for herself. Although obviously scared to death, Wanda had enough of her wits about her to grab up their loose clothes and shoes and then started running after Johnny. Harmony and I ducked low back behind the bushes as best as we could with the hopes of not being seen by Johnny and Wanda as they went running past us, with Johnny at least twenty yards ahead of Wanda by then. If they saw us they never let on and picked up their pace after passing our hiding spot. When they were out of sight, Harmony and I peeked back over the bushes to see if what had scared them had come out into the open where we could see it. Much to our surprise we saw a large, wild boar snorting and stomping around in somewhat of a frenzy where they couple had been making out. These animals were fairly common in some of the woods around southern Florida and occasionally could be found in central Florida. This particular boar appeared to be female, at least five feet long, probably weighed in around three hundred and fifty to four hundred pounds and she wasn't any too happy about having had her domain invaded by foul smelling humans. She no doubt had some piglets somewhere nearby to protect.

Are those animals very dangerous, James?

I think they are more scared of humans than humans need to be scared of them, but my next door neighbor's uncle got gored pretty bad one time by a wild boar that he walked up on and surprised on his farm. If we stay quiet it will probably just go away in a few minutes. Whatever we do, we do not want to scare it, because then it might charge us.

We could probably will it away with telepathy, James.

If it doesn't leave soon, then you are welcome to give it your best try, Harmony.

About that time the wild boar seemed to start settling down some and started moving off back in the direction that it had come. My guess is that it smelled and heard Johnny and Wanda and didn't like them being so close to its piglets, so it charged them to scare them off. After it had disappeared back into the woods, I asked Harmony if she wanted to continue our walk or head back to our picnic site. She indicated that she would rather go back to the safety of our picnic spot and be closer to my car in case the wild boar decided to follow us anyway. I agreed and we headed back to where we had left our blanket and picnic basket.

Chapter Twenty-four

We walked hand in hand quietly back to the "safety" of what would now be "our quiet spot" and Harmony communicated to me, ***Maybe we should use telepathy so the wild boar will not hear us, James.***

That is a great idea, Harmony. Do you want to stay here for a while, go somewhere else, or head back home?

As strange as this may sound, James, I think that as long as we are on the blanket mother gave us to use we will be safe. Has anyone ever found you when you have been here in this spot in the past?

No, and I have spent as much as a half a day out here before, especially on Saturday mornings. I think it is too far away from the water for fishermen to wander in this direction and it never looks like anyone has been here besides me.

Do you think that couple we saw came this way?

They ran off in a different direction, so I do not think that they came this way. Johnny is the hood that comes into the service station occasionally, but I don't ever remember seeing him with that particular girl. You sound concerned about our safety, Harmony.

Not our safety, silly, our privacy.

Oh, and I know I was blushing as what Harmony meant sank in quickly. *We could go further back into the woods if that would make you feel better.*

It would, James. I really do not want us to be interrupted or surprised by people or animals or anything else.

How about your parents being able to read our thoughts and know where we are whenever they so choose?

Have you felt their presence in your mind today, James?

Now that you mention it, Harmony, no.

That is because of the implicit trust that Voreshs have among themselves, James. Although you and I, because we are now together for the rest of our lives, will always be, as you put it, tuned into each other all the time, my parents, the Elders, and all other Voreshas will always respect our privacy and not invade our thoughts nor we their's.

But we do not have to observe that rule with other people who are not Voreshas?

That is correct, James. So, why don't we move to an even more private "quiet spot" where we can be assured that we are alone and will not be disturbed by man or beast?

Gathering up the blanket and the picnic basket I took Harmony's hand and led her back deeper into the woods about another one hundred yards until we found a very secluded spot under the branches of an extremely large live oak tree. This live oak was so large that it's limbs scraped the ground all around it and it was almost like entering a cave when we ducked under the branches and settled into a spot so private that we couldn't be seen by anyone on the other side of the limbs. I sat the picnic basket down and together we spread out the blanket on the bare ground and reclined close together in the middle of the blanket. Even though the ground in this spot was hard-packed clay, it felt like we were on a very thick and soft surface instead of a thin piece of cloth.

Whether it was the blanket working its magic or just being in the presence of this beautiful girl, I was beginning to have a feeling of pleasurable anticipation as I gazed into Harmony's deep entrancing eyes and saw there an expression of unfulfilled longing. I was so mesmerized that I wasn't sure what was happening as we moved closer together and embraced and my lips met Harmony's full, sensual mouth and I sank into the mysterious world of love on her side, now our side. We broke our kiss briefly and she laughed her affective laugh and pulled me back to her and I knew at that moment that I loved Harmony Beckham with a pure, unadulterated joy that I had never experienced before. Harmony's caresses and kisses were enveloping me and drawing me deeper and deeper into her Voresha mind where I saw myself as a hitchhiker who was being given a ride down an endless road of physical and emotional love that is impossible to explain in mere human terms, although I will try to elucidate it here. Imagine guys, if you will, being embraced by the softest, most beautiful female that you have ever dreamed about. Imagine feeling the ecstasy, the rapture, the exhilaration, and the euphoria that only your dream girl could possibly offer you. Then imagine those feelings coursing through your arteries and veins and bones, straight up your spine and through your mind to your very soul and beyond at the speed of light and at the same time the speed of a snail. And imagine that when it was over knowing that it would never really be over, but that these physical and mental feelings would stay with you forever.

When I opened my eyes I felt as if I had been completely renewed and refreshed again and I looked over to see if Harmony were asleep and if I had been dreaming all of what I thought had just happened. Harmony was reclining on one elbow and gazing into my eyes while gently stroking my temple and communicated to me, ***Did you enjoy our conjoining, James?***

Harmony, I am not sure exactly what happened, but it was the most wonderful thing I have ever experienced!

That is the Voresha way, James. Love for us is something far beyond the physical and verbal pretensions that humans exhibit. Love in the human world is only a concept and something that no human who hasn't crossed over will ever truly experience.

Is that what I just experienced with you, Harmony?

And I with you, James. Although as a natural born Voresha I was taught what to expect when this actually happened, but I had never experienced it before either.

Can I ask a stupid question, Harmony?

Nothing you could ask would be stupid, James. You are not yet expected to know everything, and neither am I.

How long did our "conjoining" last?

Once again, Harmony coyly giggled and replied, **We were in that state of love for nearly two hours, James**.

Wow!, once again, was all I could think or say.

It is starting to get dark, especially here in the woods, James, and I think we should be getting back to my house before too long.

We gathered up the blanket and the picnic basket and started back to my car, which was about a ten-minute walk away. We had only gone a short distance when I looked down and then over at Harmony and realized that we had been fully clothed when I awoke. Without thinking, I blurted out loud, "How did you put my clothes back on without me waking up, Harmony?"

"Silly boy," she started, "first, you were never asleep, just recovering from your 'wonderful' experience. Second, we did not disrobe or have sex, James. That can not occur until we are married."

"Really?" I exclaimed more than said as a question. "Will my puny human body be able to survive Voresha sex?"

Harmony laughed her contagious laugh and explained, "James, you already forgot that you now have a Voresha body, silly?" She laughed even harder and I joined in as we walked back to my car hand in hand, although I wasn't sure why we were laughing or if it was a good thing.

Chapter Twenty-five

I woke up Monday morning feeling both tired and refreshed at the same time, but with my head still spinning from the day before and the experience that Harmony and I had had out in the woods near my quiet spot. I was in such a hurry to pick up Harmony for school that morning that I lied and told my mother that I was still full from her wonderful picnic lunch and skipped out on breakfast. I knew that she loved to be complimented on her cooking and that she wouldn't argue with me about breakfast if I did so. Actually, I was starving, but I wanted to see Harmony more than I had ever wanted to eat something, even my mother's banana pudding! Harmony had asked me when I dropped her off at her house the night before to pick her up about a half hour early the next morning. She didn't say why and I didn't bother to ask her why, besides it meant spending a half hour more that Monday with Harmony than I would normally have spent with her on a school day. I was so anxious to see her that morning that I broke the speed limit on every street and did a few "slow-and-go" coasts through stop signs driving to her house. Harmony was already standing out by the street when I turned the corner and headed toward her house. I pulled up, stopped, and was getting ready to get out and open the door for her when she motioned for me to stay put and then she got in the car.

"James," she began as I pulled away from the curb, "I asked you to pick me up early this morning because I wanted to talk to you about what happened yesterday when we were out in the woods."

"Did I do something wrong, Harmony?" I asked very concerned about her wanting to talk to me about what had happened. "Because if I did, I sincerely apologize."

"James, James, James," she said exasperatedly. "Love, you were more perfect than I could have ever hoped for in a man that I am going to marry in the very near future. What I want to talk to you about is to explain to you that each experience like that that we have will be more and more intense. It is the Voresha way, so that when we are married, our first time will be the ultimate emotional and physical experience."

"Does that mean that we have to take it easy until we are married, Harmony?" I asked.

"No, silly," Harmony answered in her very sexy voice, and I know that my heart skipped a beat or two with the possibilities that that suggested. "The more time we spend together like we did yesterday, the more wonderful our first time will be when we are married. I want us to have many, many similar experiences before we are married next August, because I want more than you can imagine for our first time to be the ultimate experience!"

"Oh, I wouldn't say that," I replied. "I can't imagine that you want that more than me! And I can't even begin to imagine what that is going to be like!" We were pulling into the parking lot at school about that time and I missed three parking places thinking about when we were going to be married and our "first time" and the more intense experiences before that happened.

"James, are you going to park or cruise the parking lot until there are not any more spaces left?" Harmony teasingly asked me and giggled.

"Sorry," I said, "I was just busy thinking about our first time."

"I know, love," Harmony responded, "but we need to get to our first classes. We can talk about all of this later."

I walked Harmony to her first class, gave her an extended kiss to make any other guys close by jealous, and then headed off to my first class. Walking down the hall toward the rear door of the building, which was the shortest path to take to get to the next building where my first class was located, I was passing two of the schools so-called bullies, Ed Encorn and Buck Dirklan. These were two of the biggest guys that any high school had probably ever seen. They were big enough to be the entire front line of any defense on any football team anywhere! And on top of that they were uglier than twin aardvarks turned inside out and poking their snouts out their butts! It isn't that they were very muscular, because the only muscle in their entire body was probably the one between their ears, just big. Anyway, as I was going past them the brighter one of the two, Ed, stuck out his size 14 clod hopper and tripped me sending me and my books sprawling all over the hallway. This was the first time that they had ever picked on me, because most of the time I just simply avoided them. My theory was that if I didn't look for trouble, then maybe it wouldn't find me.

Picking myself up and staring directly into Ed's eyes I said, "Pick up my books and don't ever pick on anyone again, little boy." Besides telling him this I was using my newly found mental abilities to place this idea permanently into the big galoot's mind.

Buck looked over at Ed and said, "That's a big laugh, huh Ed? Want I should box the little fart's ears?" At that, Buck laughed out loud so everyone gathering around could easily hear him.

Ed reached over, grabbed Buck by the collar of his dirty tee shirt, which read "Cow Tipping Anonymous," and slammed him so hard up against one of the metal lockers that the door caved in about two inches. Holding Buck there against the locker Ed said in a calm but deep, menacing voice, "You will never tease or pick on anyone ever again, butt head, especially James. Is that clear, butt head?"

"Crap, Ed," Buck replied, "what's gotten into you?"

At that remark, Ed literally slung Buck across the hallway and into the lockers on the other side of the hall denting one of them as well. "You'll do as I say, jerk off, or I'll stomp your sorry ass into the floor," Ed yelled at Buck. "Do you understand, butt head?"

"Awright, Ed," Buck replied sitting on the floor beneath the dented locker and rubbing his shoulder that Ed had rammed into the locker. "Awright!"

Ed turned around and looked at me and said, "We're sorry, little buddy. From now on we'll be nice to everyone, especially to you, James. Now me and Buck will pick up those books for you."

By this time a crowd of about fifty students had gathered to see what was happening. When they saw what Ed had done and heard his apology to me they just turned around and headed off to their classes without saying a word. Ed and Buck picked up my books and handed them to me and then he pushed Buck down the hallway and they headed outside without saying another word, probably to skip most of their classes again that day, especially since they had been humiliated in front of so many other students.

As I started out the door to head to my first class, that I was already ten minutes late for, Harmony turned in, ***That was a remarkable exercise in mental control, James. You are gaining telepathic abilities and learning our ways at an extraordinarily fast rate.***

Thanks, Harmony. I didn't want to get my butt stomped, so I thought I would give the old "power of suggestion" a try.

Before long, James, you will not have to worry about getting your butt stomped as you put it, because all Voresha, especially males and including crossovers, develop amazing psychokinetic abilities.

Psycho who? Sounds like something I should be locked away for doing, Harmony.

You can be so silly, James. Psychokinetic abilities allow us to manipulate things. Remember when I moved your chair?

So, Harmony, if someone like Ed or Buck decides to pick a fight I could just make them fall down and cry like a baby?

That is funny, James, and I would love to see that happen someday to those big bullies. Although Ed will not be picking on anyone anymore, because you have implanted that idea into his mind, do not discount Buck. He is not the brightest bulb in the pack, as you so eloquently put it.

More like a burnt-out bulb that someone put back in the pack!

Stop it, James! I am going to start giggling in class and then the teacher will think I am just an airhead. Besides, aren't you late for class?

Yes, yes, I know. I can't wait for the public humiliation from Mr. Bregala.

See you at lunch, love, and good luck with Mr. Bregala.

Thanks, Harmony. See you at lunch.

About that time I was just outside the door of my first class, so I sneaked up to the door and peeked in the small window from an angle hoping that Mr. Bregala wouldn't see me. I didn't see him sitting or standing at his desk, so I moved cautiously to the other side of the window to see if he was wandering around the classroom. Much to my surprise the classroom was empty. No Mr. Bregala, no students, and no desks!

Ok, if this wasn't out-of-the-ordinary, then I didn't know squat! And there were probably a few teachers who would collaborate that. I tried the door-knob of Mr. Bregala's classroom and the door swung out easily, so I entered the room being careful to glance quickly in both directions down the walls so that I wouldn't be caught off guard by anyone or anything A quick glance around the room confirmed to me that no one was there, just Mr. Bregala's desk. Being the para-noiac that I was known to be, I very slowly and cau-tiously slid along the wall next to Mr. Bregala's desk to peek behind it and see if something was hiding there under it. Say, something like a banshee disguised as a beautiful, ample-breasted blond who was waiting to jump out and scare me to death. Yeh, I know that isn't what banshees usually do, but, hey, remember that I was a very paranoid kid with a vivid imagination, es-pecially when it came to hot, dangerous, women with ample breasts!

I moved stealthily around to the back of the desk and didn't find any monsters hiding under it nor did I see any indication that Mr. Bregala had been there that morning. There wasn't any note on the door about class being canceled for whatever reason and, besides, why would all of the desks have been removed from the classroom? I know, I thought to myself and snick-ered under my breath, they must have sent the desks out to the desk wash place to get cleaned and polished.

I don't think this is a time to be funny, James.

Harmony! Do you have any idea what is going on here?

No, James, but it obviously cannot be good.

Thokiths? Semaj? Freyfacs?

I don't get any feeling or sense of any of those beings, James, but I find it highly unusual that the room is empty except for Mr. Bregala's desk.

Ditto that, love! Wait, Harmony, there's a note taped over in the corner of the blackboard. Still being cautious, I walked slowly over to where the note was taped to the blackboard and pulled it loose. In the typical Latin fashion that Mr. Bregala liked to use on his students, "SCHOLIUM," was printed across the top of the piece of paper. I knew that the word meant "note" or "comment" only because Mr. Bregala always told us what the Latin words he used meant every time he used them (even though "scholium" was originally from the Greek). Anyway, getting back to the note, handwritten on it were these words that I read out loud to myself: "Think thou and act; tomorrow thou shalt die." I didn't know if those were Mr. Bregala's words or a quote from some book he had read, but they scared me nonetheless. Then down at the bottom of the piece of paper written almost too small to notice were the words, "Turn me over." I read these words out loud and then slowly turned the piece of paper over as if I expected something to materialize and jump out at me. In the middle of the other side of the piece of paper was written in very large, bold, capital letters, "LILITH."

Harmony? Are you there?

Yes, James, and that quote scares me very much as well. It is by one of your favorite artists, Dante Gabriel Rossetti. Does the handwriting look like Mr. Bregala's?

It does not look like anything that I have ever seen written by him, Harmony. It is much neater than the way he usually writes. Does the name or word "Lilith" mean anything to you?

Lilith was a Mesopotamian storm demon who was thought to be the bearer of disease, illness, and death. Her image first appeared nearly 6,000 years

ago in Sumer. I really do not like the looks of this, James.

Well, love, that makes two of us. What should we do about this?

I think that the first thing you should do, James, is go to the school office and find out what you can about Mr. Bregala not being here and why the desks are missing from the classroom.

That's the best plan I've heard so far, Harmony. I'm on my way to the school office now. Talk to you later.

Chapter Twenty-six

Harmony didn't answer, which I thought was a little unusual, but I took off to the school office at a good jog to see what I could find out about the situation I encountered in Mr. Bregala's classroom that morning. When I entered the office, Miss Dutrip was standing behind the front desk and turned around immediately to see who had literally burst into the office slamming the door against the wall. Before the student receptionist working the front desk during that first class period could ask me my business, Miss Dutrip gave me a suspicious look and said, "Shouldn't you be in class, young man?"

"That's why I'm here, Miss Dutrip," I said trying to catch my breath.

Before I could explain, Miss Dutrip dropped her shoulders a little and said, "You're not in trouble again are you?"

"No, ma'am," I answered, "at least I don't think so."

"And just what is that supposed to mean?" she asked cocking her head slightly to one side and continuing to give me that suspicious stare.

"Well," I began, "when I got to Mr. Bregala's class this morning I was about ten minutes late, but I have a good reason for being late, and when I opened the door no one was there! All the student desks were even missing! Only Mr. Bregala's desk was there and this note taped in one corner of the blackboard!"

"Slow down, young man," Miss Dutrip said. "Let me see the note you found."

I handed the note to Miss Dutrip and then glanced over at the girl manning the front desk during first period. Although I didn't even come close to knowing all of the students at KSHS, I usually recognized them from having seen them around campus and I would surely have noticed a looker like her. As Miss Dutrip carefully read and reread the note the girl at the desk just smiled coyly at me and then, turning away, pretended to be working on something lying on the top of the desk.

"Come with me, James, and let's go have a look around Mr. Bregala's classroom," Miss Dutrip said. "If what you are saying is true, then something is definitely amiss." Looking over at the girl sitting behind the desk, Miss Dutrip said, "I'll be back in a few minutes, Lilith. Can you manage while I'm gone?"

"Yes, ma'am," the girl replied and coyly smiled at me again.

It didn't hit me until Miss Dutrip and I had walked out the door what Miss Dutrip had called the girl. "Holy, crap!" I exclaimed. "Her name is Lilith?"

"Yes, James," Miss Dutrip responded, "but I'm sure that is just a coincidence and has nothing to do with the name on the back of the note."

"It's creepy if you ask me, Miss Dutrip," I said.

"Well, I can understand what you are saying, James," Miss Dutrip replied, "but I do not think that the girl in the office had anything to do with this, nor is she some sort of female demon."

"I certainly hope you are right, Miss Dutrip," I replied, but remembering what Harmony had communicated to me, "but why would you say she wasn't some sort of female demon?"

"Oh, nothing important," she said. "It is just a mythological reference to the name Lilith."

We had arrived at the math classroom by that time where Mr. Bregala taught all of his classes and the door was still standing open like I had left it when I rushed out a few minutes earlier. Miss Dutrip entered the classroom and as much as I hate to admit it, I cautiously entered behind her instead of leading the way.

"Well, I'll be damned!" Miss Dutrip exclaimed.

"Miss Dutrip!" I said not believing what I had just heard come out of her mouth.

"I'm sorry, James," she apologized, "but this is the damnedest thing I have ever seen!"

"Well, at least I'm not crazy," I said.

"No teacher, no students, and no desks," she echoed what I had told her in the school office. "And you have no idea what is going on, James?" she asked me sounding a little suspicious.

"No, ma'am," I answered. "This is what it looked like when I got to class this morning. At first, I thought that maybe Mr. Bregala had taken the class outside, but then I wondered why all the student desks were missing."

"I'll be damned!" she exclaimed again. "Even if the class were meeting outside, Mr. Bregala would not have removed the desks from the classroom, nor would he have made the students carry their own desks outside. As a matter of fact, it is strictly forbidden to remove furniture from classrooms without written permission from me. And what is up with this strange note that was taped to the blackboard?"

"I wish I had some answers for you, Miss Dutrip," I said, "but I don't have a clue as to what is going on here."

"It's times like this that we need to have some security guards around this school," she stated, "but the county budget won't spring for the expense. I don't even know where to start looking or who to ask questions of about this, James."

I just stood there in silence waiting for Miss Dutrip to have some sort of epiphany about this, but she, too, just stood there staring at the empty room for several minutes. I was also expecting Harmony to chime in at any moment, but then maybe this was one of her tests for me and she was waiting to see how I would handle the situation. Quite frankly, I was too dumbfounded to think straight.

"Miss Dutrip," I began, because I actually had a real idea, "what if we ask teachers and students in adjoining classes if they saw anything unusual this morning before classes began? Maybe somebody saw Mr. Bregala or the desks being removed. Maybe when Mr. Bregala arrived this morning the desks were already gone and he canceled class to go look for them."

"Well, James, I am certainly glad to see that at least one of our students has his head screwed on right," she stated. "Checking with the other teachers and classes is a very good idea and those are certainly interesting suggestions about what may have happened. Why don't you go down the hallway one way and I'll go the other way and we will meet up in the middle and report on what we find out?"

"I'm on my way," I replied and started off to the next classroom. Several minutes later, Miss Dutrip and I met up about half way down the other side of the hallway to give our reports to each other.

"Well, James, did you find out anything that might help solve our little mystery?" Miss Dutrip asked first.

"I'm sorry to report that no one seems to have noticed anything out of the ordinary, Miss Dutrip," I answered. "A few students said that they saw students entering Mr. Bregala's classroom this morning, but that was all. No one seems to have even seen Mr. Bregala this morning."

"Same here, James," Miss Dutrip told me. "In all of my years in this business of education, I have never experienced anything even close to this. Let's go back down to Mr. Bregala's classroom and have one more look. Maybe there is another note that we missed explaining what is going on around here. It isn't like him to just up and cancel a class without notifying the office first and if he went off on a field trip without proper authority to do so, he is in big trouble."

"Lead the way," I said and we walked back to the mysteriously empty classroom to have another look.

Miss Dutrip and I spent the next 20 minutes or so combing over Mr. Bregala's classroom for any evidence of any kind that might help explain the situation. I was prowling along the back wall and Miss Dutrip was examining the window sills when I looked up, gasped, and exclaimed, "Holy crap!"

Miss Dutrip's head jerked up quickly and she looked at me and asked in a very startled voice, "What's wrong, James?"

All I could do was point at the blackboard at what both of us missed and what wasn't there when I entered the classroom the first time that morning and said, "Look!"

Miss Dutrip slowly followed my finger to the front of the classroom and she, too, gasped and brought her hand up to cover her mouth. Written on the blackboard in perfect block letters that covered the entire length of the blackboard was one word: "LILITH."

"This is getting a little too creepy for me, Miss Dutrip," I said. "That was not there when I came in here the first time this morning."

"I believe you, James, and it was not there when I came back here with you a few minutes ago either," she replied, "but who wrote it there during those few minutes we were going around to other classrooms?"

"Does this school have any ghosts that students don't know about?" I asked.

"Don't be silly, James," Miss Dutrip answered. "There are no such things as ghosts or demons or any of that nonsense you kids read about in your stupid comic books. I want you to go to study hall until your next class, James, and do not, I repeat, do not say anything about this to anyone else. Do you understand me?"

"Yes, ma'am," I answered, "but everyone in this building already knows that something strange is going on."

"Oh, crap!" Miss Dutrip exclaimed. "That's right and I am sure it will be all over school within the hour. Well, you just go on to study hall until your next class and I'll see if I can come up with some kind of explanation for this and try to intercept any panic that might arise among the students."

"Yes, ma'am," I said again and headed off to the study hall.

Ok, Harmony, what's going on here? I thought hoping that Harmony had been tuned in to all of this business. When I didn't get a response from Harmony after about 30 seconds I tried again, *Harmony, are you there?*

Yes, James, I'm here. What do you want now?

Excuse me for bothering you, but do you have any idea about what is going on with the disappearance of Mr. Bregala and the students and the desks?

I am really busy right now, James. We will have to talk about your problem later. Now, if you do not mind, I have more important things to deal with.

Harmony? Harmony? Nothing. My frigging problem? I thought we were supposed to share our problems and solve them together. Maybe she was having her "period" and was just cranky. She could be certain of one thing, I would bring this up later in our regular study hall time. Someone had some explaining to do and it wasn't me this time. Maybe it wasn't Harmony's place to explain it either and maybe it wasn't anything I should have to deal with, but somehow I still felt like I was deeply involved in this "little mystery."

I was filled with a lot of mixed emotions during the next thirty minutes in study hall while waiting for my next class. First, I was at a loss for how Harmony had responded to me and called all this mess "my problem." I had been convinced that no matter what kind of trouble came our way that we were always in it together and would always come to each other's rescue. Her comment about this situation being "my problem" had left a cold, hollow spot in my heart and quite frankly I was feeling pretty lonely right now. On top of that, of course, was the situation concerning Mr. Bregala's classroom and the seeming disappearance of him, the students in his class, and the desks that had been in the classroom. I kept thinking about the name "LILITH" being spelled out across the length of the blackboard and that the name referred to some sort of female demon, according to both Harmony and Miss Dutrip. Well, all of this certainly wasn't going to help me concentrate much in the rest of my classes that day and I was not looking forward to my confrontation with Harmony later in study hall.

The strange thing about the rest of the day, before getting to study hall, was that I did not hear one person even mention what had happened that morning in Mr. Bregala's classroom. I didn't say anything about it either, because Miss Dutrip had asked me not to say anything. That was very hard to do since I saw nearly everyone in my math class during the rest of the day, including three or four in study hall, which simply meant that the students didn't disappear along with Mr. Bregala and the desks. Between my last class and study hall I went by the school office to see if Miss Dutrip had found out anything concerning the situation that morning in Mr. Bregala's class. The student manning the front desk, not the girl called Lilith this time, sent me right in saying that Miss Dutrip was expecting me.

I entered the principal's office and said, "Hi, Miss Dutrip. The girl at the front desk said that you were expecting me. Did we have an appointment that I forgot about?"

"No, James," she said, "I just figured that you would want to know if I had found out anything and since this was the best time for you to come by my office, I just sort of expected you."

"Oh, ok," I replied. "Did you find out anything out about this morning?"

"Sadly, no, James," she answered. "Mr. Bregala is still MIA even though most of the students have been seen in their other classes."

"I have seen most of the students in my math class during the course of the day as well. Have you interviewed any of the other students who are in the class?" I asked.

"I have not, James," she told me, "because I was really hoping that Mr. Bregala would show up and explain this whole matter to me. Since that has not happened, I plan to come to your class in the morning and talk with all of you together to see if anyone else has any idea about what happened this morning."

"Maybe someone will know something," I said, knowing that Miss Dutrip wasn't going to get any answers from any of the other students either.

She was obviously thinking the same way as she replied, "I hope so, James, but I really rather doubt that any of the other students are going to say anything even if they do know. Young people today are awfully secretive about what goes on in their lives and very reluctant to talk about anything with adults who are in authority."

I thought to myself that maybe I could influence that interview some by reading the other students minds and, if I read something in anyone's mind that was of use, I should be able to get them to speak up and tell what they were hiding.

"Well, I hope that you find out something in the morning, Miss Dutrip," I said. "I better get on to study hall before I'm too late." I left the school office and when I got outside I stopped, took a deep breath, and reconsidered going to study hall to face Harmony. I wasn't ready to have a confrontation with Harmony, especially in front of everyone else in study hall.

Chapter Twenty-seven

As I pulled out of the school parking lot in my 'Cuda I didn't have any idea where I was going, but I knew that I needed to get as far away from KSHS as possible for the rest of the day. I needed to be alone and I certainly wasn't ready to have a confrontation with Harmony. I thought about just going home and crashing in front of the television, but at that moment I didn't even want to be in what I used to think was the security of my own house. There didn't seem to be any place that was safe if some alien entity wanted to get to me. I now knew that I had the ability to protect myself from other people, but my abilities were not well developed enough to keep me safe from invaders from outer space, especially the kind that you couldn't see. Maybe Captain Kirk and Mr. Spock could come to my rescue from the future in the Starship Enterprise and then take me back to the future with them and train me to mop the floors of the Enterprise as we sped far, far away from earth. Mopping floors was one of those "chores" that I had been "trained" to do at an early age and that my mother still expected me to do on occasion. That would be all the responsibility I would want since I was wishing to escape from my new exciting life on the planet earth. Star Trek was a new science fiction show that had started on television back the first of September and being a science fiction fan I was hooked. I would have even been happy to go back in time to one million B.C. and let Carole Landis drag me around by my hair! And next year in 1967, I would have been even more willing to let Raquel Welch do the same thing to me in the remake of One Mill on B.C. Of course, so would every other teenage boy in 1967.

As usual, I digress, but at least those images of Carole Landis from 1940 helped to push all of that morning's events out of my head for a short time. Because I had been doing all of this fantasizing, I had not been paying any attention to where I was heading as I aimlessly drove around. I had just been driving with no destination in mind and no concern for how far from town that I went. When I looked around at the passing landscape I realized that I was driving south on U.S. Highway 98 and had already left town and was headed toward the county seat in the next the town. I knew at that moment where I was going to go for the rest of the day and when I got to the county seat I turned on to U.S. Highway 27 and headed toward the next town over from there where there was a park-like setting and a carillon. I had only been to this place a couple of times with my parents and had recently thought about taking Harmony there for another picnic "experience." I figured I had enough daylight left to get there, find a good quiet spot, and just watch the wildlife and listen to the birds singing. The meandering gardens at the park were the achievement of some famous landscape architect, who had died nearly nine years before. My favorite spot was at the end of the reflecting pool looking toward the magnificent 205-foot high, neo-Gothic and art deco carillon. The tower had been designed by a famous architect and built back in the 1920s, and the decoration on the tower was made out of sculpted stone. If I were lucky, I would also be treated to one of the famous carillon concerts while I was lounging at the end of the reflecting pool and contemplating my navel.

I parked my car and meandered back toward the tower to the end of the reflecting pool. There were only a few cars in the parking lot and the people who were around were not in this particular spot where I wanted to be alone, hoping to lose all of my worries from that morning at school. I parked my skinny little butt on a concrete bench at the end of the reflecting pool and just simply stared at the majestic tower, losing myself in the sounds of nature all around me. As I was hoping by coming to this spot, it was very quiet and the few people wandering around seemed to be heading back toward the parking lot to leave. I deliberately forced myself to study the tower and listen to all the different birds singing, with the hope of freeing my mind from both my problems and the problems of the world that I often caught myself worrying about. Recent bad events around the world made all of my problems together look extremely insignificant. Those recent bad happenings included ninety-eight British tourists dying in an airplane crash in Yugoslavia, Senator Charles Percy's daughter being stabbed to death at the family mansion in Chicago, a DC9 that crashed in Oregon killing all eighteen people aboard, and a landslide of mining debris in Wales that killed one hundred and forty-four people, including one hundred and sixteen children in the village primary school.

On the other hand there were many good things going on in the world as well and some of you would say that my crossover was one of them, even though at that moment I wasn't too sure about it. The classic science fiction television series, Star Trek, debuted with its first episode entitled The Man Trap, the Metropolitan Opera House opened at the Lincoln Center in New York City (not that I was an opera fan by any stretch of the imagination), the Baltimore Orioles defeated the Los Angeles Dodgers in game four of the World Series to sweep the series (which was a good thing unless you were a Dodgers fan), and Grace Slick performed live for the first time with Jefferson Airplane after getting her start with The Great Society. Since I loved to read the news in the newspapers and even watch it on television, I could recount lots of recent happenings and fill my head with these as I stared at the tower and listened to the birds.

I was almost in a self-induced trance gazing at the reflection of the tower in the water and listening to the birds singing when I was startled out of my half-conscious state by a voice that was obviously very close to me.

"Isn't this the most beautiful place you have ever seen?" the soft, melodic voice said. At first, I thought that maybe one of the birds could talk and was speaking to me because I had invaded its space. Of course, I came to my senses and realized that the type of birds found in that park couldn't talk and that the voice I heard couldn't be good.

Jumping up and spinning around I expected to see some reptilian alien thing that looked like Monica, but that was starting to look like a big lizard, getting ready to devour me in one big gulp. Instead, standing before me dressed in a long, flowing white dress was an exquisitely beautiful young female with full, red lips and waist-length, blazing red hair who was gazing and smiling at me with a look almost as entrancing as Harmony's. If she hadn't been gently swaying back and forth making swishing sounds with her long flowing dress, I would have sworn I was looking at a painting by one of the 19th-century romantic realists that I liked so much. I was so mesmerized by this vision of ideal beauty that I didn't even realize that I was staring wide-eyed in wonder at her.

Breaking the spell that her beauty had cast over me, she asked, "Do you come here often?"

Shaking my head back and forth to make sure I wasn't in some sort of wonderful dream and trying to get my senses back, I answered, "This is actually only my third time to come to the park. The last time was about seven or eight years ago with a church group. My name is James, by the way."

The next word out of her mouth startled me so much that I took two or three steps backward, which was one too many, and fell butt first into the reflecting pool. The reflecting pool was deeper than I had expected and I went completely under, but surfaced quickly, stood up and realized that it was only a little over knee deep. "What did you say?" I asked with a shiver in my voice.

"I said my name is Lilith," she answered. "I'm sorry if I startled you, James."

"Th-that's ok," I replied as I started to climb out of the reflecting pool, but keeping a close eye on this beauty who called herself Lilith.

"Here, let me give you a hand," she said as she seemed to float around to my side of the concrete bench and extended her hand to me. I reluctantly took her hand and after helping to pull me back up on to dry land, she said, "You had such a look of fright on your face when you fell in the water. Again, I'm sorry if I startled you, James. I wouldn't have approached you except that I don't see many people our age enjoying this beautiful spot."

Standing there close to this magnificent creature and dripping wet, I said, "It's just that I had a very trying day and that wasn't the first time today that I heard the name Lilith."

"How very strange," she replied. "I always thought my name was too old-fashioned to be used very much anymore. I have always thought about changing it, but my parents would be furious if I even mentioned it. It seems that it was one of my great-great grandmother's names."

Not knowing what I should say to this beautiful young woman, I flirtatiously offered this and immediately started to blush, "I think it is a beautiful name for a beautiful person."

"Well, aren't you the flirt," she said. "Would you like to come back to my house and get dried out? I just live on the outskirts of the park over that way," and she pointed in the direction opposite the tower and reflecting pool.

Still being caught up in her voice and beauty I replied, "I would certainly hate to get back in my car soaking wet, so I guess I'll take you up on your offer."

"Come, follow me," she said and began to seemingly float off in the direction she had pointed and from which I guessed she had come. I was obviously still mesmerized by this gorgeous creature, but at the same time I was also quite leery around strange, beautiful, young women, remembering some of my past experiences with them.

Following her, I became almost hypnotized by her long, beautiful, red hair swaying back and forth behind her. Trying to keep my wits about me, since I didn't know if I was walking into some sort of trap or not, I continued our conversation, "Living so close to the park, Lilith, I would guess that you come over here often."

"I do," she replied. "Where you were sitting is my absolute favorite quiet spot and I go there almost everyday after school and just sit and listen to the birds and try to find peace with myself."

"I have two or three quiet spots closer to home where I do the same thing," I told her. "If I lived closer to this park, I would probably come here all the time, too, especially if you were around."

About that time we were leaving the boundary of the park and entering into a neighborhood back yard. "This is where I live," Lilith said. "I hope you don't mind waiting on the back patio while I get you a towel. My parents aren't home yet and if they came home and you were inside I would get grounded for a month."

"No problem," I said. "I wouldn't want to go dripping wet through your house anyway."

"Be right back, James, with a large bath towel for you," she replied and disappeared inside the back door.

I was actually very glad that she didn't ask me to go in the house with her, because I was already finding it hard to say no to her. To say that I was a little more than anxious about this situation and the fact that her name was Lilith would be the understatement of a lifetime. While she was in the house getting me a towel I was torn between being polite and waiting for her to return and turning around and running as if giant alligator was after me. Several minutes had passed and I was beginning to think something fishy was up when the back door opened and Lilith stepped out with a towel, only now she was dressed in a bikini and looked as if she had just stepped out of the 1963 movie, Beach Party.

"Hope you don't mind, James," she started to explain as she handed me the towel, "but when I get back from my walk in the park I always change into my bikini."

"Mi-mind?" I said questioningly as I began to dry my head and arms, but unable to take my eyes off her. "Wh-why would I mind looking at a be-beautiful girl like you in a bikinini, uh, I mean bikini? Yo-you put Annette Funicello to shame, Lilith!"

"Not only a flirt, but a flatterer as well," she replied. "A girl could start to like a boy like you, even though he does stammer."

"So-sorry," I said. "I must still be a little chilled from being wet." But I was pretty sure that she knew I was just a shy, nervous kid who hadn't been around too many beautiful girls who seemed to be interested in him.

Lilith moved over to one of the chaise lounges on the patio and reclined on it as she watched me rub myself down, clothes on of course, in an attempt to get as dry as possible. I needed to get my senses back about me and get headed toward home since it was nearly an hour drive away and it was starting to get dark. "I have a long drive back home," I began to explain to her, "so I really need to get started back. I really appreciate the towel and it was certainly a pleasure meeting you, Lilith." I was still somewhat anxious about this "coincidental" meeting with a beautiful girl named Lilith, so I wanted to get away as soon as possible.

"I was glad to be there to help you, James," she said as I started to walk back toward the park and my car. "If you're ever back this way, look me up."

"Will do," I replied. "See ya."

"Bye," was all she said and I hurried off to the parking lot at the park entrance.

I couldn't believe that something bad hadn't happened to me with this stunningly beautiful creature named Lilith, that is, worse than falling in the reflecting pool, which was just a stupid knee-jerk reaction on my part. Could this have been fate? Could there actually be a beautiful, normal girl named Lilith who went to the park everyday to be alone in her quiet place, who didn't mean to scare me, who wanted to make amends for doing so by offering to help me, who seemed as shy as me, and who genuinely sounded like she would like to see me again? Naw. Coincidence, maybe, but beautiful girls never looked twice at me, with the exception of Harmony, of course, who seemed to have the rest of my life planned out in service to her. Lilith, if that was really her name, was probably laughing so hard at me right now that she rolled off the chaise lounge. I didn't think at that time that I would be coming back to this park any time soon, not because I was really afraid of her, but because I had made such an ass out of myself.

Amazingly enough, my car was still parked in the same place and nothing had happened to it. Although the park was officially closed, they left the gates open until after sunset. I pulled back out onto U.S. Highway 27 and sped off toward home having my usual doubts about what had just transpired in the park. I started thinking about Harmony again and how I was going to have to confront her about the way she had treated me earlier in the day at school. And, no doubt, she was going to have plenty to say about my little encounter with Lilith, especially concerning what I had been thinking about her. The amazing thing was that Harmony hadn't communicated with me at all since I had left school and even though I had tried a couple of times to tune in to her wave length, I came up empty. She had obviously closed me out of her thoughts since earlier in the day. I was not looking forward to tomorrow at school.

Chapter Twenty-eight

My mother didn't question why I got home after dark that day. She probably assumed that I had been with Harmony after school and I didn't tell her any differently or offer any other explanation. If I had told my mother that I had been out driving all over the country side for over two hours, she would have read me the Riot Act on wasting gasoline and putting excessive mileage on my car. To keep the conversation away from where I had been and what I had been doing. I jumped in and helped her fix our dinner and afterwards I said I was tired and went on to bed even though it was only around 8:30. I was tired, but I wanted to just have some alone time to go back over the day's events. I still had not heard from Harmony and had decided on the way home from the carillon park that I was not going to try and contact her and beg for some sort of communication. My feelings that night were very mixed about Harmony and even more so because of my encounter with Lilith late that afternoon at the park. I would almost bet that Lilith was simply a nice person being helpful to a person who needed some help at that particular moment and that our encounter meant nothing to her. But with all the crap that had been happening when Harmony was around, I was just about ready to go back to my boring old human life. Harmony, on the other hand, had "chosen" me to be her mate on her side, which, now that I thought about it, didn't seem to have the same significance for me that it did initially. I kept thinking about all of this and also what might have happened to Mr. Bregala and his classroom that morning. I fell sound asleep and didn't seem to dream about anything that night, at least that meant I didn't have any nightmares.

I woke up the next morning before my parents, but I was not in any hurry to get to school and have to face Harmony, so I took my time getting ready and ate my breakfast at snail speed. I could tell that my mother noticed something wrong, especially since I usually woofed my breakfast in a few minutes, but respecting my privacy, she didn't inquire as to what was bothering me at the breakfast table that morning. She had to remind me twice that I was going to be late for school if I didn't get my butt in gear, especially if I was going by Harmony's house to pick her up. I finished my breakfast, said bye, and headed off toward Harmony's house wondering whether or not if she would be waiting for me. When I pulled up in front of her house I didn't see any sign of Harmony, so I put the car in park and jumped out to go up to the front door and see if she were waiting inside for me. I rang the doorbell and waited for about a minute with no response before I rang it again. There still wasn't any response after a couple of more minutes, so I returned to my car and headed for school thinking that she could have at least had the courtesy to communicate with me that she didn't want me to pick her up that morning.

I was about fifteen minutes late getting to school and had a hard time finding a place to park, so I ended up having to park way out by the athletic fields and had to run to class so that I wouldn't be more than twenty-five minutes late to my first class. When I got to Mr. Bregala's classroom I once again found it empty except that Miss Dutrip was there waiting for me to show up.

"Good morning, James," she began. "I hope you have a good explanation for being late this morning. I have been patiently waiting for you for the past thirty minutes."

"Not really, Miss Dutrip," I admitted. "I guess I was dreading the possibility of coming back to this empty classroom this morning."

"Well," she replied, "I appreciate your honesty, which is much better than some lame excuse like most students would try to use. As you can see there are still no desks, nor does anyone have any idea what happened to them, and no Mr. Bregala."

"What about the students?" I asked.

"Strange thing," she answered, "they were all here on time and seemed, or at least pretended, to be surprised about what they saw or, in this case, didn't see. I questioned them about what had happened yesterday and they all played dumb and said they didn't remember anything about yesterday morning. A few of them even said they didn't remember being at school yesterday."

"That's really weird," I replied. "So, those who did remember being at school pretended that everything was ok yesterday morning?"

"That is what it seemed like to me," she answered. "What do you make of it, James?"

"Is it possible that Mr. Bregala just up and decided to leave school without telling anyone?" I asked.

"Well, he and I have talked recently about his retirement," Miss Dutrip informed me. "It was supposed to be a secret, but I never thought that he would just up and leave as you put it. However, that still does not explain the disappearance of the desks and why the students will not admit to something being wrong yesterday."

"What if someone came in late at night and stole the desks as a prank?" I asked. "I remember last year when someone let all of the snakes out of their cases in the biology lab and scared the janitor so bad when he went into the lab to clean that he quit the next day."

"That is a very good postulation, young man," Miss Dutrip replied. "I had not even given that a thought. Sometimes it takes a younger mind to come up with possibilities."

"By the way, Miss Dutrip," I began, "where are the other students who are supposed to be in the class?"

"Since none of them seemed to have any idea about what has happened here and since your teacher didn't show up, I sent them all to study hall for their first period," she answered.

During this conversation with Miss Dutrip, I kept wondering if Harmony had come to school that day and why she still had not communicated with me. Even though I was still somewhat angry about the way she had treated me the day before, I was now beginning to worry about her and if she and her family were ok. After leaving Miss Dutrip and supposedly heading to study hall until second period, I decided to give in and try to contact Harmony. After all, she had probably been listening in on everything I had said or thought for the past 24 hours anyway.

Harmony, are you out there somewhere and have you been listening in on what has been happening? I waited for a couple of minutes and got no response. *Harmony, if you are listening, did I do something to make you angry with me?* There was still no response from Harmony after I was silent for a couple of minutes. *Ok, Harmony, at least tell me to go to hell or we're through or something! Some people would consider this to be cruel and unusual punishment.* I stood outside staring up at the sky as if I expected her to appear out of one of the clouds and elucidate the whole situation. Of course, that didn't happen either and I just kept standing there staring at the sky like an idiot. I did think I saw a cloud shaped like a dragon floating casually by over the school. If only Lilith could read minds, I could communicate with her and carry on some kind of conversation.

I can read minds, James.

Lilith? Is that you or is it Harmony or a Thokith playing a trick on me?

It's Lilith, James, and I can read minds.

Holy crap! Ok, please tell me, even if it's a lie, that you are a Voresha and not a Thokith.

I wanted to tell you yesterday, James, that I am Voresha, but I knew that you had enough to think about without me throwing that at you as well. I just wanted our first face to face encounter to be pleasant.

That's very considerate of you, Lilith. So, that means that you knew about what had happened at my school and why I was somewhat shocked to learn that your name is Lilith?

Yes, James, I knew all of that. As I indicated yesterday, Lilith is an old family name and not necessarily my choice, especially since it is associated with evil and female demons.

Are you at school right now, Lilith?

Yes, I go to LWHS, but I was thinking about skipping the rest of the day and going to my quiet place at the park. Would you like to do the same and meet me there? We can manipulate the minds of everyone at our schools to make them believe that we were at school all day. It won't hurt anything or anybody and I have a lot to talk to you about, James. I would much rather talk to you in person.

That sounds like the best plan I've heard in a long time, Lilith. And, by the way, I still think Lilith is a beautiful name regardless of what anyone else might think.

Thanks, James, that's very sweet. I'll meet you at the reflecting pool in about an hour.

See you there, but if for some reason I am a few minutes late, don't give up on me, Lilith.

I will be there waiting, James, no matter how late you might be. See you in a bit.

I casually strolled out to my car, looked around to make sure no one had seen me, got in and quietly drove off campus and headed back to the carillon park. It took me about an hour and fifteen minutes to get there because of morning traffic in the first town where the county seat was located. When I finally arrived at the park, I parked my car, and ran back to the reflecting pool to meet up with Lilith. I had not tried to communicate with Lilith on my drive over and was hoping that she hadn't given up on me. As I was approaching the carillon and the reflecting pool I saw Lilith sitting there staring up at the tower. So as not to scare her, I called out to let her know I was approaching, "Hi, Lilith, I finally made it"

She turned around and smiled at me and said, "Hi, James."

"I'm sorry I'm late, but I had to be careful leaving school so that no one would see me leaving and traffic wasn't very accommodating."

"I know, James," Lilith replied. "No problem, however, I knew you were on your way and that was good enough for me."

"That is so very nice of you, Lilith," I said. "I have a question for you that I was thinking about on the way over here."

We sat down on the concrete bench next to each other and Lilith said before I could ask my question, "Yes, James there are more Voresha on earth than you were led to believe. As a matter of fact, there are about three dozen Voresha families in the state of Florida alone."

"You're kidding, right?" I asked. "I was led to believe that Voresha were few and far between.

"No, James," she answered, "I am not kidding. It is true that young Voresha females are searching for suitable human males to mate with, but those human males selected must make the crossover before mating can happen. It is also true that there aren't any young Voresha males left for the females to mate with, only older males who are mostly either our fathers or Elders."

"May I ask who you have chosen, Lilith?" I asked her.

"It isn't that simple, James," Lilith answered. "I haven't chosen anyone yet, because, up to recently, I had not found the right human male who would be the right mate for me and, as it turns out, he was chosen by another Voresha female before I could make my move."

Not putting two and two together, I asked, "Do you think that you will be able to find another human male around here who is right for you?"

"I think I have, James," she answered, "but in this case it's going to have to be up to the former human male to decide to leave the Voresha female who first chose him to be with me."

"Not having been on your side for very long, I'm afraid that I'm not following you," I told Lilith." I knew that I didn't always catch on quickly, but my brain must have been taking a nap right then.

"The male that I have chosen has already made the crossover for another female, James," Lilith said to me while looking deep into my eyes.

"You mean," I started but didn't finish.

"Yes, James, you," Lilith told me with a desircus tone in her voice and a longing in her beautiful eyes.

"Holy crap!" I exclaimed. "You're saying that you have chosen me and that I have to choose between you and Harmony?"

"You do not have to choose, James," she answered. "You can stay with Harmony and we can just be friends, but know that you were also my first choice."

"And what would happen to Harmony if I were to choose you, Lilith?" I asked.

"According to Voresha law, either Harmony or I would have to leave this area, probably this state and find another mate somewhere else," she answered. "Voresha are fundamentally a peaceful species, especially among themselves, and the Elders wouldn't allow two females who had vied for the same human male to live in the same area. Don't take this wrong, James, but the Elders don't trust the emotional state of humans, even if they have crossed over. Until you are married to Harmony, James, you still have a choice, especially if another Voresha female is vying for you. Once you have married a Voresha female, however, you are not permitted to ever go back to either being a human again or to choose a different mate."

"Why didn't Harmony explain all of this to me?" I asked Lilith.

"Dear, James," she began, "I am afraid that I am going to have to be very honest with you about your situation with Harmony and hope that you don't think that I am trying to undermine her and win you over, but you are entitled to know the truth."

"Go on, I think," I replied.

"Well, James," she began again, "Harmony, nor her parents, have been exactly up front about things concerning you and your crossover. If you will remember back to that Saturday when you and Harmony first made contact, she was somewhat surreptitious with you. To confuse you, she gradually imparted bits and pieces of information to you knowing that your human curiosity would get the best of you and that she could string you along until she and her parents decided it was time to act."

"That really makes sense now that I think about it," I responded. "So, basically, what you are saying is that I have been manipulated by Harmony and her parents, including rushing up the crossover?"

"That is correct, James," Lilith said. "I'm sorry that it happened that way to you and, I'm afraid, I may have had a part in your crossover being rushed up."

"How so?" I asked.

"Even though we were at different schools in different towns, I was actually considering you for my choice before Harmony considered you."

"Really?" I said.

"Yes, James, really," she said. "Harmony had been playing little miss rich girl and strutting around looking for a rich human male to choose, but she wasn't having any luck finding just the right candidate. All of the rich boys she tried for either weren't interested in her money or what sounded to them like a ridiculous idea about crossing over. Not only was she getting frustrated, she then realized that I was looking at you and not to be outdone by a 'middle-class' Voresha, she acted on you before I had the chance to figure out a way to meet you. The part that really bothers me is that she just toyed with you and your emotions making you think that she was something extra special."

"Lilith," I began, "why did you call yourself 'middle-class'?"

"You've been to Harmony's house, James," she started to explain, "and you have even called it a mansion. You have also seen my modest house next to the park."

"Gotcha!" I replied.

"Mr. Beckham operates a fake business that is scamming many people out of their money," Lilith began explaining. "Voresha are not supposed to appear to be so ostentatious, but he and his wife seem to have gotten caught up in the Capitalist dream of wealth in this country. My parents are living a comfortable, yet reserved and quiet, life the way it was meant for us to do. Over the thousands of years that Voresha have been on earth, none have ever brought attention to themselves like the Beckhams. It is just not the Voresha way and the Elders, at least most of the Elders, are not very happy about what the Beckhams have done."

"I'm glad that we are talking out loud about all of this, Lilith," I said. "I don't mind being able to read minds and control people's thoughts and actions, but I feel so much more comfortable talking with you out loud. I was beginning to think that Voresha spent most of their time communicating telepathically."

"Communicating telepathically is really only necessary when we have some special activity that needs to be taken care of and that would look suspicious if we were overheard by others," she explained. "I always enjoy talking out loud when it is normal conversation. We really prefer to live more like humans and not have to use our telepathic powers."

"I know that this is a terrible way to put it," I said, "but if I were to dump Harmony for you, would we have to move out of state? It isn't that I would mind moving if it meant being with you, but I really do like Florida."

"First, James," she began, "there is something you need to know about the Beckhams. Both they and the Elder who did your crossover are in very serious trouble with the main Elder council, both for deceiving you and for living such an ostentatious lifestyle. As a matter of fact, the Elder who was involved in your crossover has already been dealt with severely."

"Can I ask what happened to him, Lilith?" I inquired.

"Because we are unable to leave earth, this particular Elder was exiled to a very remote and secret place that only the Elder council knows about. He will live out his remaining life there."

"What will happen to the Beckhams?" I asked Lilith.

"That's another matter all together, James, and probably why you haven't heard from Harmony the past couple of days," she answered. "The Elder council has put up with their inappropriate behavior for all this time because they thought the Beckhams would eventually realize the error of their extravagant lifestyle and quiet down some. The straw that broke the camel's back, as humans say, was using their daughter to seduce you away from me, tricking you into rushing ahead with the crossover, and not being completely honest with you about the conditions of the crossover."

"Will the Beckhams be exiled?" I asked.

"No, James," Lilith replied, "but I'm hoping that they will be the ones who are required to move to another state or even to another country."

"So that we can be together?" I continued with my questions.

"That is up to you, James," she answered with that look in her eyes that girls get and that always melts my heart. "However, if you choose to stay with Harmony and they have to move away, you will have to go with them, probably to a very remote and small town or community."

"Right now, Lilith, I'm thinking that won't be such a hard decision," I said.

"I hope that means what I think it means, James," she said and continued to give me that heart-melting look.

"I think you already know the answer to that," I offered. "So, Lilith, is there anything else I need to know or do before I make a final decision?"

"There is, James," Lilith started, "and I was getting ready to bring this up before you went any further with trying to make your decision between Harmony and me. I have been honest with you in telling you what happened to you in dealing with the Beckhams and I hope that you believe me in light of the lies and misinformation that you have been told by a few deceitful Voresha so far. And I hope that you know that I have not told you these things because I am trying to get even with Harmony, but that I really do, in the true Voresha way, want you to know the truth. Besides that, however, I will admit that I hope you choose me."

"I have always been a sucker for believing what people tell me," I replied, "and this instance with Harmony isn't the first time it's taken a big bite out of my butt."

"Your sense of humor is just one of your endearing qualities, James," Lilith said.

"So, what is it that is so important for me to know before we go on from here, Lilith?" I asked.

"Brace yourself, James," she said. "I don't want you falling in the reflecting pool again."

"Oh boy," I said and let out a big sigh. "I have a feeling I am not going to like this."

"Probably not, James," Lilith replied, "but it is necessary for me to inform you about something that Harmony nor her parents might never have revealed to you if they could have kept it a secret from you."

"Fire away!" I exclaimed. "I think you have been honest with me and that I can take almost anything you throw my way.

"Voresha, James," and Lilith paused here for a few seconds, "are a type of psychic vampires."

Chapter Twenty-nine

I didn't fall off the bench, but I did scoot over on the bench about a foot and gazed wide-eyed at Lilith as if she had just turned into a cobra. I couldn't believe that I had just heard such frightening words coming out of that beautiful mouth, but I didn't notice her canines being any longer or sharper than normal. She was watching me carefully and I knew she was reading my thoughts, but I was both so dumbfounded and a little scared by her confession that I was both speechless and without a thought for a few minutes. As we continued to sit and stare at each other a million things were racing through my mind so fast that I couldn't concentrate on any one of them. Lilith had just confessed to me that she was a vampire! Ok, a psychic vampire, but I didn't know that from any other vampire. I guess if I believed in aliens, I could wrap my mind around the reality of vampires.

Finally, Lilith broke the silence, "James, there is nothing to be afraid of from me or most other Voresha. What Harmony and her parents did to you is very rare among our species and those that act inappropriately are always dealt with severely by the Elders. I promise you that all of the Beckhams and, in this case, the Elder who performed your crossover, will be severely punished"

Finally, I was able to get something to exit my mouth in the way of intelligible language, but which was obviously avoiding what Lilith had just told me about being a psychic vampire. "Why is sending the

Beckhams to another state considered severe punishment, Lilith?"

"Because," Lilith began, "all of their riches that they scammed others to get will be taken away and they will be forced to live a very austere lifestyle, probably in a very remote area of the country or a very poor small town where the luxuries they have been used to will not be available to them."

"Oh, ok," I replied still avoiding Lilith's confession about being a vampire.

"James, please don't keep avoiding what I told you a few minutes ago about being a psychic vampire," Lilith said in a beseeching voice.

I sat in silence for a couple of more minutes staring at Lilith before getting up the courage to follow up on what she had told me about being a psychic vampire. Swallowing hard to get what felt like a lump of coal out of my throat, I said, "I don't know what to say or how to respond, Lilith. The word vampire is more scary than 'reptilian alien thing'."

"It was very important to tell you that, James," she replied, "because, as I have indicated, we are a very honest species. For Harmony not to have told you about Voresha being psychic vampires was abominable!"

"Ok," I started, "during the crossover did they suck all of my blood out of my body and am I now one of the 'undead'?"

Lilith, not being to help herself, started to giggle and then just simply broke out laughing. "I'm sorry, James," she replied, "but when I explain to you what psychic vampires are, you are going to find what you just said funny as well."

"Well, Lilith," I said, "right now it isn't all that funny. I don't know whether to laugh or run for my life!"

"I understand how humans feel about vampires and the misconceptions they have concerning vampires," she said. "Vampires who feed on the blood of living creatures are strictly mythological or at best folk lore, James. They have never existed here on Earth or anywhere else in the entire known universe, which extends far beyond the most imaginative of human minds."

"So, Lilith, you are saying that Voresha are not the blood-sucking undead that I've read about in books or seen in movies," I said trying to get my mind around this new concept of vampires.

"The only true 'vampires', and understand that term is a misnomer," Lilith continued, "are Voresha, but also understand that there never have been, nor will there ever be, intelligent creatures in the universe that fit the profile of what humans call vampires. We have been given the title of 'psychic vampires' by those few humans who have encountered us, but who still do not believe that we exist. A more proper name for us in human terms would be manas volitionaries."

"Ok, Lilith," I said showing my exasperation and ignorance, "I'm trying to understand all of this, but you are going to have to speak in plain English until I have been better educated as a Voresha."

"Manas is an early Buddhist term that usually indicates the general thinking faculty," she explained, "and a volitionary is someone who can will others to do things and who make choices for humans by exercising our will over them. However, we are never supposed to will humans to do bad things or to will them to succumb to dishonorable and underhanded desires."

"Then if I am understanding you correctly," I responded, "Harmony and her parents 'willed' their choices on me and made me believe that I was some sort of special human who had been hand picked by Harmony."

"That is exactly what happened, James," Lilith said.

"And all of my interactions with Harmony, her parents, and the Elder had nothing to do with what I really thought or wanted, but rather were their thoughts willed upon me to believe?" I asked.

"And you said that you didn't understand," Lilith said jokingly and giggled.

So, is everything that is happening between you and me being willed upon me by you?" I asked matter-of-fact.

"Think about it, James," she replied. "If I were doing that, I wouldn't allow you to come to those conclusions. Once again, please believe me when I tell you that the true Voresha way is not to make humans do things they don't want to do, unless it is to correct their wrongs or make them better people. When you were told that that was our charge on earth you were being told the truth."

"So, what I did with Ron Cotworthy was in the Voresha way?" I asked.

"That is a perfect example, James," Lilith confirmed. "Why do you think I have tried to be so honest with you? If I were as insensitive and uncaring as Harmony, I would not have told you all of this but, rather, I would have used her tactics to seduce you."

"You wouldn't have to try very hard to seduce me, Lilith," I said and blushed my favorite color of carmine lake red.

"You are certainly the flirt, James," she replied, "and thank you."

"Just trying to be honest like a good Voresha should," I said. "So, if Voresha females do the choosing, can I assume that you have or will choose me?"

"That is what I want, James," she answered, once again giving me that heart-melting look, "but I cannot make that decision until you have renounced Harmony."

"How do I go about the process of renouncing Harmony and how soon can it happen?" I asked.

"If that is what you want to do," she began to explain, "then I will call a member of the Elder council, my parents, and Harmony and her parents into our minds and you will have the opportunity to make that announcement. Are you positive that you want to renounce Harmony, James?"

"I honestly feel like you are actually giving me this choice and not willing it on me, Lilith," I replied before answering Lilith. "I have never been one to think about things for very long before plunging head first into something that I thought would benefit me in some way or that I believed in without question. I have already benefitted tremendously from the crossover to become a Voresha and am anxious to start my new life with a Voresha female who really wants me, especially one as beautiful as you, Lilith."

"In that case, James," she said, "what is your decision?"

"Don't think that I am avoiding this decision, Lilith," I continued, "because I am pretty sure that you already know what I am going to do, but I just need to hear myself out loud if that makes any sense."

"I understand completely, James," Lilith replied.

"If I were still on the other side," I said, "I would be madder than an old wet hen who just had her eggs stolen by a stinky old raccoon!" Lilith giggled at this remark, but didn't say anything as she sat there next to me patiently waiting for me to end my discourse with myself. "But now, I am on your side and I only feel sympathy for that pathetic little tramp that calls herself Harmony and I only wish her to be completely out of my life. I am definitely ready to move on with you, Lilith."

I paused and after a couple of minutes of silence while Lilith seemed to be off in another time zone, Lilith said, "James, the Elders and my parents, and the Beckhams are all telepathically with us now. Are you ready to make your announcement to all of us?"

"One more question," I said. "You know my full name, but I only know you as Lilith. What is your last name?"

"I thought you would never ask, James," Lilith replied. "My last name is Lhuv" (pronounced like love).

"Lilith Love," I repeated. "I could get used to that in no time."

"You have the pronunciation correct," Lilith said, "but I see in your mind that you are spelling it incorrectly. It is spelled L-h-u-v, and that would change to your last name after we are married."

I let my mind roam around for a couple of seconds and discovered the thoughts of all six other Voresha present that Lilith had summoned telepathically to hear my announcement. *Hello, everyone. From reading the myriad of thoughts going back and forth among all of you, I see that you are aware of why you have been called here by Lilith. Before I make my announcement however, I would like to say to Harmony that your conniving ways have really hurt and disappointed me.*

As usual, Harmony couldn't keep her biting remarks to herself, ***Oh, get on with it, jerk, so we can get back to what we were doing before being so rudely interrupted.***

Harmony! Mr. Beckham exclaimed. ***Keep your thoughts to yourself before you get us into more trouble than we are already in!***

Continue, young man, the Elder instructed me.

Mr. and Mrs. Lhuv, I want to say to you that I think you have the most beautiful daughter any couple could ever have, not only her physical beauty, but her inner beauty as well. Before I met Lilith, I mistakenly thought that Harmony was that person, but Harmony's outer beauty, which can't even come close to Lilith's, is the total opposite of her inner being which is the most ugly thing that has ever crossed my path.

James, you are embarrassing me, Lilith said.

James, if you go through with your announcement today, you and Lilith have mine and Lindsea's blessing, Mr. Lhuv communicated.

Thank you, Mr. Lhuv. Everyone, you have been summoned to this telepathic conference, if you will, to hear this: Harmony, I formally renounce you as my future Voresha mate and proclaim my love for Lilith Lhuv. Because you have treated me like a lifeless puppet, I ask that you never venture into my physical or mental life ever again.

I knew that everyone had heard me, but for a few seconds that seemed like minutes, all was eerily quiet. Mr. Beckham broke the silence, **Harmony, it is your duty as a Voresha to acknowledge this renouncement**.

Yes, father. All I have to say is good riddance, James. You have been more trouble than your puny little brain could possibly imagine! I should have known that a poor, backwards, jackass like you wasn't worthy enough to polish our servant's boots! Even if you become a full-fledged Voresha, you will still have to rely on your Voresha female to rescue you every time she turns around.

Silence, Harmony Beckham! James, this is Elder Oqu Ezhu Thegh. Your renouncement has been heard by all concerned and has been accepted by all concerned. The Beckhams will now remove themselves from the state of Florida immediately and re-settle to their new home as previously directed by the Elder council. Failure to do so will result in their joining Cudur Mus Noslen in his exile. Now, begone with you. Landan and Lindsea Lhuv, I would be

proud to be witness to the marriage of Lilith and James at that time that they decide to marry.

Thank you, Elder Thegh, Mr. Lhuv replied.

You mean Lilith and I get to decide when we are to be married?

Yes, James, it was Mrs. Lhuv. ***You only have to wait until you are both 18, and Lilith's birthday is only four days after yours, so your wait will not be that long after your 18th birthday.***

I think Lilith and I have a lot to talk about before then, but I am hopeful that you are as anxious as I am to be joined in marriage, Lilith.

I am so ecstatic that I don't know what to say right now, James. I am so happy that you picked me over Harmony. This wasn't hard to believe, because as I gazed into Lilith's face her beautiful eyes seemed to be shining with excitement.

I thought you chose me, Lilith.

Another misleading thing put in your mind by Harmony. Although Voresha females choose a human male to be with, it is entirely left up to the man to decide one way or the other whether he wants to become a Voresha or not. Many human males over the centuries have declined the offer and have been allowed to go own their way. Of course, their memories of any contact with Voresha was erased.

Well, Lilith, this was no doubt the easiest decision of my life! Because of the things that happened to me back in 1963, during the summer that I turned fourteen, I never thought I would ever be with anyone, much less someone as beautiful and nice as you.

You, James, are undoubtedly the nicest human male who has ever walked the planet earth, and Harmony is the biggest fool who ever walked the planet Earth.

As the late afternoon sun illuminated the tops of the distant orange trees and then cast long, full shadows beneath the weighted down branches full of nearly ripe fruit, I asked Lilith, "Can we talk out loud now?"

"Absolutely, James," she replied. "I'm sorry to have kept communicating telepathically with you."

"Oh, I don't mind communicating that way, Lilith," I said. "I just like talking to you out loud, because it's the way we first communicated and I like hearing your voice."

"Then I have a question for you, James," Lilith said.

"Yes?" I asked.

"Would you like to seal our relationship with a kiss?" she asked.

"As you said earlier, I thought you would never ask!" I exclaimed.

"After this," she said and moved closer to embrace and kiss me, "we don't have to ask each other."

Chapter Thirty

Our embrace and first kiss were as exhilarating as my first kiss with Harmony, if not more so. There was just something about the way a Voresha female kissed that cannot begin to be compared to a kiss by a human female, not that I had had that much experience kissing human females or females of any species. When we stopped kissing, Lilith looked deep into my eyes and I could see myself reflected there and she said, "Another thing that you were told by Harmony that is true, James, is that we cannot engage in sexual activity until after we are married. I hope that you aren't too disappointed with that."

Well," I began, "as I told Harmony, as a human male it would be difficult to control my urges, but now that I am a Voresha I believe in and will abide by Voresha rules. As long as I now know that I am with someone who is honest and really wants to be with me, I am more than willing to wait."

"It is very exciting to me as a Voresha to think that we might live the next three hundred and fifty years or more together, James," Lilith confided.

"That is still mind boggling to say the least, Lilith," I replied. "To think that I might be able to live another three hundred and fifty years sounds like something out of Edgar Rice Burroughs' Mars Series of books in which Martians could live to be a thousand years old."

"You're interested in science fiction?" she asked with enthusiasm in her voice.

"I've been interested in science fiction since I was in the sixth grade," I answered. "Besides Burroughs, I like Keith Laumer, Isaac Asimov, Robert Heinlein, H.G. Wells, and Harry Beam Piper among others."

"I love the Mars Series," Lilith replied. "I also like all of those other authors as well. It's kind of strange that we like science fiction and are now living it, or so most humans would think."

"I have thought about that a lot," I responded, "and I am still having a little bit of a hard time believing that I have actually been involved with beings from other planets and galaxies."

"I can understand how that would be difficult for humans to understand and accept," she said, "but I am so glad that you are ok with the reality of the situation, James."

"Reality and science fiction being the same thing. Who on earth would have ever imagined that?" I said. "Back to us, Lilith, how often do you think we will be able to see each other since we live in different towns about an hour apart and go to different schools?"

"I'm glad that you brought that up, James," Lilith replied. "Funny thing, my parents and I actually discussed what our situation would be if you chose to go with me instead of Harmony. Now that everything has been cleared up and you have chosen me over Harmony, my parents and I are moving close to your high school and I will transfer to KSHS as soon as next week."

"No way!" I exclaimed with joy.

"It's true, James," Lilith said. "With Harmony and her parents out of the way, my parents and I are permitted to take their place in your town so that you and I can be together all the time."

"Well, let me tell you that that makes me the happiest camper in the universe!" I exclaimed.

"After me, of course," Lilith replied.

"So, starting next week we will be able to see each other at school every day," I said and then asked, "Do you want me to pick you up for school everyday and take you home as well?"

"Of course I want you to pick me up and take me home every day," Lilith answered, "especially in that cool car of yours. And not only will we see each other at school everyday, I will be in the same classes as you so we can even sit next to each other."

"Hot damn!" I exclaimed with the excitement in my voice mounting. "I'm really glad that you like my car, Lilith, and I can't believe that we are going to be with each other all day every day at school stating next week! But what are the other students going to think about me having a new girlfriend and Harmony not being in school any more?"

"Sometimes, James," Lilith began, "we have to adjust people's minds so that sudden changes in their lives go unnoticed by them. It not only makes life simpler for them, but it makes our job on earth much easier as well. As far as everyone at your school is concerned, including the teachers and staff, we have always been together. Harmony will have been completely erased from their memories and they will believe that I have always been there instead of her."

"Once again, that is really great!" I said. "I keep forgetting that Voresha have that telepathic ability. It may take me some time to get used to changing things for the better, especially where others are concerned."

"Always remember, James," Lilith continued, "as long as how we change other people's minds isn't harmful to them, unless they're criminals, and it is for the best all around, it's ok. Your experience in changing Ron Cotworthy's way of thinking and reacting is a prime example of that. You not only made his life better, but also the lives of everyone who has contact with him, especially his parents. And it is quite possible that his change averted something tragic happening to Miss Mutchan."

"It is amazing how nice and calm he has been lately," I replied. "So, Lilith, it's getting a little late and I didn't leave any note with my parents as to my whereabouts, so I guess I should be getting back home soon," I explained.

"I know, James," she replied. "Me, too. I probably won't see you until next week since we have a lot to do to get moved before school on Monday next week."

"What days are you planning to make the move?" I asked.

"Well, my parents have a little house all picked out near the school," she answered, "and we will probably move a few things each evening until the weekend when we'll make the big move."

"I'm not working at the service station now, Lilith," I said, "so I could help you in the evenings when you get to your new house. And this weekend I could help all day both Saturday and Sunday. Of course, I've got to come up with a good story for my parents, especially my mother, about Harmony and me splitting up and me getting a new girlfriend so quickly."

"That would be great, James," she said. "I'm sure my parents will be very happy for the extra help in moving. And about your parents, as far as they are concerned you have been going steady with me all along. I hope that doesn't upset you too much."

"Upset me?" I stated more than asked. "That just about solves all of my problems. You are the best, Lilith!"

"Well, my parents didn't think it would be a good idea for your parents to think that you were jumping from one girlfriend to the next every few weeks," she replied. "I'm so glad that you aren't upset, James."

"Not at all!" I exclaimed. "I am so excited I am about to wet my pants!" I saw the beginning of a giggle forming at the corners of Lilith's mouth at that remark. "You will let me know where your new house is located and when you get there so I can come over and help you and your parents with moving," I said.

"Absolutely, James," Lilith replied. "We will probably bring the first load of stuff over tomorrow night. I will let you know sometime tomorrow where and when. We had better say goodnight and get to our respective homes."

We hugged and had another long kiss and then headed off to our separate homes. I was in such an excited state driving home that night that instead of listening to the radio in my car, I sang Happy Days are Here Again out loud all the way home. When I got home my mother didn't even say anything about me being late. She had waited to cook my dinner and seemed very happy to do it, even though she had been on her feet all day at work. When I came in the kitchen door, she asked me how Lilith and I were getting along, which initially caught me off guard for a few seconds. I told her that I had just come from Lilith's and we were getting along famously. She seemed very pleased to hear that and then set about fixing our dinner of fried pork chops, mashed potatoes with milk gravy, and spinach; of course, we had banana pudding for dessert. After dinner, my mother and I talked for a little while and I went to bed early because I was quite tired from all of the day's activities and excitement. All I could think about when I went to bed was being with Lilith the next evening helping her and her parents to move to their new house near KSHS and then being with her constantly starting the next week.

I awoke in the middle of the night thinking someone was calling my name and then realized that it was Lilith trying to contact me. I turned over, sat up and looked at the clock to discover that it was about 3:00 in the morning.

James, I'm sorry to wake you up, but I am so excited about us that I haven't been able to get to sleep. Please don't be angry with me.

Lilith, you can wake me up anytime you want. I'm very excited, too, but I can usually get to sleep when my excitement is about good things that are happening.

My father is the same way, James. He can sleep through the most exciting times for my mother and me. When I got home my mother was so excited about you and I being together that she was already thinking about our wedding. My parents had gone to the local newsstand and she bought several magazines about marriage and brides and couldn't wait to show me.

How cool is that? My mother seemed to be very happy when I got home and even asked me how you and I were getting along. As you indicated, there obviously wasn't any recollection in her mind concerning my former girlfriend.

Thanks for not mentioning your former girlfriends name, James.

The sooner I forget that bitch, the better.

Such language, James!

Sorry, Lilith.

No problem, James, I totally agree with you.

I'm really excited about helping you and your parents move and seeing your new house, Lilith.

I hope you won't be too disappointed in our humble dwelling and our simpler ways, James.

Well, it couldn't be any worse than this house I live in, Lilith, and, besides, I was really uncomfortable being around rich people. My parents have been hard working lower middle-class people all their lives and probably won't do any better than that. My mother only had a fifth-grade education and my father barely made it through high school, but they have always put a roof over our heads and food on the table.

My situation is very similar, James. Although Voresha are educated at home to be very knowledge-able about many things, especially concerning the universe and other beings, we rarely get beyond a high school education. You will find that your know-ledge base increases substantially now that you are officially a Voresha.

I can't think of anyone that I would rather learn from than you, Lilith.

Your former girlfriend, James, was such a fool not to realize what a sweetheart you are and to use you the way she did.

I think I'm turning red again, Lilith, but I can't tell for sure sitting here in the dark.

Well, I think I am finally beginning to get a little sleepy now, James. All the excitement yesterday and the news about moving have kept me awake. I'll let you get back to sleep and we'll see you tomorrow evening at our new house. Goodnight, James.

Goodnight, Lilith. Just think, before long we'll be saying that to each other in person in our own bed!

Well, now I may not get to sleep at all tonight thinking about that!

Me either, Lilith. At that, we cut off communica-tion, but Lilith was right, I didn't get to sleep the rest of the night.

Chapter Thirty-one

When my mother saw me looking so sleepy-headed the next morning she asked me if I slept ok. I told her that I had not slept much because I had a big test at school that day and I hadn't studied very hard for it. She admonished me for that, but wished me good luck on my test as I went out the door. I thanked her and said that I hoped she had a quiet day at work. I had the local radio station on in my car on the way to school and although I didn't really believe in fate, all they played were Paul Anka love songs. Tell Me That You Love Me, You Are My Destiny, Put Your Head On My Shoulder, Puppy Love, Love Me Warm and Tender, and Love (Makes the World Go Round) all played before I got to school. Of course, when they started playing Paul Anka songs on the radio that morning I started driving a little slower. I didn't know if Lilith was listening to the same station or not, but I was convinced that hearing all those love songs wasn't merely coincidence. For one thing, you hardly ever heard a Paul Anka song on the radio and to hear six in a row was unbelievable.

You're right, James, it wasn't a coincidence that they played all of those Paul Anka love songs while you were driving to school this morning.

Lilith! Good morning.

Good morning, love. I'm glad that you enjoyed the songs.

Did you have something to do with the radio station playing all of those Paul Anka songs, Lilith?

Yes, James. I telepathically contacted the DJ at the radio station and told him to play those particular songs and then I got you to turn your car radio on to make sure that you would hear them.

I knew it had to be more than a coincidence that they played all Paul Anka love songs while I was driving to school.

They were all from me to you this morning, James, since I can't be there with you until tonight.

Well, Lilith, you have certainly made my day more bearable since I won't see you until later.

Just talking with you this morning will help me to get through the day, James.

Dear God, I hope you're real and that this isn't a dream!

I heard a little giggle in my mind. *You will know very soon when we are together everyday for the rest of our lives that I, and my love for you, James, are very real and will be for the rest of our lives.*

Trust me. Lilith, that was just a saying. I truly believe this time that I am in love with someone who is just as in love with me. I believe that with my entire being, heart, soul, and mind. By the way, what's your new address and what time should I meet you and your parents there tonight?

My parents will have a small truck loaded down with boxes of things and will pick me up from school and head on over to the new house. We should be there by 4:00 or a little after at the latest. Can you be there that early?

Not a problem, love. See you then.

See you, James.

Lilith had given me the address of her new house and it was only about one mile from school, so I could loiter around school and the neighborhood when I got out of study hall until it was time to meet Lilith and her parents. The day was off to such a good start and with

Harmony out of my life, I couldn't imagine that anything bad could happen. And, once again, I was wrong on both counts. As I was walking up to the main sidewalk to head for my first class, I tripped over something, stumbled a few steps, and then went to the ground with pain shooting through my right ankle. I had dropped my books and was grabbing at my ankle and trying not to scream out too loud with the pain throbbing through my foot and lower leg. I looked to see what I had tripped over, but there wasn't anything there except level ground. Miss Dutrip had been walking down the sidewalk when I fell and heard my painful cry. When she saw me writhing on the ground she came running over and knelt beside me asking, "James, what on earth happened? Are you ok?"

With tears forming at the corners of my eyes, I managed to squeak out, "No ma'am, I twisted my ankle and it hurts like hell!"

"Poor, boy," she said trying to console me. "Can you get up?"

"I think so, Miss Dutrip," I answered. "Sorry about my foul mouth."

Helping me to my feet, or at least to my left foot, she replied, "That's not half as bad as what I would have said in the same situation, James. No, let's see if we can get you to the school nurse and have her take a look at that ankle."

Without saying anymore, Miss Dutrip helped me to hobble along to the nurse's office and they both helped me get up on the examining table. My ankle was still hurting pretty bad, but the throbbing pain seamed to be getting better. My ankle had started to swell some and the nurse suggested that I take it easy for about an hour and she put an ice pack on it and gave me some Bayer aspirin for the pain. Miss Dutrip asked me a few questions about how I managed to trip and twist my ankle and wrote the information down on an accident report form. She wanted to know if she should contact my parents and I told her no since neither of them could leave work to come and get me. The school nurse, Miss Crablatroan, told Miss Dutrip that she would report on my condition in about an hour to see if I could walk, but that someone needed to let my teachers know that I might not be in my classes that day. Miss Dutrip said she would take care of that and left the nurse's office wishing me well as she went out the door.

I had never been in the nurse's office before or even met Miss Crablatroan, but unlike what I had pictured it was decorated with pretty wallpaper and had some personal pictures of Miss Crablatroan and some her friends hanging on the wall. Miss Crablatroan was a little on the heavy side and was wearing a white uniform with a white nurses cap attached to her hair with booby pins. She did, of course, have the usual posters hanging up that dealt with the usual high school maladies such as colds, herpes, eye problems, and sexually transmitted diseases. Miss Crablatroan hadn't said much to me except to find out what had happened and where it hurt until Miss Dutrip had left the office.

"James, isn't it?" she asked.

"Yes, ma'am," I answered.

"No need to be so formal when Miss Dutrip isn't around, James, " she said. My name's Florence, Flo for short."

"It's very nice to meet you, Flo," I said, "but I wish it had been under different circumstances."

"Well, unfortunately, James," she said, "the only time I usually see any of the kids is when they are sick or hurt. I think that the swelling of your ankle should go down pretty soon, but I would guess that it is going to be very sore for several days. You would be wise to stay off of it as much as possible for at least three or four days."

"Oh, crap!" I said. "I have got to help a friend and her parents move over the next few days."

"Well, James," she replied, "that would probably not be a very good idea. I can loan you some crutches to hobble around on, but that isn't going to work very well with moving things. I think from the bruising that has started that you have a torn anterior talofibular ligament and putting weight on it is not going to help it heal faster."

"An anterior what kind of ligament? Isn't there anything that I can use besides crutches?" I desperately asked. I was already thinking how disappointed Lilith would be if I couldn't help them move.

"James, I'm going to wrap it up tight with some wide bandages and suggest that you wear a half boot or cowboy boot if you have something like that in your closet," Miss Crablatroan told me. "That will help some, but I am afraid that you are still going to be in some pain. And the talofibular ligament is the ligament that goes from your outside ankle bone to the bone at the top of your foot."

" Oh, that ligament," I said. "It would be great if you could wrap up my ankle, Flo. I've got some boots at home that would probably be perfect for that. They're not cowboy boots, but I used to wear them at the service station when I worked there."

"Well, James," Flo said, "if you insist on walking around on that ankle very much for the next week, I would highly recommend that you were those boots. Now, just lie back and take it easy for the next hour and I'll check on you every so often to see how the swelling is doing. If the swelling goes down enough, you can borrow the crutches and go to the rest of your classes today."

"Thanks, Flo," I said and she left the examining room and went back to her office. I fluffed up the tiny little white pillow on the examining table and reclined with my hands behind by head for extra support to think about how I managed to fall and twist my ankle. I was just about to doze off when I was rudely interrupted.

Well, how do you like that, James?

Harmony? I thought I told you to stay away from me, including telepathically!

Yeah, well, good luck with that jerk! In case you haven't figured it out yet, you're little fall was my doing and that's just the beginning of what I'm going to do to you!

Wait a minute. Aren't you supposed to be in some other far off state in some remote location?

Well, smarty pants, my parents weren't too happy with that judgment and neither was I, so we just moved to the next town and we're going to make life as miserable for you as we can.

Elder Oqu Ezhu Thegh, I hate to bother you, but if you're out there listening, please come in!

Good luck with that you little wussie! When I get through torturing you no one, including that bitch, Lilith, is going to want your ugly carcass!

James, Elder Thegh, here. Did you call me?

Yes sir. The Beckhams have not left Florida and Harmony caused me to trip and injure my ankle a short time ago. She was just in contact with me and is making all kinds of threats against me.

Hold on for a few minutes, James, and I'll be right back.

Yes sir. About five or six minutes passed and then Elder Thegh came back to me.

I have located the Beckhams, James, and since they did not heed their instructions to leave Florida and leave you and Lilith alone, I have sent a group of enforcers to escort them into exile with former Elder, Cudur Mus Noslen. They will be picked up soon and

be on their way and will never bother you or Lilith again.

Thank you, sir. I want you to know that I was as concerned for Lilith as myself, but as far as I know, Lilith hasn't been approached by Harmony since my announcement.

James, I have been close friends with the Lhuv family for a very long time and since you are about to join that family, you are now my close friend as well. Know that I will always come when called. And to ease your mind, Lilith is safe and sound, James, and you need not worry about her safety or your safety any more. Over the next few days, while the Lhuvs are moving and you are helping them in that endeavor, I am personally going to take you under my wing and increase your telepathic powers to match those of a natural-born Voresha who is seventeen years old.

Wow! Will I be aware of this happening, Elder Thegh?

Not while I am working, James, but as you progress you will become aware of your new powers.

I'm not sure how much help I am going to be to the Lhuvs with their moving since I hurt my ankle.

First of all, that was not your fault. That was Harmony Beckham's doing. I want you to lie back down, James, close your eyes, and concentrate on the beautiful image of Lilith. Can you do that for me?

No problem there, sir. I did as instructed and within a few seconds I had either fallen asleep or had been telepathically hypnotized in some way. I wasn't sure how long I had been in a state of stupor, but I awoke to nurse Crablatroan shaking me and calling out my name.

"James, are you awake?" she asked me as I came to. "You gave me a fright there for a minute when I couldn't get you to wake up."

"Yes, Flo," I answered. "I guess I just fell into a deep sleep from the trauma and pain."

"Well, let's take a look at that ankle, young man," she said. "I didn't want to check it before you woke up in case I startled you and you kicked me."

"If that had happened, Flo," I said, "it wouldn't have been on purpose."

"I know, James," she responded, "but I still didn't want to take any chances of ending up with a broken nose or black eye. Imagine me trying to explain that to the principal." Flo moved to my ankle and very gingerly began to unwrap the bandage holding the ice pack in place. When she had removed the ice pack, she exclaimed, "My word! The swelling is completely gone down and there isn't even any bruising! I've never seen anything like it before."

Your ankle is completely healed, James. You won't need a crutch or special boots and you will be able to help Lilith and her parents move.

Wow! Thanks, Elder Thegh.

No problem, James. Now back to nurse Flo.

"I guess it must be a miracle," I said in response to Flo's amazement.

"Miracle, smiracle!" she exclaimed. "You must have remarkable recuperative powers. Can you stand on that ankle yet?"

"Let's see," I said and having faith in the Elder's powers, I jumped off the table and landed flat on the floor with both feet. Then I raised my left foot and stood on my right foot. Since I didn't feel any pain I started hopping around on my right foot and said, "Looks like I'm as good as new, Flo. You're one heck of a nurse!"

"Flattery will get you everywhere, young man," Flo said and we both laughed. "I still cannot believe that you don't have any pain or swelling or bruising."

"Feels fine," I said. "Can I get on back to my classes now?"

"I don't see any reason why not, James," Flo answered. "I'll let Miss Dutrip know that you made a miraculous full recovery."

"Thanks, Flo, you're the best!" I said and left the nurses office.

Chapter Thirty-two

When I got outside, I noticed that it was getting close to time for my second period class to be over, so I decided to wait and go to my third period class. I was standing outside the classroom building where my third period class was held and decided to try and contact Lilith about what had just transpired.

Lilith, are you listening by any chance?

I'm here now, James. Elder Thegh just contacted me a few minutes ago and told me what happened this morning there at KSHS. I'm so sorry, James, that you had to suffer that pain because of you-know-who.

Thanks, Lilith. I guess I should have known that if she could find some way to interfere with us, she would. Did Elder Thegh tell you that the Beckhams were being sent into exile with former Elder Noslen?

Yes, he did, James, and that is the best news I've heard in a long time. I am so glad that you are ok and will still be able to help us move. Even if you couldn't help, I would still want you to be there with us.

One way or the other, Lilith, I was going to be there, even if I had to hop on one foot all the way.

I heard that cute little giggle in my mind. **You are so funny, James. It is rare to find a teenage boy with a clean sense of humor. James, I am sorry that I couldn't be there to help you or that I wasn't in contact with you when you had your mishap this morning. You-know-who had managed to put a block on my thoughts about you and actually had me in somewhat of a trance during those events. People around me at school thought I was spaced out on some kind** *of drugs and my first period teacher sent me to the school nurse to have me checked out.*

I hope your school nurse is as nice as Miss Crablatroan here at KSHS, Lilith.

She was nice, James, but very suspicious until I came around. She prodded and poked and talked at me like I was a zombie, which I guess in one way I was acting like one.

Well, Lilith, at least she took the time to wait and see if you were ok before calling in the authorities.

Yes, James, that's for sure, because my mind wasn't clear enough to change what they were thinking at the time. When I finally came around, I told the nurse that one of my medications sometimes had that effect on me, especially when I didn't take it with food. She instructed me to be more careful and sent me back to class, which is where I am right now.

I'm just waiting for third period to start. There wasn't much time left in second period and I didn't want to listen to all the questions and ribbing about falling over my own two feet. I have decided to skip study hall this afternoon and head on over to your new house early. I will probably be there before you get there, Lilith.

This is so exciting, James! I can't wait to see you this afternoon. Well, there's the bell to end second period. I'll be talking to you later. Bye for now, love.

See you later, Lilith.

The bell to end second period had just rung at my school, too, so I began to head toward my third period class. Either the word hadn't gotten out that I had tripped over my own two feet that morning or everyone's mind had been blocked from that knowledge, because no one ever mentioned it to me. The rest of my classes that day went as smoothly as Peggy Fleming gliding across the ice last year as she won the 1965 U.S. Championship in figure skating. As I had indicated to Lilith, I skipped out on study hall knowing that Mrs. Tinmoor wouldn't have anything to say about it. I drove straight over to the Lhuv's new house, but they had not arrived there yet. There new residence looked a lot like my parent's house, one level ranch style brick that probably had three bedrooms instead of two and maybe two bathrooms. This house also had a one-car garage and a slightly larger front porch than the front stoop at our house. The lot size was about the same except being in an older and more established neighborhood, there were probably 12 or 14 trees on the property including five medium-sized live oaks. The rest of the trees were evergreens of one type or another and had dropped a lot of pine needles on the ground around them. Although the house looked to be in good repair, it didn't look like anyone had lived there for several months, as the yard definitely needed mowing. Since I had a lot of experience mowing yards I figured I could at least offer to mow the yard for the Lhuvs.

I had parked out on the street next to the curb and was just strolling around the yard when a small moving van pulled up and backed into the driveway. Lilith was riding next to the passenger side door and when she saw me she jumped out of the truck, almost before her father had stopped it, and ran up to me giving me a big hug and kiss. "I am so glad that you are ok, James," she told me as her eyes started to tear up.

"Thanks, Lilith," I replied. "You and me both. I didn't want to disappoint you by not being able to help you and your parents move, but Elder Thegh took care of my injury in addition to dealing with the Beckhams. He is really a very nice man and said that he was now my friend as well."

"He is one of my parents' best friends and was a good friend of my grandparents, too," Lilith told me.

About that time Mr. and Mrs. Lhuv had gotten out of the moving van and walked up. "Good afternoon,

James," Mr. Lhuv said. "It's so nice of you to help us move."

"Hi, James," Mrs. Lhuv said. "I certainly second that. We were so sorry to hear about what happened to you at school this morning, but we are very glad that you are ok and that Elder Thegh has made sure the Beckhams will never bother you or Lilith or anyone else again."

"That is a greater relief to me than you can imagine," I told them. "I would feel really guilty if I couldn't help you move after offering to do so. I'm just glad that you are letting me help you so that Lilith and I can spend some time together before next week."

"Our little girl is our future, James, and her happiness is paramount to us," Mrs. Lhuv said.

"We would not have held it against you, James, if you hadn't been able to help because of an injury," Mr. Lhuv said, "but when Lilith asked us if it was ok if you helped us move we couldn't possibly have said no."

"Thanks, again," I said. "It means a lot to me to be so readily accepted by you and Lilith."

"Well, then," Mr. Lhuv began, "this truck isn't going to empty itself. Shall we get started?"

"I am at your service," I said. "You tell me what to get and where to put it."

Most of what the Lhuvs had in the moving van were carefully packed boxes of miscellaneous items and clothing along with small pieces of furniture like a coffee table with a glass top, six mismatched lawn chairs, a coupe of night stands, a wicker hat rack, an older white enameled and wood kitchen table with four matching chairs, and a Montgomery Ward lawn mower very similar to the one we had at home and that I had given a lot of use to since 1963. With four of us unloading the van it didn't take long for everything to be put in the house or garage. It was only around 5:30 when we finished unloading everything and Mr. and

Mrs. Lhuv invited me to have dinner with them, their treat, at the local Howard Johnson's, which was only a few minutes away. Wanting to be with Lilith that afternoon for as long as I could, I readily accepted and Lilith and I followed her parents to the restaurant in my car.

About once a month, my father would take my mother and me to Howard Johnson's for dinner on his night off from the service station to give my mother a break from always having to prepare our meals. My two favorite dishes there were the beef burgundy and stuffed flounder. Not wanting to embarrass myself by trying to eat the noodles that came with the beef burgundy, I ordered the stuffed flounder with my favorite side dish of spinach. The Lhuvs seemed a little surprised by my combination of foods, so I explained that the stuffed flounder and spinach were what I usually ordered when I came there with my parents about once a month. Mr. and Mrs. Lhuv said they had never known a child who liked spinach, but were glad to see that I was eating a healthy meal. Mr. and Mrs. Lhuv both ordered steaks done medium well with baked potatoes loaded down with butter and sour cream and Lilith went with a Swiss steak with mashed potatoes and brown gravy.

Everything went smoothly at dinner and it was about 7:00 when we said our goodbyes and headed off home. I agreed to meet them the next evening when they came with another truckload of boxes and small items. Mr. Lhuv said that they would move the larger furniture on Saturday and Sunday and was very happy to have another man to help him with those heavier items. It had certainly been an interesting morning, but the rest of the day turned out fine and to top it off I got to see Lilith. All I could think about driving back home was how long it would be before I saw Lilith late the next afternoon.

Chapter Thirty-three

After I had gone to bed that night, I decided to try and contact Lilith to talk about some things that were on my mind, but which I didn't want our parents to be in on just yet. *Lilith, I hate to bother you, but if you are tuned in, I need to talk with you about some things.*

I'm here, James. I will always be here for you no matter what, especially when we don't want anyone else to know what we are communicating about. What do you want to talk about tonight?

I was thinking about art school again and was wondering if that was still part of the plan for us like it was with me and you-know-who?

I really don't mind using Harmony's name now, James. I truly believe that you are over her now and that you and I were meant to be together from the beginning. Besides, she and her parents are now far, far away from here and will never be able to interfere with our lives again. One of the reasons that I chose you, James, was because of your interest in art. You see, I have also been interested in art for as long as I can remember and was hoping to attend an art school as well, although I had not decided on one yet. The only problem that both your parents and my parents have is finding the money to send us to a good art school, like the one in Sarasota where you want to go.

That is so cool that you are really interested in art as well, Lilith! I knew that Harmony wasn't really interested in art or going to Sarasota with me to attend art school. She never really showed much enthusiasm about the idea. As a matter of fact, I had suspicions that she was going to stay here in town while I was away at school. Concerning money for me to go to school, my folks are planning to take out a loan to send me there and I really hate that, but at the same time I really want to go to art school in Sarasota.

I was planning to talk to you more about this next week, James, when we were moved and settled into our new home and me in my new school, but let's go ahead and talk about it now.

Thanks, Lilith. As I said, I hate to bother you to-night about it, but I couldn't get to sleep for thinking about it. I was just wondering if going to art school was going to be part of our future together or if there were other plans for us.

Are you saying that you would change your plans about going to art school just to be with me, James?

Absolutely, Lilith! Like you said, I believe that we were the ones who were meant to be together and I will do whatever is necessary to make that happen, even if it means changing my art school plans. I would even be willing to go back to work at the service station with my father if necessary.

Harmony was right about one thing, James.

Really? What's that?

That you are undoubtedly the most honest, sincere, and caring human male on the face of this planet.

You're making me blush, Lilith. I can feel the blood rushing to my face.

You are easily embarrassed, James, and I heard that cute giggle in my head. ***Concerning art school and our future together, my parents and I talked about this before we made contact since this was something that both of us were thinking about doing. My parents, too, were planning to take out a loan to***

send me to art school even before we met. As grateful as I am about that, it bothers me as well that they are willing to make that sacrifice for me.

I wish that we could come up with some way that we could both go to art school and our parents wouldn't have to go in debt to send us, Lilith.

Me, too, James. I have been thinking and thinking about it, but I haven't come up with a good idea yet. At least Harmony's parents had the money to send both of you to art school so your parents wouldn't have to worry.

I would rather not go to art school, Lilith, than to even think about that scenario again!

I'm sorry, James, it just doesn't seem fair that some kids get everything and some, like us, have to struggle.

Well, Lilith, now she is the one who is going to have to struggle, along with her parents!

That's at least some consolation, James. They will never be able to prey on unsuspecting people ever again thanks to my parents' friend, Elder Thegh.

I am so thankful that he came to my rescue, Lilith, because there is no telling what Harmony had in mind for me.

Lilith, James, Elder Thegh here. Did you call me or did I just hear my name mentioned?

Sorry, Elder Thegh, Lilith and I were just saying how grateful we are that you intervened on my behalf when Harmony Beckham was trying to harm me. We didn't mean to disturb you tonight.

As I indicated to you before, James, you are now as good a friend of mine as the Lhuvs. Never consider contacting me as bothering me. Everyone thinks that the Elders are always very busy, but between the two of you and me, we are actually very bored. We really don't have that much to do anymore except watch out after our kind and there are plenty of us to do that

without getting overwhelmed. So, you two are always welcome to contact me anytime day or night.

Thank you, Elder Thegh. James and I were just discussing our future plans and trying to figure out a way for both of us to go to art school without sending our parents to the poor house.

So dramatic! I think you should consider a career in acting, Lilith.

I'm sorry, Elder Thegh, it's just that James and I both feel bad about our parents borrowing money just to send us to an art school. I mean, it's not like we are planning to study something useful like business.

You have both studied art enough to know that without art there would be little beauty for us to behold from the worlds of the past. Artists are a very important part of human culture and creating art is just as important as running a business or inventing things to make life more enjoyable. Never, you two, put yourselves down because you want to be artists!

Yes, sir, we both chimed in perfect two-part harmony.

Now, if the two of you think you can be quiet for a few minutes, I have a proposition for you. Neither of us said anything and the silence was almost deafening. *Good. When bad Voresha are exiled or banished to parts unknown because they made a lot of money by taking advantage of people, that money doesn't just disappear and they do not get to take any of it, not one cent of it, with them to wherever it is they are sent. As a matter of fact, when a Voresha is exiled he or she has to work in a commune like setting to help support the others who have been exiled with them. If they refuse to do as they are instructed, then they are dealt, how shall I put this, a more final punishment. The Beckhams had approximately one million dollars in the bank when they were sent into exile. They were the only Voresha on the planet who had amassed such wealth, because it is not the Voresha way to live extravagantly. Along with helping those who need our help in one way or another, living well and working in human society to make a living to support one's family is part of the Voresha way.*

Sir?

Quiet, James, I am not through!

Yes, sir.

There have only been four or five times in all of Voresha history here on earth, and that has been thousands of years, that anyone of our kind amassed wealth comparable to what the Beckhams had amassed. In all of those cases, the riches were ill gotten and the Voresha were dealt with severely. Now, I suppose that the right thing to do would be to try and give all that money back to the people from whom it was scammed. However, that would prove to be almost impossible and certainly a daunting task to say the least. The Elders do not have any special needs, but since the first time that a Voresha amassed such wealth, the Elders decided that they would use the money to support themselves very modestly, almost in a monastic way, thus giving them time to tend to the needs of all other Voresha. We live so modestly that we are all able to get by simply on the interest income from the millions that are invested and still put part of that income back in investments. On occasion there have been worthy causes that members of our little flock have had or circumstances where Voresha needed a little extra help and the Elders have provided extra funding to those individuals. I know it is getting late, but are the two of you still with me?

Yes, sir, we replied in unison once again.

I thought maybe I had your undivided attention by now. As I understand it, both of you are interested in art and want to attend an art school in Sarasota, Florida. Is that correct?

Once again, we both answered in unison, *Yes, sir.*

One of the things that you young people will achieve when you get to be my age is the ability to carrying on more than one conversation at the same time. While I have been communicating with you I have also been in contact with the Elder council who has been in contact with all of the other Elders and we have all voted in agreement to help the two of you out financially by using a little of the Beckhams' former money to send you both to art school.

Oh my, God! Lilith, we are going to go to art school and our parents won't suffer the financial consequences of our selfishness!

Oh, James, I think I am going to cry!

Settle down, you two. There is a catch.

Anything, Elder Thegh, I said.

Yes, anything, Lilith echoed.

The two of you have to promise the Elders that you will spend your lives creating art that shows the beauty and pleasantness of the world so that all humanity can know that this isn't such a bad planet after all. With the help of the Elders, your artwork will be shown in important galleries around the world and your income will come from the sale of your work.

I'm sorry to be so dense, Elder Thegh, but are you saying that all Lilith and I have to do for the rest of our lives is create beautiful art work to share with the rest of the world?

And they said you were slow, James, Elder Thegh said and started laughing and then Lilith joined in and so did I. *It is very refreshing to know that you both have a sense of humor and can laugh at yourselves! And, yes, James, that is exactly what I am saying.*

Lilith, can you believe this? This is the most incredible thing that I have ever heard, besides, of course, being chosen by you!

It is very hard to believe, James, but we can completely trust Elder Thegh.

I don't know how to express the gratitude that I am feeling right now, Elder Thegh, but I think I can speak for both Lilith and myself when I say we will work hard at doing the best we can at art school and in doing the work that you and the Elders have charged us with doing.

I know you will, James, and I know that Lilith will, too. I can't imagine a more perfect couple to carry out this very unique and important assignment. You will be the first Voresha in history to be charged with creating beautiful art for all the world to enjoy. Now, if you will excuse me, I am getting a little tired and need my beauty sleep. Goodnight to you both and I will be in communication with Lilith's parents tomorrow and they will then communicate to your parents, James, that financial arrangements have been made for your educations after high school.

Goodnight, Elder Thegh, and thanks again, Lilith and I both said.

Lilith, I don't know if I can sleep now or not.

Me either, James, but we both have a big day ahead of us tomorrow so we better try and get some sleep. See you tomorrow afternoon. Goodnight, James.

Goodnight, Lilith.

Chapter Thirty-four

I'm sure that you would like to hear that I had some more dangerous encounters with some sort of aliens that were not so friendly to humans as Voresha or that Harmony escaped from her exile and came back to do me more bodily harm or undermine me in some other way. However, much to my delight things went smoothly for the rest of the week and through the weekend. The Lhuv's move into their new house about a mile from the KSHS campus couldn't have been easier. Both my time helping Mr. and Mrs. Lhuv and Lilith with the move and the private time that Lilith and I got to spend together over the weekend were quite enjoyable. Lilith's parents were the two nicest people I had met in a very long time and they treated me with respect and welcomed me into their inner circle as if Lilith and I were already married.

Elder Thegh had been in contact with the Lhuvs about the financial arrangements concerning Lilith and me going to art school and Mr. Lhuv had contacted my parents with the good news. My parents were thrilled with the idea that some "foundation" had given both Lilith and I scholarships to go to art school and that all of our expenses, including tuition and room and board, would be paid by the scholarship. It was Elder Thegh's idea to tell my parents that it was a special scholarship fund that Lilith and I had applied to through Mr. Lhuv's work. After all, even if we had told my parents the truth they wouldn't have believed it and probably would have sent me off to the looney bin, or worse, made me work as a gas jockey the rest of my life. To say that Lilith and I were excited about going to art school in Sarasota together after we graduated would be putting it mildly. The only subject that hadn't resurfaced where my parents were concerned was the fact that Lilith and I would actually be married when we went off to art school and that our "room and board" would be our own small, private apartment near campus. They would find that out in due time. The Lhuvs thought it would be better to wait until Lilith and I had graduated high school the following May before springing that on my parents.

The end of the Fall term at KSHS seemed to come sooner than expected and everyone was excited about the Christmas and New Year's holidays. Lilith and I couldn't have been getting along better and having every class together just brought us closer and closer. My buddies were all still dumbfounded by the fact that I was dating the most beautiful girl in school and that we had somehow managed to get all of our classes together. To top off the end of the Fall term, the Lhuvs had invited my parents and me to their new house for both a Christmas Eve dinner and to see in the New Year. Christmas day, of course, Lilith and I spent with our parents at our own houses, but Lilith and I exchanged gifts on Christmas Eve at her house. We all gathered around the Lhuv's television set and watched the newly released How the Grinch Stole Christmas on CBS, featuring the voice of Boris Karloff as the Grinch. Everything was going right and nothing was going wrong, Lilith and I were falling more and more in love, and our parents were getting along famously. I just kept hoping that I wasn't having a dream this time either or that this was just a long continuation of what I thought had been a dream back in 1963.

The subject of marriage, going to art school, and our future together creating art were all Lilith and I could talk or think about, except, of course, when we were making out. Christmas was a blast and New Year's found us sneaking outside to welcome in 1967 with a long and wonderful kiss. Lilith had gotten me The Beach Boys new album, Pet Sounds, that had come out back in May and which had our new favorite song, Wouldn't It Be Nice, on it and their new hit single that had been released in October, Good Vibrations, a song that would eventually become number six on Rolling Stone's 500 greatest songs of all time. Lilith had told me that all she wanted was some "Tigress" perfume by Faberge, but that she had never bought any because her mother thought it was a little too suggestive for a young girl. I asked her what her mother would think if I bought her the perfume for Christmas and she said that since we were to be married soon and since she had become a young woman that her mother had said it would be ok. So, Lilith got a one-ounce bottle of Tigress cologne splash from me for Christmas and we were both very happy, especially since she wore the perfume only when we were together.

Lilith and I spent nearly every day of the Christmas break from school together spending lots of time at the park near her former house. We would drive over to the park and take long walks through the woods and sit on the bench where we first met and make out when no one else was around. We saw several movies over the holidays, most at the Silver Moon Drive-In, including Alfie, which starred Michael Caine and Shelley Winters, Born Free, which starred Virginia McKenna and Bill Travers, Boy, Did I Get a Wrong Number!, which starred Bob Hope and Elke Sommer, and Frankie and Johnny, which starred Elvis Presley and Donna Douglas, who was probably better known as Elly May Clampett on the television series, The Beverly Hillbillies.

It was an especially warm Christmas season in Florida and Lilith and I took advantage of that by taking a couple of day trips to Daytona Beach to enjoy the sun and water. I was just starting to get interested in surfing and we rented surfboards and tried our hand at the east coast surf. Fortunately, I didn't decide to become a professional surfer! We also made one trip to Sarasota to look around for available places to rent when we arrived for art school the following Fall. I had been to the Sarasota area a couple of times with my parents, because my father wanted to try out the area for fishing. I always tended to wander away and prowl up and down the relatively deserted beaches in search of unusual sea shells or other interesting specimen from the Gulf of Mexico. I once came across a shark that was probably about six feet long, but whoever had caught it had cut its jaws out and left it to rot on the beach.

Once again I digress. Lilith and I continued to talk about our future as it got closer to time for the Spring term to begin at KSHS. With Harmony and her parents out of the way Lilith and I were hoping that the Spring semester would be quiet and not involve any non-friendly aliens trying to get at me. And I kept hoping that all of this wasn't going to turn out to be a dream.

The End

…..for Now